WHERE EVIL LIVES

A DARK SECRET. A HIDDEN CURSE

ELLIE DIAS

Editing, design, and distribution by Bublish

ISBN: 978-1-64704-796-2 (paperback)
ISBN: 978-1-64704-794-8 (eBook)

Dedication

To my beta readers Steven Lubarsky, Paul Duquette,
Lori Coutu, Judi Epstein, and Pat Egan.

To my copyeditor, Cheryl Malandrios, and my
developmental editor, Tracy Lawson.

To Marychris Bradley/The Book Team for her tireless work in
helping me fine-tune the cover and creating a stunning video.

To Bublish Inc. In additon to support and insight,
their expert publishing team guided me through
my manuscript and readied it for print.

My deepest thank-you to all for helping me get to the finish line.

"The scariest monsters are the ones that
lurk within our souls . . ."

— Edgar Allan Poe

1

SAM
JANUARY 1965

IT WAS ALMOST seven, and twenty-six-year-old Sam Middleton was ravenous but lost his appetite when he read the note on the stove.

> The chicken casserole will be ready by the time Dad gets home. Homemade bread on the counter. Volunteered for the evening shift. Love you, Mom.

In an obvious nudge to force them to spend time together, she had set their plates on the table next to each other. He moved them farther apart.

Growing up, unpredictable harassments doled out by his father had spoiled mealtimes. A picky eater, if he had caused a scene about what lay on his plate, his father would say, "You're not leaving until everything is off your dish."

If she wasn't working, his mother would come to his rescue and tell his father to back off. His most vivid memory involved a night when he had been alone with him.

A wedge of shepherd's pie had occupied his plate. Unable to eat more, he had pushed the dish away. His father shoved it back.

"Eat."

The menacing stare on his dad's face had driven him to take another bite. Choking it down, Sam glared at him. "I'm done." Before he could stand, he had felt the heat of his dad's breath on his neck when he came over and pressed both hands on his shoulders.

"You're going to sit here until you finish."

Another bite and he had vomited.

Eighteen years later, the taste of that meal stayed with him. When his father walked into the kitchen, he tensed for a moment before he said, "Mom made your favorite. Enough to feed an army." He slipped on the oven mitts and placed the casserole and cutting board with the bread and knife on the table. His dad took his seat and dug in. No greeting. No conversation. *At least I don't have to fake being pleasant.* Sam inhaled his food, put his dishes in the sink, and was halfway to the door when his dad spoke.

"Wait."

Sam's shoulders sagged. *So close to a clean getaway.*

"Here, for your trip."

He tried to conceal his surprise when his father handed him a check. "Thanks. I'll put it to good use."

"Better not spend it on booze."

"You always have to bring up the *one* night I came home drunk. How about I remind you of what *you* did to me?" A chill ran up his spine as he watched his father's fingers grip the bread knife. "What are you going to do? Throw it at me? Stab me?" He drew himself up to his full height and stepped closer to the table. "What's stopping you?" He watched his dad's Adam's apple bob as he swallowed his words. He released the knife and let it clatter to the floor.

"I'm sorry, I . . ."

Sam picked the knife up, pierced the check, and jammed it into the table a breath away from his father's hand. "I don't want a red cent from you. I just want out."

As he passed by the mirror in the front hall, he stopped to stare at his reflection. The blond hair, the sapphire color of his eyes, and the irregular-shaped birthmark on his left temple that turned red with anger were carbon copies of his father's. He'd finally stood up to the old man but shuddered to think they might have more in common than their looks.

Back in the kitchen, Sam sat eating a slice of his mother's homemade chocolate cream pie when she walked in. He smiled and patted the chair next to him. "Sit, unless you're too tired."

She tousled his hair. "I'm never too tired to talk to you. Catch me up on your last registration exam. How do you think you did?"

His knuckles tapped the side of his head. "Sometimes my brain has to work harder, but I did well, all things considered." He saw deep lines appear across her brow.

"I wish things had been different for you. Easier, the way it was for other kids. I should have done more."

"After all the misery I put you through, no way. You never got mad when I went nuts and shoved my books and papers on the floor every time I had trouble reading and writing. If it weren't for you, I doubt I would have ever been able to apply and be accepted at architect school." He wanted to add, *My anger is nothing compared to Dad's way of reacting. He'd raise his hand and tell me to stop acting like a baby. And if I couldn't control myself, or refused to obey him, he'd threaten to punish me.* So many times he'd asked his mom why he was treated so badly. But she never gave him a straight answer. When he got back from Paris, he intended to find out why. Something he should have done years ago.

"I've always had faith in you." She sighed. "I'll miss you while you're gone."

"It's only a semester." He watched as she swiped a tear with the back of her hand.

"I know."

He stood, folded his arms around her and kissed her cheek. He felt responsible for all the years she'd spent defending him while trying to bridge the gap between him and his father. *I hope with me out of the picture, your life won't be so stressful.*

Sam sat across from Joe in the Logan International Airport terminal, rereading the *Boston Globe*. Splashed across the front page: Teen Found Guilty of Fatally Stabbing His Father.

"Hey, what's so interesting?"

He thrust the paper at Joe. "Did you see this?" As soon as the words left his mouth, he thought of last night and the knife incident with his father. *Was it a learned behavior or something more sinister?*

"Pretty sick, but that can't be the only reason you seem—I dunno—pissed off. What gives?"

"My dad gave me his nicest send-off."

Joe asked, "What did he do now?"

"More like what I did, and you don't want to know."

"Christ, he's still a dickhead after all these years."

"Tell me about it. I should be used to his craziness, but it still irks me how I rattle his cage whenever we're in the same room."

"Once you're in Paris and surrounded by all the fabulous architecture, you won't have time to think about him. Not to mention all those hot French chicks you'll meet."

"No time for that." Sam watched him make the sign of the cross.

"Sounds like you missed a higher calling."

"If you weren't my best friend, I'd punch you."

Joe put one arm across his gut. "Let's hope I'm never on the other side of those fists."

Sam smiled. "Just trying to keep you in line, my friend. Now that we've made it and will be officially licensed, maybe you can check out some places for us to hang out our sign. How does Middleton and Rossi sound?"

"I like the name, but we'll have to duke it out about whose goes first."

Sam looked at him. His olive skin, dark-brown hair, and coffee-brown eyes made him a perfect specimen of Italian descent. It was a stark contrast to Sam's thick crop of ash-blond hair, fair skin, and eyes the color of deep sapphire. At six four and built like a football player, compared to Joe's five-foot-four, chubby frame, they were an unlikely pair. Their personalities similarly contrasted. Everyone wanted to be around Joe because of his gregarious disposition. Shy and reserved, Sam wished he could be more like him.

Close-knit allies since grammar school, Sam loved the guy like a brother. Humor and honesty went hand in hand with Joe. And if Sam was about to make a bad decision, Joe gave his opinion no matter how harsh. Most of all, Sam counted on him to listen whenever he needed to vent about another go-round with his dad.

Sam felt a jab hit his side.

"Get a load of that redhead."

He glanced at the gate, turned back, and gave Joe a slight shove. "Go on, get out of here. They're lining up to board."

"I want a postcard of a different architectural building every day. Well, not every day, but at least once a week."

"Sure thing." He slapped him on the shoulder and headed to the gate.

Sam felt the release of tension in his body as the plane took off. He was excited to experience the landscape, food, customs, and architecture, and Paris would be the perfect getaway from being the target of his father's wrath. When the flight attendant came around with snacks, soft drinks, beer, and wine, he thought, *To hell with my father. I may have one of each.*

As soon as they were able to move, he walked to the lavatory. While he waited, he faced the cabin. One individual wasn't hard to miss—the girl with the striking red hair. He decided to take a cue from Joe's playbook. Stop and say hello on his way back. But once he was closer, he returned to his seat. *What's the point? I'll never see her again, and my history with girls stinks.*

In high school, he'd dropped girlfriends the minute they got serious. In college, he'd dated the same girl for three years. She was beautiful, smart—a real catch by any guy's standards. But when she pushed for more, he broke it off. There was a reason he never wanted to commit: the miserable relationship between his parents and the fear he'd be quick to anger, like his dad.

Satiated, he fell into a deep sleep and woke with a start when the pilot announced they would land in ten minutes. He rubbed his eyes, looked out the window, and held his breath. The weather had cleared and made visible a structure no bigger than the size of a fingernail. He'd seen the iconic metal tower in pictures and movies. Soon, he'd be able to view its magnificence and touch it.

The energy was palpable as throngs of people crisscrossed Charles de Gaulle Airport. A lightness in his step, Sam headed toward baggage claim. Tracking the carousel for his bag, he recognized the redhead a few feet from him. He frowned. She had a desolate look in her eyes. How could anyone feel anything but excitement in one of the most popular cities in the world? With a swift kick to the side of the conveyor belt, he thought, *Stop wasting your time trying to puzzle out a stranger.* Almost missing his duffel bag, he heaved it off the track.

When he looked up, she had disappeared into the crowd. Outside the terminal, the frigid January air bit his skin. He slipped on a jacket and hailed a cab.

"Bonjour, monsieur. Where can I take you?"

He leaned forward. "Bonjour. The Sorbonne."

2

MADDIE
JANUARY 1965

STANDING IN THE kitchen, twenty-one-year-old Maddie O'Dell's eyes held a sheen of unshed tears. Laugher and joy had been lost to a pall of darkness that emerged from every corner. She knew she could never live in a place that no longer felt like a home. Painful memories of the family she'd lost would be sure to resurface when she had to choose which room to clear out first.

To stall, she opened the refrigerator to force something into her empty stomach. It held nothing but an outdated carton of milk, two slices of spoiled lunch meat, and cheese. She sucked in a long breath. *Everything is an effort—grocery shopping, cooking, eating, getting out of bed.* Releasing a strong exhale as she closed the door, the phone ring. It was Julia, her roommate since freshman year at Northeastern University.

"How is it going?"

"I can't get motivated."

"Take a break. Meet me at the coffee shop in half an hour."

When Maddie had first met Julia, she'd been taken aback by her unrestrained joy and high spirit. Contrary to her own leaden view of life, Maddie had thought, *This is going to be disastrous. I need a calmer roommate.* But underneath the fun-loving exterior, Julia had a heartfelt compassion for all things, big and small. In her, Maddie had found a best friend and confidante—someone she'd learned to trust with the tragedies that befell her.

In the past, she'd tried everything to make sense of what had happened. Reading about the four stages of grief, talking with a therapist, attending group therapy, which left her more depressed, and the fury she'd felt when the parish priest said, "God took them home. They're in a better place." Julia had responded differently. She'd listened, really listened, and never once offered unhelpful platitudes.

Last week's nor'easter brought six inches of snow, making Maddie shiver as she trudged through it. When she opened the door, the harsh wind blew her into the coffee shop. She stamped her boots, found a corner booth, and pulled off her hat and coat. Sitting with two coffees and two chocolate covered jelly donuts, the tension in her body evaporated the minute Julia burst through the door.

Julia plunked down her body. "I hate this damned New England weather."

"When you're baking in India's stifling heat, you'll be wishing for the cold."

"Can you believe it? Me, in India?"

Maddie rolled her eyes. "That doesn't surprise me after seeing you stroll around campus dressed in colored peasant blouses and striped bell-bottoms. Each time I walked into our room, you were in a crossed-legged position, eyes closed, humming a chant that made no sense to me. I still can't piece together how a Bible-reading Irish girl did a three-sixty."

"You're not the only one. It's been a drag listening to my family lecture me on how irresponsible I am for wasting my psych degree by traipsing through a third-world country. All they want is for me to get married and give them a dozen grandkids." She paused. "I'm an inconsiderate idiot for ragging on about my parents when you don't . . ."

"Any other time, hearing about them would make me laugh, but I've dreaded the thought of going through all the rooms in the house." A fist against her cheek, Maddie said, "I had such good intentions, but maybe it's too soon. I don't know what's worse: box everything before I leave or deal with them when I come back."

Julia reached for her hand. "The change in scenery, exciting classes, visiting all those wonderful places, meeting new people—it's the best medicine to help you deal with everything you've been through. If I could, I'd stay and help you, but I can't change my flight."

"I'll be okay. What choice do I have except to move forward? And you're right, it should be good for me." Intuitive as her friend was, Julia didn't catch the uncertainty in her voice.

Maddie stared out the window. She squeezed her eyes shut to keep a wave of tears from coming. *It's been ten years, and the past still haunts me. Will it ever end?* A blanket on her lap, she rested her head against a pillow and thought about Paris and the dream of visiting landmark sites, studying art, and painting. Would Paris be the game changer? Give her a new perspective? Renew her faith in humanity?

Her mother's voice floated in her head. *Maddie, life is precious. Never waste a second of it. This is your trip of a lifetime. Take it all in for both of us.* She whispered, "I'll try, Mom. I'll try." She reached into her bag and unwrapped the Christmas present from her father. It was a magenta, brocade journal with her initials etched in gold on the cover. She used the silk, silver ribbon to open it. A sealed pink envelope from her mother's stationery lay there. In her father's right-handed scrawl, he had written, "To the best daughter a father could ever wish for." She took out a folded letter on the same delicate paper.

My dearest Maddie,

I remember your mother spending hours talking to you about Paris and her desire to go, but she unselfishly gave it up for her family. My heart tells me she'll be smiling down on you as you fulfill her dream. Use this journal to write about all the wonderful things and places you'll experience. Feel her presence wherever you go, especially at the top of the Eiffel Tower. When you return, I'll be waiting with open arms to pull you into those bear hugs you love. Have a wonderful time and remember not to let the past rule your life like it did mine for so many years. Keep your heart and mind open. There is still so much good in the world waiting to receive you.

Love,
Dad

Tears sprang to her eyes. *Oh, Dad, if only you were still around to hug me.* When the sounds of unbuckled seatbelts blended with the buzz of excitement, she slid the letter back in the envelope. The plane had landed, and a voice over the intercom announced, "This is your captain speaking. *Bienvenue à Paris.* Welcome to Paris."

Weaving through the congested terminal made her light-headed. Taking a seat by enormous paned windows, she rested her head between her knees. If she couldn't get through the airport, how would she manage alone in a strange city? *This won't work. I should turn around and fly back home. But to what—a grief that would swallow me whole again?*

When the symptoms subsided, she looked around. Everyone seemed to move with a purpose. With single-minded determination, she thrust her chin high, picked up her bags, and left.

Holding the door open with a foot, Maddie grappled with her belongings. The lobby of the low-budget hotel desperately needed a drastic overhaul. Four orange, plastic chairs and a battered coffee table sat stationed in front of a garish yellow-and-red-plaid couch. A petite woman in a tired black dress stood behind the counter. The sparse gray bun on the top of her head was drawn so tight it overarched her eyebrows.

"Bonjour, madame. My name is Madelynn O'Dell. I have a reservation."

Dull, beady eyes glowered at her. When she spoke broken English, the tone had the edge of a steel blade.

"You a college girl?"

"Yes."

"I told my husband not to rent to you kids, but he never listens." A bony finger wagged at her. "No parties allowed inside the lobby or your room."

Itching to get away from the frosty sneer, Maddie asked, "Where is the elevator?"

"Behind you."

She pointed to the suitcase, a canvas bag with art supplies, and a portable easel. "Can anyone help me?" The woman shooed her away with a brusque *no*.

When the metal door slid open, she yelped. "What in the world?" The inside was so narrow, she had to sit on top of the suitcase and adjust the rest of her belongings on her lap. Her hands pressed against the walls, the elevator clattered. When the door cleared, she hopped off and scrambled to get everything out. Weighted down, she lumbered along the gloomy hallway and unlocked the door to 365. It was as bleak as the lobby. A lifeless room, painted a sorry blue, housed an uninviting twin bed, a bedraggled nightstand, a pockmarked desk, and another orange, plastic chair. Nothing could disguise the brown-stained carpet. *I've got two weeks in this seedy place before I move into the apartment. Thank you, Dad, for the extra money.*

Careful not to bring too many clothes, she'd packed only the essentials to get through the changes in weather. A minimalist for makeup, a mesh purse held a pink lipstick and a compact of blush. For sentimental reasons, she'd brought the three-piece brushed-nickel dresser set embossed with an ornate design her mother had bought. It was meant to control her untamable mass of red hair. She smiled. *You should have saved the money.* When she turned and saw a view of the Eiffel Tower outside the window, her eyes smarted with tears, and the smile dissolved. *Mom, you should be the one here.*

3

SAM

AS SOON AS Sam got squared away in the dorm, he walked outside to find a café and order a double espresso. The sky was overcast with clouds, and the temperature felt like it was below zero. Relieved to get out of the cold, he entered Café de Flore near the campus. He'd read about this place, the oldest coffee shop in Paris, and couldn't wait to try it.

The moment he opened the door, thick, acrid swirls of smoke and a myriad of indistinguishable languages assaulted his senses. As he waited in line, his eyes scanned the room. Mirrors over the red-upholstered booths reflected understated lighting and made the mahogany paneling glow. It definitely had an Art Deco vibe, and he found it easy to imagine this as a hangout for writers and musicians back in the roaring twenties.

He wove between occupied booths in search of an empty seat. In a far corner, he approached a guy dressed in a black turtleneck, black slacks, and a matching beret. The man pointed to himself and the chair.

"*Oui. Soit mon invité.*"

He knew what *oui* and *invité* meant. Using the best accent he could muster, he said, "*Merci.*"

"*Mon nom est Antoine.*"

"I'm Sam," and shook his hand.

"*Ravi de vous rencontrer.*"

Unable to decipher what he said, Sam looked at him sheepishly and shrugged. Silence followed until Antoine stood, nodded, and left. *This is the last time I go anywhere without my French pocket dictionary.*

On his way back to campus, he wandered the tree-lined streets of the Latin Quarter and noticed a variety of architectural styles in the buildings and churches. The city would be his laboratory, a place where he'd test ideas and garner inspiration. And when classes started, he'd be able to study the sites with the eyes of an architect. The opportunity to see rich historical architecture of every period, from the Middle Ages to the twentieth century, escalated his excitement.

Passing an old movie theater, quaint shops, and a cafe on every corner, a secondhand bookseller caught his eye. Packed with an eclectic group of people, he strolled in and browsed through the aisles.

When he walked by two girls engrossed in a photography book of Paris, he said, "Are you students at the university?" They smiled, nodded yes, and shifted their attention to another girl who greeted them. About to leave, he spotted the redhead in a corner, looking at postcards. Undecided about whether to put himself out there, Joe's voice popped into his head. *Don't be a wuss.* He wandered over and said, "Hello."

His breath hitched when she looked up. The glow of her emerald eyes mesmerized him. *God, she's even more stunning up close.* The postcards fell to the floor, and when they bent down, his fingers tingled as they grazed hers. When they stood, he said, "I recognized you from the plane." She left the postcards on the counter, mumbled a thank-you, and walked out. *That went well,* he thought dryly.

Back in the dorm room, someone had settled in. Tossed on the bed was a white hoodie with Norway spelled in red and blue above the country's flag. *Whoever he is, I hope he speaks English, or it's going to be a long four months.* As soon as he finished his thought, a tall, brawny guy with a large forehead, a slim, pointy nose, disheveled light-brown hair, and hazel eyes shot through the door and skidded to a stop. *Here goes nothing.* Extending his hand, he said, "Hi, I'm Sam."

"Good to meet you. I'm Kristoffer. Kris to my friends."

He laughed. "You speak English."

"Looks like you do too." His answer accompanied a grin as wide as his shoulders.

"So," Sam asked, "what brings you to Paris?"

"The architecture and the girls."

"In that order?"

"Depends on the girl. How about you?"

"Same as you . . . architecture."

"What, no girls?"

"Not sure. Depends on my hectic class schedule."

"I give you a week and you'll change your mind."

"We'll see. Where did you go to school?"

"Oslo School of Architecture and Design. I convinced my parents to let me do my last semester here. How about you?"

"An architecture school in Boston. I have my license, but I wanted to take a few European courses. Paris seemed the best placed to do it. I noticed one of the books on your bed. We're in the same class."

"Great. If I don't make it, I can get your notes."

"I don't come cheap."

"Some days it might be worth it."

A reminder of Joe's cheerfulness and humor, he felt the weight of his dad's constant anger and disapproval melt away.

On the first day of the history of Parisian architecture class, Sam was dressed and ready to go before Kris crawled out of bed. He poked his shoulder and said, "Get a move on. You're going to be late."

He pulled the covers over his head. "I'm not a morning person. It was stupid to sign up for this class."

"Ever hear the quote by Shakespeare?"

"Don't tell me."

"Better three hours too soon than a minute too late."

"Ugh. I'm living with a nerd who quotes a dead guy at seven-thirty in the morning. Go on. Get out of here."

He was partway out the door when Kris said, "Besides being a nerd, are you always on time?"

"Yep." He had learned from his father that if he didn't show up at the dictated hour, he'd suffer the consequences. It had been a hard-won lesson but proved to be prudent now. "See you in class."

Sam made a quick stop at the campus dining hall, bought two coffees, and entered the auditorium. Like the Café de Flore, it was a melting pot of foreign languages. To stay alert, he knocked back the caffeine. All night, he'd lain awake, trying to figure out how to sleep through the sounds made by his roommate. Flung pillows did nothing to halt the loud snores that came in fits and starts.

The noise level in class dropped several decibels but shattered when the door banged open. Swiveling around, Sam watched Kris bulldoze his way inside. He waved and gestured to the seat next to him and handed him a coffee.

"Thanks, pal. I needed this."

"Not more than me."

Kris joked, "Tough time sleeping in a strange bed?"

"More like a rotten night sleeping with someone who sounds like a freight train coming through the walls."

"It happens when I'm on my back. Next time, give me a shove and I'll roll over."

"If that doesn't work, I'll hit you with one of your size thirteen shoes. Those things are big enough to ski on."

Conversations stopped when the professor marched in with a lit cigarette suspended from his mouth. Short and stout with a handlebar mustache, he wore a black beret, dark-navy tweed suit, and a white shirt with a skinny blue necktie. Sam whispered to Kris, "Crap, I hope we can understand him." His concern abated when the professor spoke perfect English with a lilt of a French accent.

At the end of class, they stood in the hallway, going over the syllabus. "This should be interesting," Kris said. "Lectures two days a week and one day for field assignments. No classes for the second half, only an individual research project."

When Sam looked up, he frowned. The girl with the red hair hurried past them. *This is the third time I've seen her. What are the odds she's in the same class?* He felt a nudge.

"Hey, you concerned about the syllabus? I think we got lucky with this one."

"Nope, I'm good with it." His eyes followed her out the door.

Kris laughed. "So much for classes being the only thing on your mind."

His face flooded with heat. "Don't be stupid. Let's get something to eat."

Before they entered the dining hall, Sam groaned, "Christ, this batshit weather sucks." He glanced at Kris, whose only defense against the cold was a sweatshirt. "Man, how can you stand it?"

"When you grow up in Oslo, the winters can get down to minus thirteen degrees. This is a heat wave for me."

In line for food, Sam's eyes took in the savory meal selections. He settled on a baguette with a pork rib in Dijon sauce and a cake made of alternate layers of puff pastry topped with chocolate drizzled sugar icing. Except for the dessert, Kris had ordered the same thing.

Kris said, "Man, I don't know about the colleges in the States, but the food where I went. . . all I can say is I survived on burgers and pizza."

"Me too. It made me miss my mom's cooking even more. Any brothers or sisters?"

"Five. I'm the only guy. Imagine what it's like living with four girls." Kris scowled. "All of them going through stupid girly stuff at different stages. I can't tell you the number of times my dad lost his temper. He loves us, but it's nice to be out of the madhouse for a while. How about you?"

"Just me."

"It must have been great as a kid. All the attention. No bickering or fighting."

"I hated it. Being an only child is nothing to celebrate."

"How come?"

Filled with heavy resentment, he said, "It was like being under a microscope. Zero got past my dad. One wrong move and I suffered for it." He shook his head. "You ready to split? My next class is ten minutes away, and you know me, I don't want to be late."

About to empty the tray, he stopped. The redhead was sitting alone, staring down at her empty plate. He took another chance and approached her. "Hi, I'm Sam. We're in the same class." In one swift move, she slid back her chair, picked up her tray, gave him an unconvincing smile, and left.

He muttered, "I got the message," as he walked away.

4

MADDIE

MADDIE WOKE TO a beam of bright sunshine. When her stomach rumbled, she realized the last thing she'd had was airplane food twelve hours ago. Ready in record time, she eyed the elevator, reconsidered, and took the stairs. The smell of freshly brewed coffee reached her nose, and for the first time since she'd arrived in Paris, she smiled.

A pot of coffee, cream, sugar, and five croissants on a platter were set up on a small card table. Grateful Marcelline wasn't there to greet her with a surly tongue, she drained her cup and polished off a croissant. Satisfied, she dug into a satchel and removed the guidebook recommended by her college professor.

A clear anchor of where to start appeared impossible with the forbidding diagrams of colored lines twisted in a chaotic maze. A one-thousand-piece Jackson Pollock puzzle would have been a more manageable challenge. Her smile fell in a straight line. *How am I going to confront this confusing city alone?* Determined to circumvent the rising panic, she thought, *Stop the nonsense. It can't be more difficult than navigating my life at home.*

Up and down streets, she roamed the city. As the early-morning sun disappeared, the temperature dropped like a stone. A chill seeped in, and the air on her face felt like frozen lace. Fingers curled in gloves, she attempted to salvage the remnants of heat. For relief, she walked into a café. Warm and inviting, she sat by the window and frowned at the crumpled map. When a server approached, she said, *"Pouvez-vous m'aider?"*

"You are American."

A blush crept up from her collar. "Sorry, it's my bad accent."

"Oh no, mademoiselle. It is perfect. I have a keen eye for anybody who isn't a local." She grinned. "Unless you are wearing black, gray, or navy, you are not considered French. We have the expression, 'Black is such a cheerful color.'"

Maddie's insides tightened. *I'll never fit in.* Black reminded her of wakes and funerals.

"How may I assist you?"

She pointed to the map. "How do I get here?"

"After crossing the Pont des Art bridge, you'll be on the Right Bank of the Seine, which is in the First Arrondissement."

She found her way to the bridge and passed through Place Vendôme, but the weather was too unforgiving to wander around the massive entrance to the Royal Palace. She decided to walk to the Louvre. When she entered, a rush of excitement sent added color to her windswept red cheeks. More impressive than she expected, it would take months of concentrated examination without sleeping or eating. Too late to check out the Impressionist gallery, she stopped to see the world's most celebrated portrait.

A handful of people stood in front of the *Mona Lisa*, which was behind a glass barrier. According to several historians, the painting marked the birth of her second son after the death of her two-year-old daughter. She wondered what message her enigmatic smile conveyed. Most people would say happiness, but her artist's eyes suggested a different emotion—a hidden sadness. A soreness crept into her throat. *Thinking about my losses, am I projecting my own feelings?* It didn't seem to matter where she was. The cutting memories kept them alive.

After a dreary evening in her room, an incalculable loneliness swept through her while she listened to peals of laughter floating from the lobby. The attempt to deflect her melancholy by writing in the journal failed. *What joy would it be to look back and read about the sad look on Leonardo da Vinci's masterpiece, or the despair I feel when I pass someone dressed in dark clothing?* As the sounds dissipated from below and exhaustion seeped in, she murmured, "Let tomorrow be a better day."

Maddie stepped outside to sunlit clouds drifting across a clear blue sky. It made the day more hospitable than yesterday's foul weather. She thought, *Not a small thing to be grateful for.* She made her way to the Pont Neuf bridge and leaned against one of the semicircular areas jutting out from the path. Several houseboats were moored next to the bridge. Others floated along the Seine. *I wonder how it feels to live in one. If I didn't mind the peering tourists, I could see the positives to living on the water.* Her home would always move, and she could change course whenever she needed to escape.

Amid the tourists and locals nudging their way through markets and cafés, she crossed the bridge and looked upward at the tall, vertical twin towers of Notre-Dame Cathedral and the Eiffel Tower. *Do these magnificent structures still register with Parisians as they hurry past them? I suppose it's easy to get stuck in a state of forgetting—something I'll never be able to do.* Her innermost thoughts conjured up a question. *What would my mother say about my incessant emotional reactions to an upended life?* Probably the same thing her father wrote in his letter. "Don't let the past rule your life." Excellent advice, but no one she cared about was here to remind her.

She turned toward a steady hum of voices that broke into boisterous cheers at a wedding couple being photographed. Her eyes crinkled, and the sullen mood was interrupted when the bride lifted the frilly white gown and flashed a pair of bright red sneakers. She whispered, "Life is short. Love like there's no tomorrow." She sighed. *Advice I can't seem to follow.*

Maddie entered the historic Latin Quarter, the bohemian heart of the city, where students with book bags huddled together in small groups. Clouds of smoke hovered over their heads from the flickering lights of cigarettes. She was suddenly leery of renting an apartment in this noisy area but had chosen it because of the closeness to the university. Now, she regretted not staying in a quieter place.

Standing in the largest square in Paris, she fussed, "Stop being an idiot. You'll be fine."

As soon as she moved her position, a ghastly color spread across her face. In front of her stood the Saint-Michel Fountain. As a child, her mother and the nuns in catechism class told her angels were a stand-in for God and that they would safeguard everyone she loved. She'd believed it. Embraced it.

When she had made her First Communion, she'd been given a holy card with the prayer of Saint Michael on the back. Wherever she went, she kept it close—in a pocket, backpack, lunchbox, or tucked under her pillow when she slept. If someone needed to be watched over, like her best friend or her baby sister, she had read the prayer out loud to make sure she'd been heard.

At eleven years old, it all changed. The idea of the archangel, the powerful protector against evil who was supposed to protect her mother and sister from a violent death, proved to be a flagrant lie.

5

SAM

A SHORT DISTANCE from the university, Sam's last field assignment was the Saint-Sulpice church. The bright sun quickly lost its power to another blast of frigid air. He tugged at the wool hat to protect his reddened ears, pulled the scarf over blue-tinged lips, and crammed his hands in his pockets. Every morning, the weather was a test of endurance and how to dress.

"Christ," Kris said. "You look like Nanook of the North. How the heck are you breathing in that getup?"

Through chattering teeth, Sam replied, "I'm not. It burns like hell when I inhale. If this continues . . ."

Kris snickered. "You should have gone to Mexico."

"Where's your sympathy? Never mind, you don't have any."

"Not for a six-four guy who's built like a brick wall. Looks like you'll have to suck it up. If we run, it'll bring in some heat."

He nodded, and they took off in a mad sprint.

The professor, suited for the Antarctic, approached the class. He waved them into a circle. "Unfortunately, much of France is still in the middle of a rare cold snap."

Sam eyed the vaporized puffs of breath swirling above his classmates' heads and joined the grunts and foot stamping.

"I can only imagine what you're thinking. Why does anyone offer this course in January? *Je n'ai aucun contrôle sur la température ou le semestre. Ca devrait durer une autre semaine.*"

Kris elbowed him. "Want to translate?"

"Sure, when I get my French degree."

Someone yelled, "He says he has no control over the schedule or the temperature."

"I will keep the lecture brief. This building took one hundred forty years to build under the direction of the most prestigious architects. It has a Baroque-style edifice and is the second largest in Paris after Notre-Dame. Notice the fifteen-foot difference in the two towers and how they're slightly lopsided. Many feel it marred the overall harmony. Do as much sketching as your fingers can tolerate. Then go inside and take notes on the interior. Anyone who is an art major, check out the painting by the Italian Renaissance painter Masaccio. Your final reminder: one week to hand in an eight-page paper on the history of the architecture, its famous builders, and your drawings. When you've completed your work, may I suggest a warm, comforting cup of *chocolat chaud vin chaud.* If you prefer something stronger, try *noel.* In English, it's called Irish Whiskey."

The drawings completed, the class moved inside and spread out. When Sam finished his notes, he joined Kris at the front of the church's gilded pulpit. "See the redhead sitting by herself?"

"Yeah, what about her?"

"Half the semester is almost over, and I've never seen her talk to anyone before or after class. And at every assignment, she's always off to the side. What do you think is going on with her?"

"Don't know. Maybe she's shy. Why don't you go talk to her?"

"I've tried and got nowhere. Maybe I'm giving off the wrong vibe."

"I'm done here, but I'd be happy to stay and put in a good word for you."

Sam gave him a light shove. "You're such a jerk."

"If you try again, at least get her name. You can't continue to call her the redhead. And if she stiffs you, several of us will be at our usual hangout. A few belts of whiskey will ease your pain."

Risking another blow-off, he stopped as he got closer to her. *Jesus, she looks like she's been crying.* As he was about to ask if she was okay, she got up and left without a glance in his direction. A distorted pamphlet about the painting *Madonna and Child with Angels* was left in the pew. *What the heck? Each time I've seen her, she's upset. Do I really want to bother with a girl who seems to have emotional issues?*

Two weeks later, the brutal temperatures melted the memory of *chilled to the bones.* The vibrancy in the city bounced back, and the warmth made it more agreeable to study outside. Sam and Kris walked to the extra credit assignment, the last one before the independent study.

Sam said, "We lucked out with the weather. How much warmer do you think it will get?"

Kris took out the pocket tourist guide. "Says here it's sixty degrees in April, sixty-nine in May, and the best part . . . spring is the perfect time to indulge in the desires of the city of romance. Fall in love with the culture, the history, the picturesque scenery—and the girls."

He laughed. "That last part is a nice addition even if it's not true."

"In my book, it is. Since we're on the subject, I've been wondering about something. We've been here, what, almost two months, and the gang we hang around with, me included, have calendars that are keeping us busy. As far as I can tell, you haven't dated since we got here. Is there a steady back home?"

He pushed a playful tone. "Nope, I'm a free agent."

"Then what gives?"

He released a long, drawn-out sigh. "The redhead."

"There are a million girls you can target. Take my advice. Stop wasting your time."

He didn't know why, but despite her strange behavior, she had this magnetizing effect on him, and it wasn't because she was heart-stopping gorgeous.

When Sam and Kris got to the public square in the Latin Quarter, Sam stood at a distance. His open-mouthed stare captured the full breadth of the Saint-Michel Fountain. Unlike other Parisian fountains, at eighty-five feet, its design used a mix of blue and yellow stone with green and red marble. Nearer to the ground were two ferocious-looking, water-spouting dragons. He moved in to get a closer look at the sculpture of the archangel holding a sword poised to strike the demon.

Architecture could communicate a hundred unique stories, but his was a personal interpretation. Growing up, it'd been difficult doing battle with his father. But the older he got, the less he'd felt like the smaller, weaker opponent facing a stronger adversary. The altercation in the kitchen before he left for Paris had proved his father no longer had power over him or his life.

"If you're finished," Kris said, "a group of us are heading over to Café Mabillon."

"I'll catch up with you later." He bought an expresso, leaned against the pedestal that supported one of the winged dragons and waited for the redhead to appear. He allowed himself to romanticize their encounter. She would be hesitant at first, but once he told her how much he'd been wanting to meet her, she'd blush and say, "I know. I've been wanting to meet you, too."

Together, they would walk back to campus and talk about how much they had in common. And before they said goodbye, he would ask her out on a date. He scowled. *How's that gonna work? In her world, I don't exist.* He thought of another approach. More direct. More forceful. *I'm a great guy. Let me take you out and I'll prove it. Right, Sam, that would be one hell of a big turn-on.*

He looked at his watch. Daylight would soon fade, and the sun would set in twenty minutes. Everyone in the class was long gone. It finally sunk in. She wasn't coming. Pissed for being such a jackass, he spun on his heels and left.

By the time Sam arrived, the cafe bustled with students and tourists. Still trying to get rid of his frustration, he found his way to his friends. He listened to conversations ranging from the Vietnam War, France's launch of its first satellite into orbit, and their favorite topic—girls. One of them said, "Who makes the best dates— French, Norwegians, Italians, Swedes, Americans, or the Irish?"

They agreed, if she was hot and available, it didn't matter. With no interest in offering an opinion, he remained silent until Kris mentioned a guy he'd met while ordering at the counter.

"His name is Rafe, and he's a grad student at the university. He invited me and anyone else to his apartment tonight. Are any of you interested?" Two of them said yes. He looked at Sam. "What do you say? I know you're not much of a party animal, but a couple of beers won't hurt, and it should be fun."

Sam enjoyed the occasional beer, but he would never forget the night he'd come home shit-faced and past curfew.

Sam had staggered into the dark foyer and felt a tight squeeze around the back of his neck. Whoever it was had superhuman strength. "Mom! Dad! Someone's broken in!" Shoved across the room, he had fallen onto the couch. When he looked up, he gasped. Illuminated by the static of the TV, his father's face had looked like a grotesque pulp of beet red flesh.

"Jesus, Mary, and Joseph," he shrieked. "What the hell is wrong with you?"

His father threw a fist in his face and said, "You're drunk."

Sam's mouth went dry, and his heart pounded in his chest. His father had never hit him, but there was always a first time. He stood, braced for the punch, and tried to gauge another way out—his mother. *Where the Christ is she?* Then he remembered— she was working. Terror and anger bubbled inside him. "Do it. You've been dying to, so get it the fuck over with!" Then he quickly changed his mind. With a body check to his father, he made a mad sprint for the stairs. Drenched in sweat, his legs like jelly, he ran to the bathroom and locked the door. Splashing water on his face, he'd tried not to look in the mirror. Every time he had, the sight of his dad's image had caused his insides to curdle.

Sam felt Kris shake his arm.

"Hey, you okay? You've got this crazed expression on your face."

He rubbed his clenched jaw. "Let's go to the party."

The apartment was in a run-down neighborhood near the campus. Up three flights, the stairwells vibrated with earsplitting, mind-numbing music. Once inside the room, the stench of cigarette smoke and the pungent smell of pot choked Sam with every inhale. When the soles of his shoes stuck to the floor from all the spilled drinks, he flattened against the wall and watched the mob spiral out of control.

Two guys in a fistfight crashed into him. As the heat of his anger drove up from his gut, he decided to get the hell out before he did something he would regret. Eyes red with irritation, clothes and hair reeking of smoke, he thought, *Dad, you were right about one thing: whoever or whatever makes you lose control leads to no good. Too bad you never got the memo.* He will never forget get all the years he'd been made to feel unworthy and not good enough. And how, whenever he looked at his father, he wished he was dead or had the means to get rid of him for good.

Seeing Kris and his friends in the middle of the pack, he pointed to the door and shouted above the madhouse. "I'm out of here." As he headed for the dorm, despite the warmth of the evening, he shivered at the thought of a dark cloud hovering over his future.

6

MADDIE

MADDIE'S INTEREST IN the history of Parisian architecture surprised her. Studying the legendary buildings and structures, she realized there was a strong correlation between artists and architects—they were both sources of inspiration. She would have enjoyed the class more if her body didn't freeze up because of a guy who kept checking her out and trying to talk to her. She had never gotten over the fear of a depraved stranger coming out of nowhere, like the one who savagely attacked her mother and sister. Since that day ten years ago, she'd never felt comfortable or safe around anyone except Julia.

The semester half over, it was disheartening the way those feelings had hindered her ability to connect with others in a city known for its beauty, wealth of art, and culture.

But her time in Paris turned around when she met Nancy—a fun-loving, outgoing California girl who had recently moved into an apartment on the same floor. She had a way of filling space with her laugher and positive energy. A reminder of Julia, it was hard to forget their first encounter in the hallway of the shared bathroom.

"Hi, I'm Nancy. I'm two doors down from you."

"I'm Maddie."

"You're the painter in number ten."

She had managed a shy smile. "How did you know?"

"Twice you left your door open, so I peeked inside. Your work is fab, but—and don't take offense—you need to do something about that outfit. Remember, you're in Paris."

She had tugged at the collar of her cotton blouse. "Really? What's wrong with how I look?"

"Everything. Hey, it's Saturday. Are you busy right now?"

"No."

"Great, I'm taking you shopping."

Unable to protest, Nancy had drawn her down the stairs and out the door. Outside a quaint boutique, Maddie had gawked at the garish sight of two mannequins draped in every color that existed in the largest box of Crayola crayons. "You can't be serious." But she was.

She had led her through a bright purple door and pointed to the dressing room. An assortment of patterned garments followed. Expected to be worn together in layers, she held each item up to her chin. Nothing matched, and there were way too many tassels and fringes. "Oh, dear Lord, it's so not me."

Excited, Nancy said, "Hurry up. I'm eager to check out the new and improved you."

When she had tiptoed out and studied her appearance in the mirror, she had erupted into a fit of laugher. *I can't see myself carrying this off, especially in public.*

"*Parfait, Mademoiselle O'Dell.* Now, you epitomize the classic boho attire."

Maddie woke, stretched her arms overhead, yawned, and kicked off the covers. Her eyes circled the one-bedroom apartment. She loved every inch of the cracked ceiling, scuffed hardwood floors, and chipped blue walls. Resting amid the blue flakes were her paintings. It pleased her how they captured the lifestyles of the Parisians by using the backdrops of her favorite places around the city. They also included three paintings she had done for inspiration at the Museé d'Orsay. When the gurgling in her stomach hinted she needed food, she quickly dressed, grabbed her notebooks, and headed out the door.

When Maddie traversed the maze of narrow streets, she stopped to check her reflection in a shop window. Decked out in a white peasant blouse belted over a floral hippie skirt, with a green beret angled on her head, she turned from side to side and giggled. Under normal circumstances, she never would have had the audacity to dress this way. It had taken a week to get used to the physical transformation, but when she decided to consider the look as a work of art, it boosted her confidence.

She ventured to other places to eat besides the campus dining hall and the food stands. But she was partial to the Shakespeare and Company Café with its magnificent views of Notre-Dame Cathedral. Tiny inside, with limited seats, it wasn't the go-to café for fresh-baked breads and crêpes sizzling in butter. It was all about the atmosphere. Never tired of looking at the decorated walls of great writers and artists, she fantasized the prickly disagreements on the right way to apply paint color, the correct style of writing, or the political issues of the day.

As soon she spotted an available table on the patio, she sat and dug into a hefty portion of a sweet potato and mushroom quiche. If there was time, she decided to spend an hour in the adjoining bookstore with Zoe. She remembered the first time she'd stood at the entrance of the bookstore's second floor and stopped at the red staircase.

Each riser had hosted a segment of the quote, "I wish I could show you when you are lonely or in darkness the astonishing light of your own being." She thought, *I'm lonely everywhere, and it's hard to believe any light is beneath all the darkness.*

It had surprised her when Zoe, the resident calico cat, came out of hiding and rubbed up against her leg. The encounter lasted only seconds before the cat scampered up the stairs. She followed. On the second floor, tucked between floor-to-ceiling shelves, there were two girls sitting cross-legged on a cot, reading. Curious, she rounded a corner, saw an overstuffed chair, and sank into it. Before she had time to select a book, Zoe was nestled at her feet. When she reached down to stroke her back, a sudden warmth washed over her and she had wondered, *Maybe this is what I need. A pet that can offer companionship and make up for the emptiness.*

7

SAM

SAM WORKED IN the library, perusing his stack of notes and sketches. By 12:30 p.m., he was bleary-eyed and famished. The only thing he'd had was an extra-large expresso at seven in the morning. Instead of grabbing lunch on the fly, he decided to take a break and eat somewhere outside the campus. Choosing the Shakespeare and Company Café, he entered the packed room, ordered two bagels thick with ham and several cheeses, a large piece of apple pie, and coffee.

Only one empty seat remained on the patio, but it held a handbag. He gripped the tray when he recognized who occupied the other chair. He couldn't help but notice the way she was dressed. Unless he wanted to stand, he had no choice but to take the seat. Her head was down when he approached.

"Nice outfit," he said.

When she looked up, red traveled from her neck to her cheeks. She wasn't the only one with a reaction. It felt as if someone had turned up his internal heater. "Do you mind if I sit before someone steals this precious commodity?" She threw him a hesitant look before she removed the bag from the seat. "Did you know we're both taking the Paris history class?"

"Yes."

So, she does know I exist. "What are you doing for the final?"

"Museum architecture."

"Which one?"

"Two. The Louvre and Museé d'Orsay."

He sought to draw her out. "I heard someone say there are a hundred and thirty museums in Paris. Why those two?"

As if somebody flipped a switch, she hardly drew a breath between sentences. "There's quite a bit of history with the Louvre. It once served as a fortress, a dungeon, and a royal palace until it became a museum. During World War II, before the fall of France, much of its art collection had to be evacuated, hauled off on trucks, and transported in wooden cases to a French chateau. When the Nazis arrived, most of the museum had been emptied. Then in the 1900s, a handyman stole the *Mona Lisa* right off the wall. No one saw it was missing until twenty-six hours later. Visitors placed bouquets of flowers in the space because they were so upset. It remained vacant until its recovery two years later."

"You've piqued my interest. And the other museum?"

"Originally a Paris railway station and hotel, I chose it because of the large collection of Impressionist masterpieces."

He noticed she never made eye contact while she talked. "The interest in art, does it mean you're an artist?"

"Yes."

"Is this the reason you came to Paris?"

"Somewhat." She stood. Gather her things and said, "I still have a lot more to do on my paper."

The sudden decision to end the conversation baffled him. "Oh, okay. By the way, I'm Sam. Thanks for letting me join you."

"You're welcome."

"Before you take off, what's your name?"

"Maddie."

He rested his knuckles on his chin. *I have no idea how that went. Then again, maybe it's a start.* Not ready to tackle the assignment, he decided to skip the library and make use of the great weather.

It was warm with the right amount of breeze to hop on the secondhand bike he had purchased a month before. Whenever the weather permitted and there was time, he explored the neighborhoods on both sides of the Seine. The postcards he sent to Joe were about the architectural designs starting with Ancient Rome and the massive structures like Notre-Dame that had taken centuries to complete. Included were the fun parts: busy cafes, his eclectic group of friends, his roommate, and Maddie. What a talented artist she was. And with her beautiful, eye-catching red hair and green eyes, he wanted to get to know her better.

As he pedaled toward Concorde Square, he recalled how biking had been the highlight of his childhood. His first bike drew a blank, but getting the second one on his seventh birthday had been magical. A shiny black Schwinn Racer, it came with a certificate, numbered and registered by the company. The bike and its parts had been guaranteed for as long as he remained the sole owner. He and Joe had ridden everywhere together. On weekends, they took off in the morning and would be gone for hours. The wind had whipped their faces as they zoomed down hills with arms stretched out like Superman. But that wasn't the best part. The bike had been his ticket to freedom. Freedom to act like a normal kid, away from the prying eyes and threats of his father.

In the center of the square stood the three-thousand-year-old Luxor Egyptian Obelisk, the oldest monument in Paris. A gift from Egypt, the eighty-foot column of pink granite and the world's biggest sundial showed the time by its shadow. His attention drifted to the twenty-one panels of hieroglyphics, and he wondered what fascinating stories they revealed about their dynasties. It made him speculate about his extended family.

As a child, he'd had some great memories of his grandparents on his mother's side before they'd died. But he'd never met his father's. They'd passed away before he was born. *I wish I had known them. It might have been helpful for understanding the insane actions of my dad.* Another conversation he intended to have when he returned home..

At the Palais Bourbon, Sam considered biking around the gardens, but the Museé d' Orsay was nearby. Maddie had talked about it, so he decided to check it out. With a color-coded map, he tried to figure out where to begin and remembered she'd mentioned the Impressionist artists. He decided to start in that gallery. When he turned a corner, he saw her standing next to an easel with an arm across her chest, holding a palette.

He walked over. "Twice in one day."

When she nodded and turned back to the canvas he thought, *Was that a hint to leave her alone?* "I'll let you get back to your painting." He drifted through several other galleries and decided to return. "I had to come back and tell you what an incredible artist you are."

"Thank you," she said, and resumed painting.

Maybe she'll talk more if I mention what I saw in the Renaissance gallery. "Have you seen Raphael Sanzio's painting, *Saint Michael Vanquishing Satan*? It's pretty dramatic and reminds me of the extra credit assignment. Hey, when you're done, why don't we get together and share notes." Her face turned ashen, and her voice sounded like a fragile thread that threatened to snap when she told him she didn't do it. Before he could respond, she hurriedly put her art supplies away, grabbed her easel, and left.

He thought, *What the heck was it about mentioning the extra credit assignment that caused such a strong reaction?* Then he recalled the crumpled pamphlet of the painting *Madonna and Child with Angels* and how it looked like she had been crying when she'd rushed out of the church. He scratched his head. *Is there something about angels that overwhelms her? Was it me asking her out? Or is it something more serious?*

8

MADDIE

ON THE PONT Neuf bridge, Maddie secured the canvas on the portable tripod. Instead of the subject in front of her, she stared at the palette. She couldn't stop thinking about her reactions to Sam in the museum and all the other times he'd approached her. *He must think I'm crazy and regrets ever meeting me.* She snatched a tube of yellow and squeezed it so hard it landed on the blank canvas. *For heaven's sake, focus on what you're doing.*

"Hi, Maddie."

She whirled around and came close to stumbling over her feet. Embarrassed by the clumsiness, she stammered, "Ahh, umm, hi."

Sam asked, "Did you know this is the oldest bridge in Paris, the first one to cross the Seine and have sidewalks for pedestrians?"

It surprised her that he acted like nothing had happened in the museum. "I didn't."

"Here's another interesting fact: on official documents, they named them *people on foot.* Sorry about that. It's a bad habit of mine. Going off like an encyclopedia with facts no one cares about."

She smiled. "I'm sure you noticed from our conversation the other day I do the same thing."

"Since this is the third time we've met, don't you think it warrants at least a cup of coffee or an espresso? Who knows what else we might have in common. What do you say?"

"I'm sorry, I can't. I need to clean up this mess and do one more painting for art class."

"Another time?"

"Maybe." When his eyebrows angled and his smile faded, she wondered if he was confused, disappointed, or fed up with her evasiveness.

Back in her apartment building, she flopped on Nancy's bed and pulled a pillow over her head. "This guy keeps asking me out, and I either act like an idiot or give him lame excuses."

Nancy pulled the pillow away. "Next time say *oui*. It's easy. Just one syllable. Wait, he's not some weirdo, is he? There are lots of guys in Paris you don't want to hang out with."

"No, he seems really nice, but I didn't come here to get sidetracked from my studies."

She laughed. "Falling in love during your semester in Paris is practically on the syllabus."

"Love? Are you crazy?"

"Fine, but going on a date is not a marriage proposal. Quit being so serious. Go have some fun."

"I'm not good in social settings." Her cheeks turned a fiery red. "Especially with guys."

"You've got to be joking. Guess not by the color of your face. So, here's the thing. Let him steer the conversation. And a word of advice before you respond—don't stay inside your head and analyze every word out of your mouth. You'll end up having a miserable time."

"I swear, you sound like my best friend who has a psych degree."

"I'm honored. One more thing. The subjects you should avoid on the first date—politics, religion, and definitely do *not* mention sex. Plenty of time for that if things go well."

What would she say if she knew I was still a virgin?

On her way to the library to return a book, an image of Sam floated in the pool of her thoughts. Disappointed when a week went by and he hadn't sought her out, she realized how nice it would have been to spend more time with him now that the semester was almost over. Dismissing it, she thought, *Just as well. No need to fret about stepping out of my comfort zone or doing something stupid.* Suddenly, she sensed movement behind her and froze until she heard his voice. She turned.

"Hi, Maddie."

The way he said her name sent an unexpected flutter through her chest.

"I don't know about you, but I've been so doggone busy with finals, it's left zero time to sleep or catch a breath. I'm glad they're finished. Now it's a waiting game until they post the grades."

He looked like he had just woken up. His hair was a mess, and he wore sweats—not his usual clean-cut, preppie attire. Having only run a comb through her wild mop of red, she didn't fare any better. She laughed. "I've been living on black coffee and junk food from the campus dining hall. All I want is something decent to eat."

"I could use a good meal. Remember what you told me the last time? You said 'maybe' about coffee."

"I did."

"And?"

Is it his persistence or the unexpected warmth I feel that makes me want to say yes? Her mouth slipped into a grin. "Yes."

"Great. Give me a half hour to get out of these clothes, and I'll meet you in front of my building."

She turned to go, and in her excitement, she realized she didn't know which dorm. "Sam, what number is it?"

"Fifteen."

The last thing she heard as she headed toward her apartment was him saying, "I can't wait."

She whispered, "Neither can I."

Maddie took a quick shower and pulled out every piece of clothing on the rack. She decided to downplay the boho style. Except for the scarf tied around her rebellious mane, she chose a pair of jeans and a yellow T-shirt. A quick peek in the discolored mirror, she said, "God, I hate my hair. One of these days, it's going to meet the tips of a sharp pair of scissors." Something in that statement made her flesh crawl. Shaking it off, she shut her door, walked down the hallway, and bumped into Nancy.

"Whoa girl, slow down. Where are you off to in such a rush?" Her eyes widened. "The hint of light pink on your lips is telling."

She shifted her weight from side to side. "I'm meeting that guy."

"It's about time."

She tugged at the scarf. "How do I look?"

"Great. I want to know every single detail when you get back."

"Wish me luck."

"You're going to be fine." She waved her finger. "Remember, don't overthink. Be your sweet self, and he'll be the one who gets tongue-tied."

As Maddie hurried to the university, the weather remained perfect. Not a hint of a cloud, the sky was a dizzying blue, accompanied by a light breeze. She speculated on where he would take her. *Coffee seemed to be his thing.* But her eyebrows lifted when she saw him standing next to two bicycles with baskets—a blanket in one and a large white paper sack in the other. It had been years since she'd been on a bike. She had a flash of her dad running beside her, holding onto the back as her legs pedaled furiously. It had taken weeks before she was confident without training wheels. Now, she prayed she wouldn't humiliate herself.

"Have you been to the Champ de Mars Gardens?"

"No."

"It's a nice place for a picnic. But there's somewhere I want to stop along the way."

After a few stops and wobbles, her confidence grew. It made her feel like a Parisian as she rode alongside him through curving pathways, hidden alleys, and courtyards.

He pulled ahead when they rounded the corner and said, "*Voila!*"

"What is this place? It looks like a fairy-tale village!" Charming, shuttered houses in soft pastel hues lined the narrow, cobbled lane. This alone would have been enough to enchant her, but she clapped her hands in delight at the sight of a painted ginger cat hunting delicately painted birds on one of the houses. "These are incredible!"

He walked his bike beside her. "I can't figure out how the artists makes them look so three dimensional."

"They're called *trompe-l'œil*, which means *to fool the eye*."

"They sure do."

"How did you find this place, and why aren't there more tourists?"

"I came here after I overheard someone say it's a place few people are aware of." He whispered, "Let's keep it a secret."

An expert at keeping things to herself, she drew her thumb and index finger across her lips.

When they arrived at Champ de Mars gardens, Maddie helped spread out the blanket and watched as he set out a variety of gourmet cheeses, buttery baguettes, a box of colorful French macarons, and a bottle of white wine. She felt her heartbeat in her head. *It seems excessive for a first date. Is he expecting more?*

He poured two glasses of wine. "If you're wondering why so much food, I wanted to make sure I covered everything."

The heat rose in her cheeks for questioning his motive. As her lips curled around the rim of the glass, she waited for him to speak first.

"When do you graduate?" he asked.

"This is my last semester."

"What's next?"

"I have an adjunct position teaching art, and if I'm lucky, one or two of my paintings will be accepted at a gallery."

"You don't need any luck. You're too talented."

Her robust laugh surprised her. "I've been told I was born with a brush in my hand."

Sam wrapped his arms around his knees and leaned forward. "Why the interest in the Impressionists?"

"They have a wonderful way of using intense colors and emphasize painting landscapes outdoors. Because of their style, angry critics initially refused to let their work be exhibited in the Louvre." Her tone turned tart. "They compared it to ugly wallpaper."

"That's nuts. I'm no expert, but when I walked through the gallery and saw Monet's collection it was . . . I don't know what words to use."

"There's only one: *masterful.*" She changed the conversation. "When do you graduate?"

"I did. Now I have my architect license. Before my partner and I set up an office for our design company, I decided to do an additional semester in Paris."

"What made you decide to become an architect?"

"The blame goes to Santa. When I got my first Erector set at Christmas, I spent hours on the floor, constructing all kinds of elaborate structures. And the weekend my mom took me to New York City, the size of the Empire State Building blew me away. We rode the elevator to the top. When I stared at the skyline with all its tall buildings, I decided that's what I wanted to do with my life."

"Do you have any favorite structures or buildings?"

"There's only one in my book—the Eiffel Tower. It's *the* most incredible bunch of steel ever erected. I'll give you the short version; otherwise, we'll be here until midnight. In the late 1800s, it was the tallest manmade marker worldwide and took seven thousand tons of iron fitted together with 2.5 million rivets."

The more he talked, the more she felt a gravitational pull. It made her nervous, but she couldn't deny how much she liked him. Every time he smiled, her chest constricted around her heart.

"Over a hundred men worked on it, and they never lost a life during construction. Parisians weren't too happy because they considered the structure unsafe and an eyesore."

He stopped. "See what I mean about the data dumping?"

"Not at all. My mother would have enjoyed all the details."

"Has she ever been to Paris?"

A wave of hurt washed over her. "No. She always wanted to, but . . ." Unwilling to offer more, she picked at the cheese in her hand.

"I bet you'll have a lot to tell her when you go home."

She looked down at the mess in her lap. "I had a nice time, Sam, but I'd like to go now." He nodded, and they packed up the picnic.

Her bike did a slight zigzag when she stole a glance at him. His eyebrows were knit together, and his mouth was pursed. *He's upset with me, and I don't blame him. He planned a perfect afternoon, and what did I do? The same darn thing. Retreat into myself and avoid anyone who tries to get too close.* With an awkward silence between them, the ride back seemed like an eternity. When they reached the campus, she got off the bike, kept her eyes on the ground, thanked him, and left before he could respond.

Too embarrassed to tell Nancy how the day ended, she scurried past her door. Sitting on the couch, she wrapped her arms around her stomach and shook her head. *I ruined the day for both of us.*

9

SAM

WHEN MADDIE GOT off the bike and left, Sam thought, *If she walks any faster, her feet won't touch the ground.* Back in the dorm, he threw the pile of clothes off the chair and slumped into it.

Kris asked, "How did the date go?"

"I'm not sure. We were having a great time, sharing stuff about ourselves. Then out of nowhere, she wanted to leave."

"That's strange. From what you told me, so is she. Did you do or say anything that might have offended her?"

"The only thing I can think of was when I asked about her mother. After that, her whole demeanor changed." *Angels, paintings, and now her mother? This girl has some major issues, and yet . . .*

"You've been driving yourself batty over a girl who doesn't know what she wants. Forget her. Loosen up. Time for some real fun before you leave Paris. I say we go somewhere to liven you up."

"Nah. Not much in a party mood."

"You sure? Moping in the room won't help you get over her."

His shoulders dropped as if all the air had left his chest. It was too late for that.

The next morning, Sam decided he had to see Maddie again. She'd mentioned the street her apartment building was on was within walking distance from the school. With no number, he stood at the corner, knowing she would need to come this way to get to the heart of the city. All morning, he watched people on bicycles and couples holding hands pass by him. By late afternoon, his back ached, and the oppressive heat made his shirt cling to his chest. When the growling in his stomach reached his backbone, he questioned his stupidity. *Middleton, you are a fucking moron for coming up with this dim-witted plan. Move your sorry ass and go eat.*

He made his way to the street vendor across from the university. As he wolfed down his food, his heart faltered when he spotted Maddie. Head down, she was digging in her handbag. When she looked up, her eyes met his. His brow furrowed as she walked toward him.

"Hello, Sam. I want to apologize for yesterday. You planned a perfect day, and I cut it short."

He could tell she was nervous by the way she moved from one foot to the other. Happy to see her, he didn't ask why. "We were both tired after the final semester push. If I had any smarts, I would have stuck with the picnic."

A faint smile tipped the sides of her mouth. "Then I would have missed out biking around Paris and experiencing that wonderful street with all those lovely houses. Thanks again. Sorry I interrupted your lunch."

Don't let her leave until you ask her out again. "If you're not too busy, would you like to do something later this afternoon?" As he waited for her answer, his breath bottled up in his chest.

"Are you okay if I pick the place this time?"

Am I okay? Does she really need to ask? Tapping down his euphoria, he said, "Sounds good to me."

"I'll come by the campus around two."

As soon as she was out of sight, he pumped his fist in the air and whistled all the way back to the dorm.

When they stood at the bottom of a hilltop village in Butte-aux-Cailles, Sam asked, "Is this how we get there?"

"Yes. It's the only way to reach the Rue des Cinq Diamants." She nudged him. "It's quite a climb. Can you make it?"

He grinned and flexed his biceps. "This body is made for endurance."

"Sunday mornings are quiet because the locals aren't awake. Afternoons get noisy when the street-art lovers arrive."

He cocked his head. "Street-art lovers?"

"You'll see."

As they wove in and out of a labyrinth of cobbled streets, she took him on a tour past small houses draped with ivy and leafy green rooftops, quirky restaurants, cafes, bars, and boutiques. What grabbed his attention were the gigantic murals of musicians, graffiti, children, and animals on the facades of every building. "These are unbelievable."

"Famous artists come here from all over the world to exhibit their work. There's a saying, 'Life happens on streets. Why wouldn't art?'"

Sam stopped in front of the mural of a beggar lying curled up on the pavement.

Maddie murmured, "This one generates all kinds of emotions."

"It reminds me of the day—I must have been seven or eight—when my mom and I were about to enter a shopping mall. At the end of the sidewalk, a man was slouched against the building. He had an overgrown beard, greasy, matted hair that stuck to his scalp, wore filthy, tattered clothes, and had oversized shoes that exposed his dirty feet. People walked by him, pretended he wasn't there or made insulting comments. Someone even kicked him."

His voice grew thick. "I remember telling my mom how disgusting he was and someone should call the police and lock him up. All she said was, 'Let's go shopping.' When we walked out, my bag had a new denim jacket and a pair of Keds canvas high-tops. She took my hand and walked over to him. Knelt beside him and gave him a bag with a few things that would keep him warm: wool socks, a sweater, gloves, a scarf, and a hooded winter jacket. Dirt was caked under his fingernails, but it didn't stop her from pressing a five-dollar bill into his hand. The man had tears in his eyes when he said, 'God bless you for your kindness.' That day had a tremendous impact on me." He noticed her eyes mist over. "I guess it wasn't the most uplifting story to share."

"It's not that. Sometimes I get . . ."

"Get what?"

"Honestly, it's nothing. Let's keep walking. There's still a lot to see."

He stood in front of her and sensed an aching fragility about her guarded exterior. "Tell me. I'd like to know."

She hesitated before she said, "I lost my mom and sister when I was eleven."

"Oh God, I'm so sorry."

"Anyway, I loved your story, and your mom sounds wonderful. I'm pretty hungry. Do you want to get something to eat?"

When she shut down, it was his cue to move on. "I never say no to a meal in Paris."

"Good. You'll need an appetite. We're going to a place known for the best Parisian crepes."

Once they were seated, a server strolled over and handed them menus. After Maddie ordered, Sam handed back his and said, "I'll get whatever she's having." When they finished eating, he pushed back his chair. "These are fantastic, and I'm tempted to ask for seconds." When she stood to get someone's attention, he put his hands up. "Another bite and I won't be able to move. So are you looking forward to going home?"

"I'm staying another two weeks."

Without thinking, the words flew out of his mouth. "No kidding. So am I." In a week, he was supposed to be out of the dorm and on a flight home. He didn't know how he'd pull it off, but one thing was certain—he wasn't ready to say goodbye.

"Any plans for what you'll do with your time?"

Sam thought, *To see more of you.* "There are a few more buildings on my list to study. How about you?"

"There are three museums I haven't visited and at least a couple more paintings to do. If you don't want anything else, I'll pay the bill to free up the table."

He reached for the check at the same time she did. "Let me get this. It's my way of saying thanks for bringing me here." Their touch lingered for only a second when she pulled her hand away, but not before her cheeks reddened.

"No, it's my treat."

"I'll agree if you'll have dinner with me tomorrow night. Ever been to Le Polidor?"

"No."

"Neither have I, but one of the guys in my dorm told me it's good, and I've been wanting to try it since I got here."

"I'm not sure about tomorrow night."

Does she regret getting so personal with me? "I hope you can, and if you do, meet me at five thirty in front of the main entrance of the school."

A quiet panic spread, causing Sam's stomach to shift. *I have to find a place—and fast—but first, I need to change my flight.* He found a pay phone on campus, called the airline, got rebooked, and checked the bulletin boards for rooms to rent by the week. After multiple phone calls, he found one above a café on a side street near Maddie's apartment. The next call wouldn't be easy.

"Hi, Mom."

"It's so good to hear your voice. I've been crossing off the days until you're home."

"Please don't be upset, but I would like to stay longer. I won't get another chance to come back, and there's so much more to see and do." By the whooshing sound of her breath, he sensed the disappointment. Never one to refuse him, she said she understood and would wire the money. "Can you call Joe? Let him know about my change in plans? He was supposed to pick me up at the airport. Tell him I'll take a cab."

"Don't do that. If I'm working, Dad will."

He didn't mean to, but his tone was curt. "I'd rather take a cab."

"Sam, I want things to be different between you and your father. He wasn't doing well a while back, and I don't want either of you to regret not trying to meet each other halfway."

I have no desire to patch up what can't be repaired. "Is it serious?"

"A heart condition, but it's under control now."

Part of him wanted to say he wished it wasn't, but that would have hurt her. "You must be relieved. Sorry to keep this short, but I've got a lot to do. I promise to keep sending postcards. Love you, and thanks again for understanding, and for the extra money."

"I love you too."

He hung up the handset, and for a second, he reconsidered what he was doing. Throwing himself at a girl who gave no sign she had any real feelings for him. But any doubts were insignificant compared to his desire to be with her.

Kris thought he was nuts when he explained why he decided to stay. His last words had been, "I hope you know what you're doing—rearranging your life with no hint of where her head is. If you get dumped and I'm still here, find me before you leap off the Eiffel Tower."

Sam kept checking his watch. At a quarter past six, he realized she'd stood him up. He muttered, *Maybe I should plunge off the Tower to end my obsession.* He kicked a stone with the tip of a sneaker and paused midstride when she rushed toward him.

"Sorry I'm late."

Is it a lie or a last-minute decision? Stop overthinking. She's here, and that's what counts. He flashed a smile. "I'm glad you came. It's a two-minute walk from here. Earlier, I did some fact-checking. The restaurant is over one hundred and seventy-five years old. The interior has remained unchanged for over one hundred years, and the bathroom is described as legendary."

"Really? What kind is it?"

"A Turkish toilet."

"Okay, I'll bite. What is that?"

"You probably don't want to know the specifics details. On a positive note, the restaurant was a popular place for artists, students, intellectuals, and even politicians from the surrounding neighborhoods. Hemmingway lived nearby and often dined there with his first wife. Except for the mysterious toilet, I love places like this. It's like opening a door to history."

Warned the restaurant would get noisy and crowded after seven, and they would have to sit with strangers, he was relieved they arrived early. When they walked in, the tables were set French style—communal dining. Four people were close enough to eat off each other's plates. *This won't do.* He saw two separated tables. One was taken by a couple. He took her hand and made claim to the corner one. It surprised and pleased him she didn't pull away.

Sam said, "I'm a little tired of having to sit with strangers. Don't get me wrong, I've met a number of interesting people, but it's nice to enjoy dinner with one person."

"I'm not big on that style of dining, so thanks for securing the last table."

"I aim to please."

"Did your friend make any suggestions on what to order?"

"Only that it's homey French food. Let's take a risk and ask the server to pick. I've already said this, but I am really glad you came. It gives me time to get to know you better. If that's okay."

"What would you like to know?"

"Where is home?"

"About an hour and a half west of Boston—for now."

"Sounds as if you're planning to move. Did you decide where?"

"Somewhere outside the city."

"Me too! My partner is supposed to find me an apartment. Since I'm on a tight budget, God only knows what he'll pick out. Will your dad be moving to be closer to you?" Her gaze broke, but not before he detected tears in the margins of her eyes.

"My dad died before I came to Paris."

"Jesus, Maddie, you lost him too?" He couldn't stand the idea of her being hurt even more. He wondered, *Should I ask if she has any family to go home to?* But he changed his mind when their dinners arrived.

"For mademoiselle and monsieur. This is the dish most requested by our diners. Bar fillet from our butcher's room with garlic roasted potatoes and green beans with almonds. *Bon appétit.*"

The rest of the meal, he chose questions that had nothing to do with family or pets.

"Will you be painting outdoors?"

"As long as it's not raining."

"How about giving me a lesson? I'm good at drawing buildings, but when it comes to people, I'm a stick-figure kind of guy." When she dawdled over her response, he thought, *Here comes no.*

"I suppose the practice would be helpful before I start teaching."

"When?" he blurted. *Christ don't sound so anxious.*

"How about tomorrow at nine?"

"Great, I'll be ready."

This time, he insisted on walking her home. She tried to protest, but he tucked her hand into the bend of his elbow. "I won't take no for an answer."

Listening to the notes of chirping crickets as the evening sun cast its long shadows across the ground, silence hung in the air. The first few times he was with her, he'd felt the need to cut the tension and keep the conversation going. But tonight, it was like the most comfortable thing in the world. He placed a hand on the small of her back when they reached the apartment. "Same meeting place?"

"Yes. I had a nice time tonight, Sam, and I loved the restaurant."

He felt an overpowering urge to kiss her. Instead, he gave her hand a gentle squeeze. "So did I."

10

MADDIE

ON HER WAY to meet Sam, Maddie's willingness to speak about her losses surprised her. But Sam's tender way of showing concern moved her to open up. When she saw him waving his hand like an excited child, a feeling of joy washed over her.. She asked, "All set?" He nodded, took her art supplies, and handed her a steaming coffee in a paper cup..

"We're near the fountain. Let's go sit and appeal to the archangel's good side to keep this sunny weather."

She stepped back, spilling the drink.

"Maddie, your hand!" He dug a napkin out of his pocket and handed it to her. "Does it hurt?"

She wiggled her fingers. "Looks like I can still paint." *I won't spoil today or let anything affect my mood. I deserve to be happy for a little while.* "Let's head over to the flower market. The hundred-year-old pavilions are hard not to miss."

"Is it considered a hot spot for painters?"

"Yes, especially this time of year. It gets really crowded on Sundays because it becomes a bird market. Kids love it. There are as many vibrant bird species to choose from as there are flowers."

"Looks like you'll have to bring me back on Sunday."

Greeted with a rainbow of colors and delightful fragrances, spring had brought an abundance of buds into full bloom. Maddie chose a small grassy spot and showed Sam a few pointers on composition. Engrossed in her painting, she almost forgot he was there. When she turned to check his progress, his eyes were fixed on her instead of the drawing.

He held up the blank paper. "I was too busy studying the subject next to me."

For a second, her mouth refused to cooperate with her brain. "I, . . . I should have realized the time. I made you miss lunch."

"Nah, I'm not hungry. I'd rather continue with my drawing."

She gave him a sly look. "What drawing? Let me get you started, and you can add to it."

Kneeling beside him, she sketched a grouping of flowers. As soon as he inched close enough for their shoulders to touch, she stood and lost her footing. He got to his feet in time to steady her. Her reserved expression returned. "You're on your own now," she said, and he released the hold.

"Thanks, now I have something to work on."

She returned to her painting and wondered, *Is this turning into something I won't be able to handle?*

An hour later, unable to put a dent in her work, she said, "With the loss of sunlight, it's probably a good idea to leave."

He held up his paper. "What do you think?"

She laughed. "I think you should stay with what you're good at—monuments and buildings."

Back at her apartment, Sam asked, "If you don't have anything pressing to do, it should be a nice evening for a walk."

11

SAM

WHEN SAM LEFT his room to pick up Maddie, he imagined what their future together would look like. His firm would be a big hit in the city, and she'd become a successful artist. They would decide what style house he would build, insisting it had to be big enough for a large family. There wasn't any doubt she would be a terrific mother, and despite not having a shining example, he was sure he'd be a good dad. Comforting. Dependable. Patient. Never say a harsh word and able to provide a safe and secure environment. And one day, they would return to Paris to retrace the path where they fell in love. Knowing his days in Paris were numbered, he didn't want to wait any longer to tell her he loved her.

Rooted outside her door with his hands jammed into his armpits, doubts wormed their way through his head. *Maybe I shouldn't be so hasty and give it more time. No, if I don't say it now, I'll go mad.* The door opened before he could knock.

Maddie leaned against the doorjamb. "I thought I heard someone come up the stairs."

His hand raked through his hair as he tried to keep the timbre of his voice measured. "We haven't spent much time together, and it's going to sound crazy, but I have strong feelings for you." He shook his head. "No, that's not true. I've fallen in love with you."

The blood drained from her face. "You what?"

Like a speeding train closing in, he rushed through the words. "I can't explain why, except it's how I feel."

"Sam, you hardly know me."

The sternness in her voice stunned him. "I know enough to mean it."

"Please go."

"Maddie, I . . ."

She backed away.. "No more," and shut him out.

Both hands against the closed door, he pleaded, "Maddie, I'm sorry if I scared you. Please let me in so we can talk."

"There is nothing more to say."

As he walked down the stairs, he muttered, "No, damn it. I'm not giving up. Not without a fight."

12

MADDIE

MADDIE REALIZED GOING out with Sam had been a huge mistake. *How is it possible that after three dates he thinks he's in love with me? Even if were true, nothing could ever come of it.*

When she heard giggling outside, she walked over to the window. In the middle of the sidewalk, a couple stood with their arms around each other's waists. Undisturbed by the people milling around, he bent his head and kissed her.

She stepped back and closed her eyes. *If I had been anyone else, that might have been Sam and me.* No way would she let herself get involved in a serious relationship. The thought of loving and losing someone again was a risk she refused to take. She remembered the day her life, as she knew it, had shattered.

Maddie had run through the house and aimed for the kitchen. She couldn't wait to tell her mom what her six-grade teacher said. "You're so young and already painting like the old masters." She hadn't been sure what that meant, but it sounded like a huge compliment. Her eyebrows arched. The house, usually filled with her sister's constant chatter and her mother's singing, had been too quiet.

Her father was bent over the countertop where her mother stood every afternoon baking after-school snacks. Her grandparents sat at the kitchen table. Both sniffling, their eyes were blood-shot, and a jumble of balled-up tissues lay scattered on the table. Maddie had knitted her forehead in confusion. "Dad, where's Annie and Mom?" When he hadn't responded, she said, "Will someone please tell me what's wrong?"

He turned and walked toward her. His face, the color of white chalk, had frightened her. *Something awful must have happened.* He put his arms around her and squeezed so tight it took her breath away. Everything got mixed up when he sat in her mother's chair. She wanted to tell him but stopped when he covered her hands with his. She loved their strength and how the size and warmth against her small ones made her feel safe and protected. But this time, they were cold and shaking.

"Sweetheart, your mom and Annie . . ."

She scrunched up her face. "What about them?"

"They were in a terrible accident."

Her heart had stumbled over its rhythm. "Are they in the hospital? Why aren't you with them? We need to be there."

Tears edged the corner of his eyes, and his lips trembled. "It's too late."

She felt an unsteady rise and fall in her chest. "Too late for what?"

"There was nothing anyone could do."

"That doesn't make sense. The hospital has doctors and nurses to make them better."

"No, Maddie. They couldn't."

Wrenching from his grasp, she had shrieked, "You're lying!" She ran to her room, slammed the door, and flung herself on the bed. With a fist to her mouth, her insides roared, *They can't be dead.* But the expression on her father's face said otherwise. Shattered and frightened, she hadn't known how she would get up every morning and face another day without them. Her head buried in a pillow, a sob had erupted. Then another and another and another.

Maddie sat in the dark on the lumpy tweed couch, mindlessly pulling the yarn and making holes in the ragged throw. A steady flow of tears trickled into the empty spaces. She moaned, "I'm so sick and tired of letting the past determine my future." But like a muscle clinging to bone, it had become a part of her. She stood to turn on the lamp when a knock on the door startled her. Since Nancy and the other girls had moved out, she was the only one left on her floor.

"You have the wrong apartment."

"It's Sam."

She put her back against the door. "Please go away."

"All I need is five minutes, then I promise I won't bother you again."

His voice bordered on begging. Against her better judgement, she let him in.

"I'm so sorry I upset you. I should have never told you how I feel."

Her lips quivered. "It's not you."

"What is it?"

"It's too painful to talk about."

He took her hand and led her to the couch. "I'm a good listener."

Her eyes settled on a spot on the floor. "I told you my mother and sister died, but what I didn't tell you was how." Her voice was heavy. "They were brutally murdered and left for dead in the park near our house. My mother"—she shook her head—"my mother was two months pregnant, and my precious Annie was five."

Sam's mouth dropped open in horror. "Jesus Christ, Maddie. I—I . . ."

"It's hard to know how to respond to something so horrendous."

Anger rose in his voice. "I hope they caught the bastard."

"The police did. Based on the evidence, they arrested a forty-five-year-old guy. He got a life sentence in a California federal penitentiary."

"That's it? He deserved to be electrocuted."

Anger etched around her mouth. "I know, especially when he showed no remorse."

"God, your dad. What it must have done to him, and then needing to tell you how they died."

She released a deep exhale. "He said they died in an accident and then he tried to keep me in this ridiculous bubble until what happened wasn't a topic of gossip. I was not allowed to go to school for a week, and he stayed home from work and shadowed me. I never got to answer the phone, the newspapers mysteriously disappeared, and he never turned on the news when I was around. It was all so pointless. When I returned to school, besides the whispers and stares, I overheard kids in the lunchroom say they were murdered."

"Jesus, what a terrible way to find out the truth. Did you confront him?"

"Yes, and when he couldn't deny it, I was furious. When I asked about the details, he told me I was better off not knowing. It made me even angrier, so I decided to find out on my own."

"How?"

"At the library, I found newspaper articles on microfilm. The murders were splashed all over the front pages, and reporters published every sick detail." Her eyes closed. She had envisioned her mother's pleading screams as she fought to protect her unborn child and Annie while being beaten, raped, and choked to death at the hands of an animal.

She pressed her fingers against her eyelids and tried to stop the tears from falling. "My mom always said nothing bad would ever happen to our family because Saint Michael would watch over us and keep us safe. She was so wrong. It left me feeling scared I would wake up one day and my dad wouldn't be there to protect me." She winced as tears coursed down her cheeks.

Sam wrapped his arm around her. "It's okay. I've got you, and I'm not going anywhere."

"That's not all. I'd never experienced a wake before, and my dad had the difficult job of explaining it to me. I was so confused when he said it was a special place for people who loved them and cared about them to say goodbye." She remembered thinking, *What could be so special about not seeing my mother and sister alive?*

He got up, covered her with a blanket, and kissed her forehead. "You're exhausted, and you need to rest. I'm going to run out and get you something to eat. I promise I won't be long."

When sleep didn't come easy, the memories of the wake and funeral reemerged.

Maddie and her father had walked up to the two white caskets decorated with delicate pink roses. She hid behind him and listened to his repetitive muttering. "Kate, I don't know if I can go on without you." When he had turned to face her, pearl-shaped tears clung to his lashes. Her elbows turned inward, and her mouth tensed. *What if the accident messed them up, like the first time I saw something dead up close?* She and a friend had been walking through a woodland path and found the body of a squirrel. On its side, eyes wide open, its fur matted with blood, it distressed her to think how much it had suffered.

"Why do we have to look at them when they're dead?"

"It's what we do, Maddie. Be a good girl and kneel at the altars so you can say goodbye."

Her head bent, she had waited until her breath settled. The sight of her mother lying on a cloud of white hadn't been so bad. She was glad someone had dressed her in her favorite church dress, but got upset to see her face caked with makeup. She pouted. *Someone did a terrible job.* Expecting the skin to be soft and warm, her fingers had brushed lightly across her mom's cheek. It felt cold and hard. Her breath became shallow. *Mom, this is not the way I want to remember you.* She leaned closer and detected a faint ring of black and blue marks on her wrists and neck. *Were they caused by the accident?* Before she could ask, her father had taken her hand and brought her over to Annie's casket. The top was closed, and several framed photographs of her sister sat on a pedestal.

"Why isn't it open?"

"There's no reason to look inside."

Her face lost its color. "Why not?" When he had turned away without an answer, her eyebrows snapped together. *What's he keeping from me?*

The procession of people, most of whom she'd never met, made her body stiffen at the unwanted hugs and repetitive comments of how sorry they were. Between the headache caused by the overpowering odor of the flowers and depressing piped-in music, she wanted to get out of there. But her father was kneeling in front of her mother's casket again. She placed a hand on his shaking shoulders. "Everyone's left, including Grandma and Grandpa. We should go too."

She had marched straight to her room as soon as she got home, changed into pajamas, and sat on the bed. When her father walked in with a haggard look, she wanted to ask if he was okay but was afraid he'd fall apart again.

"Honey, I'm sorry you had to be brave for me."

She tasted resentment. *How would you know?* He had been completely unaware of how much she was suffering and how duty bound she felt not to shed one tear for his sake.

"We have one more day to get through—the church service and the cemetery, where we can say our final goodbyes."

What is he talking about? One more day and then what? Everything will be back to normal? She plucked at her eyebrows to keep from crying. "What's the point? They won't hear us."

"Many people think they do."

"Do you?"

He lifted his shoulders. "I'm not sure, but it can't hurt to try. It's late, and we both need to get some sleep. Is there a prayer you'd like to say before I turn out the light?"

"No." She had remembered some of the things she used to pray for. *Don't let our house burn down. Let my mom be all right when she goes to the hospital to have her baby. Please keep my family safe.* When he left, she had gotten on her knees and folded her hands. "God, please take me with you next time you go to Heaven."

The next day, she sat between her father and grandparents and had looked around the grim, spooky graveyard where hundreds of people were buried. Soon her mother and sister would join them. When the priest said they had been called home, it made her angry because the rule should have been for old, sick people. *What kind of God are you? Why were you so cruel and selfish taking them away? I hate you, because I never got to tell them how much I loved them, and I hate every one of your angels—especially Saint Michael.* When her father had handed her two white roses, this time there was no holding back. Her grief had crested as a flow of tears splattered onto their caskets.

By the time Sam returned, scrunched up tissues circled Maddie. Her nose was red, and her eyes were puffy.

"Christ, I should have never left you."

"My head feels like I have a massive hangover, not to mention how I must look."

He put the food and drinks on the table, sat beside her, and winked. "In my book, you never looked better."

She almost laughed. Instead, she said, "I don't know what came over me. It was a terrible mistake to burden you with all that wretched stuff."

"No, it wasn't. You mean everything to me, and I want to be here for you. Whatever I can do to help you deal with it, I will."

A heaviness wrapped itself around her body. "I'll never get over this. You deserve better than what I could ever offer."

He ran his thumb down her cheek. "What I see in front of me is a person with amazing courage and great strength."

When he brought her in close, she rested her head on his chest and felt the rise and fall of his breath. "My whole life I've lived in fear of what's around the corner."

"If you let me, I can fix that."

"I'm not sure you can."

"I am."

Heat rose from her stomach when he lifted her chin and kissed her. There was an urgency in her response.

He pulled away. "We don't need to do this."

The protective shell around her heart had been punctured. She whispered, "I want to."

13

SAM

SAM AND MADDIE spent their remaining time meandering around Paris, eating breakfast and lunch at street venders and dinner at their new favorite restaurant, Le Polidor. They talked about the classes they had taken, compared notes about professors, and talked about their interesting friendships with Nancy and Kris. He made sure the conversations never strayed to anything dark or serious.

One afternoon, they strolled along the Champs-Élysées, the shopping haven for the wealthy. Sam stopped to peer into several expensive shops. "I guess there aren't any budget stores on this avenue."

Maddie told him, "There's one across the street that meets our meager pockets. Don't move. I'll be right back." She sprinted into a store and returned with a black beret.

He tried to back away, but she stood on her toes, lifted her arms, slanted it on his head, and waved a finger back and forth.

"Don't you dare remove it. Dressed the way you are, it's the only thing on you that cries French."

It took a second for him to register a playful side she kept hidden. A beam of amusement stretched across his face. "Looks like I have no say in the matter."

She laughed. "Not this time."

They spent the rest of the day outside the city walking around Bois de Boulogne, the largest park in Paris. When they settled on a bench, she turned to him.

"Tell me about your mom and dad."

"My mom and I are really close. If not for her patience and support, I'm not sure I would've gotten as far as I did in school. My dad was all over the place when it came to me. One minute, he'd be aloof and distant, the next, he'd be rip-roaring mad at me."

"I can't imagine anyone getting angry at you."

"It started in first grade. I struggled with math and reading. Frustrated, I had some serious meltdowns. I acted out. Cried. Threw my books on the floor. My mom did her best to console me until my dad intervened. He'd yell and threaten that if I didn't stop he would spank me. To protect myself, I'd hide behind my mother or crawl under the table."

"That must have been awfully scary for you. Did you ask your mom why he acted that way?"

"Plenty of times. The only answer she gave was something to do with his upbringing."

"Was your mom able to stop him?"

"She'd get mad. Cussed at him a few times and accused him of being the problem." He exhaled a contemptible sigh. "Then he'd put the blame on her. Told her I was coddled too much. If that wasn't bad enough, I overheard him tell her their life would have been better without me."

Through closed doors, he had heard his father say, "Edie, I hate when Sam gets out of control. Doesn't it scare you he might be capable of doing something bad?"

"No, and I'm fed up listening to you go on about this."

Fuck, he's at it again. Why the Christ does she put up with the jerk?

"Ever wonder if our life would have been better without kids?"

The sharpness in her tone had cut through the air like a bolt of lightning. "What a despicable thing to say. My son *is* the most important thing in my life. You would be wise to remember that."

He had charged out of the house, hopped on his bike, and rode hard until his legs could no longer pedal. Despite the antagonistic relationship with his father, it had devastated him to find out he never wanted or loved him.

Maddie reached for his hand and squeeze it. "I'm so sorry you had to grow up feeling that way."

Sam forced a smile. "I'd like to believe he was different before I was born. Otherwise, why would my mom marry him?" He pulled her in close and ached to tell her again how much he loved her. It had to be before they left Paris. He decided it would be tonight, at the perfect spot.

Atop the Eiffel Tower, Sam put his arm around her waist as they watched the sun set against a brilliant pink and orange horizon. Under the glow of the moon hanging in velvety darkness, he faced her, cleared his parched throat, and let the words tumble from his mouth. "I love you, Maddie. You're the best thing that's happened to me, and I want to share my life with you."

She let out a jagged exhale. "Sam, I . . ."

He placed the tip of his finger to her lips. "Don't say anything. All I ask is that once we're settled in Boston, I can see you. If you decide I'm not . . . if it's not what you want, I won't pursue it."

14

MADDIE

MADDIE PRESSED HER forehead against the cool glass of the plane's window. She watched it fly above the canopy of ribbon-shaped clouds and thought about the kaleidoscope of feelings. They were so different from four and a half months ago. In the same seat, she had been filled with an inexpressible sadness. For too many years, the fear of another loss had kept her insulated. Now, Sam's words infused every cell in her body. *I love you. I want to spend the rest of my life with you.*

Everything about him was perfect. Sensitive and thoughtful, his lovemaking had been so careful and tender when he'd realized it was her first time. She remembered how he brushed her lower lip with his before he kissed her. And when his mouth shaped to hers, she melted into him with no reservations. It wasn't only physical. She felt the strong emotional ties and trust that rose between them. Maybe it was because of their shared losses—her family and his lack of a father who loved him.

Maddie stood on the doormat. The word *Welcome*, scarcely visible, had given up its invitation long ago. As she turned the doorknob, her temples thudded like a bass drum. She took one step inside and was besieged by a silence that had thickened while she was away.

Because the house had been sold, she had three weeks to get it ready before the closing and move into an apartment a realtor found. The same feelings she had before she left for Paris rose to the surface. When going through personal items, she didn't know how prepared she would feel handling the painful memories. Maybe she'd be lucky and happier ones would cancel out the hurtful ones.

In the kitchen, she boxed the contents of the cabinets and put aside the flatware and her mom's royal-blue Currier and Ives dishes, keeping two sets—one for her and one for Sam when he came to her new place for dinner. She left the corner cabinet drawer for last. Years ago, her father had collected a plethora of unusable items. The stash included outdated receipts, empty matchbook covers, a partial deck of cards, corroded batteries, three sticks of gum, and the receipt for a toaster. Unable to recover the top drawer, her mom gave up and labeled it, "Dad's useless stuff." An amused smile spread across Maddie's face. "You were quite the collector."

On the yellow Formica counter was the *World's Greatest Dad* coffee mug—a birthday present bought with her first allowance. A brown, crusted coffee ring had formed at the bottom. Unsure whether to discard it, she filled it with water and a dash of liquid soap.

Inside the pantry door hung her mother's bright-blue apron with white pockets. Underneath was an identical one with *Maddie* sewn on it. Splatters of chocolate chip cookie dough stains had endured multiple washings. She held both aprons to her chest. *How can I get rid of these and the happy memories of fun afternoons learning to bake? No,* she thought. *What's the point of hanging on to something you can't bring back to the way it was?* She decided to toss the aprons and her father's castoffs into a trash bag.

Thirsty, she grabbed the last item left in the pantry, a warm can of soda, and looked in the freezer. A thick layer of ice had collected inside. She pulverized it with a forgotten knife under the sink and released a tray stuck to the side.

She parted the ivory ruffled curtains and stared out the kitchen window. The backyard was small but large enough for the perennial garden that had flourished under her mom's watchful eye. She could picture the arrangement. Tall clusters of yellow black-eyed Susans with bulging black cones in the center. The bright-purple bearded irises, a beautiful contrast to her mother's prized lavender and fuchsia peonies—their blossoms as wide as dinner plates. And the eye-catching beds of colorful daises surrounding red roses. The area had become the home to countless bees, birds, and butterflies. All that remained was a myriad of weeds, dried stalks, thorny bushes, and a broken bird bath. She slid to the floor and sighed. *I feel like that godforsaken garden.*

Maddie's gaze lingered on the iconic red cat clock hanging above the window. In another life, its googly eyes had rolled back and forth with every ticktock of its wagging tail. It had stopped at three o'clock—the exact time she'd walked into the kitchen and heard the news her mother and sister were dead. Her eyes shiny, she resisted the tears that threatened to slip out and focused on the memory of how her mom had not been impressed the day her father brought the clock home.

"John, for heaven's sake, you can't be serious."

"Kate, it's the hottest item in all the stores. I had to wait in line to buy it." He had lifted the clock from the box and added two batteries. Standing on a chair, he banged a nail on the wall, hung it above the window, and stepped back. "This is the perfect spot. Watch the eyes and tail move, Maddie."

She had squealed and clapped her hands. "Daddy, it's magic."

He turned to Kate. "What do you think, Mommy?"

She had given him a single-sided smile. "Maybe the store will run out of batteries."

Like a slow bleed, another memory drew Maddie back to the weeks following the funeral. It was a difficult time filled with resentment toward her father. Because of his inability to act like the parent, she'd been left to handle the household chores. Going to work had been the only consistent thing he was able to manage.

Each morning she'd wake up hoping to follow the scent of crispy bacon with chocolate chip pancakes smothered in thick pads of butter and dripping with gooey maple syrup. Instead, only the stale smell of day's-old coffee had reached her nose. Hungry and mournful, she'd plod toward the kitchen to find a rumpled blanket thrown on the couch and the noticeable imprint of her father's head on the pillow. Every night, she had heard him wander and release pitiful moans. Overcome with grief, she would cry out, *Mom, I can't do this without you. I hate you for dying, and I hate how Dad acts like he wants to die.*

When she had found the cupboards scant and the refrigerator cooling outdated milk and juice, she'd gone ballistic. Holding up three fingers, she said, "Darn it, Dad, count them. Three times this week I told you we've gone through most of the food and groceries your friends and our neighbors delivered. At the end of the week, we won't have anything to eat for breakfast, nothing to make my lunch, and a big fat zero for dinner. I want you to take this list and go to the store today."

When he kept forgetting half the items, she had solved the dilemma after watching a commercial for TV dinners. A mother, surrounded by her family, displayed each food item in separate compartments inside an aluminum tray. A man in the background said, "No work before. Just pull them out of the freezer. Pop them in a heated oven, and dinner for the entire family will be ready in twenty-five minutes. No extra dishes, and no pots and pans. Then eat right out of the same tray."

The best part—she had several selections to choose from. Unsure of how her dad felt about anything, she had played it safe and added an assortment of dinners to his list. What ended up in the freezer was a stockpile of the same mystery meat swimming in disgusting brown gravy, accompanied by a watery vegetable medley.

The first time she had taken a bite, her face contorted into an ugly grimace followed by a gag. Eyes watering, she snuck a side-glance at her dad and hoped he didn't see her spit the chunk of meat into a napkin. Too preoccupied, he pushed the untouched meat to the edge of the tray and focused on separating the peas, corn, and carrots into tiny piles.

The frozen dinners left uneaten and tossed in the garbage, she had to figure out something else. She found her mother's *American Woman's Cookbook*, full of color photographs and appendages with detailed instructions. She realized cooking wasn't any different from painting. Start with a blank canvas. Select the material. Prep it. Mix it and work it until you had a finished product. But after a week's worth of making dinners and doing the housework and her homework, she went off on him again.

"I'd like to sit around and be miserable missing Mom and Annie, but I can't. I'm too darn busy taking care of you."

When he had finally decided to take on some of the chores, it turned out to be catastrophic. If he ironed, he ruined his shirts. Her school uniforms hadn't fared any better. The hem on one of her plaid jumpers got scorched, and the sleeves of a blouse wore imprints from the tip of the hot iron. Zealous about bleach, he had done a number on the wash when he mixed the colors with the whites. Everything, including her Monday through Sunday panties, had been marked with a rainbow of blotches. Desperate to protect her clothes, she hollered, "I'll do it myself, like everything else." Not by choice, she had became the reliable caregiver. It led to a silent despondency that had settled between them.

Maddie surveyed the living room—mint-green walls, beige carpet, and furniture covered in ivory chintz. Once a warm and inviting space, today it gave a nod to the weather—overcast and bleak. She ran her hand along the couch and chairs. *Should I take them to the apartment?* No need to debate the answer. The furniture only held spilled tears and anguish. *They won't be coming with me.*

As she pulled books from a wooden cabinet, she found two scrapbooks titled *This Is the Story of Your Life* with *Annie* and *Maddie* written underneath. Hers was filled with dated photographs from the day she was born, plus all the milestones—baptism, first tooth, First Communion, first days of school, every holiday, and every birthday until her eleventh. In one of the empty plastic inserts, she found a letter.

> *Dearest Maddie,*
>
> *The evening you were born, my life changed forever. Even now, I recall the sweet smell of your breath and the precious beat of your heart against my chest. I was uncertain what lay ahead of us, but I knew we would be on this journey together. I made you some promises that day. Never to let you forget how special and loved you are. And, the most important one—to protect and keep you safe. If, my darling daughter, life becomes too difficult, I will be at your side to see you through it. As you come into your own, always remember to hold fast to your dreams until they come true.*
>
> *Love,*
> *Mom*

She sat back on her heels, took a breath, but had trouble getting it all the way into her lungs The absence of her mother's physical presence felt stronger than ever. Gone were her hugs, her smile, and the way she lit up a room.

Her fingers traced the outline of Annie's name. It included all the momentous occasions. In every picture, her sister looked like a ray of sunshine. In the last photograph, taken on September 27, 1955, she wore a party dress—an early birthday present. Her delight hadn't lasted twenty-four hours. She'd been savagely murdered the next day. The gaping hole in Maddie's heart grew wider. Like her mother, everything about her beloved sister was gone—too soon.

Before she closed the cabinet doors, she noticed a set of keys tucked in the corner—the same ones her father had hidden. It was still fresh in her mind the first time she'd tried to open the doors to her parents' and sister's bedrooms.

"Dad, why are the doors locked?"

"I decided it was for the best."

"Not for me. Being around their things will make me feel closer to them."

"Maddie, it will only make you sadder."

Her face had erupted into angry splotches of red. "You won't listen to me when I want to talk about them. You removed all the pictures from the walls and hid all their photographs. It's as if you're trying to erase them." When he tried to take her hand, she had pulled away and fired back. "I don't have anything anymore. Not even you."

"I'm trying to make things easier for you."

"Well, you're not. I hate you!" She yelled, and stomped out of the room. It didn't matter she saw his face veiled in sadness, his voice toneless. She had lost her security, his love, and her place

in his life. That day, she had vowed to ignore him the way he ignored her.

Three days later, she had found the keys and entered her sister's room. It had taken only seconds to realize he had been right.

Maddie knew it would be hard to enter Annie's room. All the
years that had followed, an unspoken decision existed between her
father and her to keep it locked. Today, there would be no choice.
Her sister's belongings needed to be sorted and boxed. She paused
before entering. Eyes closed, she inhaled through her nose and
exhaled through pressed lips. It took several breaths before she
inserted the key and twisted the doorknob. Straight ahead, her
brain collided with the unwanted memory she would never forget.

At the end of the canopy bed lay a bunched-up, pastel, mul-
ticolor bedspread and a floral eyelet nightie turned inside out—
remnants of Annie's last morning alive. She stepped back as the
dull ache of grief struck again. To avert a meltdown, her fingernails dug into the fleshy part of her arm and forced her to
refocus her attention on the floor. Crayons with worn tips, open
coloring books, and half-dressed baby dolls were scattered on the
safari-patterned rug. On top of a toy chest rested *the* prized possession—a Country Rose nine-piece china tea set—the one she'd
passed down to Annie. The corners of her eyes crinkled at the
memory of handmade invitations for their parents and the hours
spent hosting tea parties.

She lovingly folded smocked dresses, cotton tops, and overalls. The closet was empty except for a pair of unworn pink
patent-leather strapped shoes and the two-layer pink-tulle birthday dress. Salty tears flowed unchecked at the vision of Annie

blowing out five candles on the princess cake her mom would have made. Swiping away the tears on her face, she turned to the dresser. On it sat her first pair of bronzed walking shoes, solidified into a memorable milestone. After a last look around, she left with the tea set and bronzed shoes—each a treasured keepsake.

At her parents' door, she rotated the key in the lock and stopped. When her heartbeat didn't resume its steady rhythm, she rested her forehead against the door. Before she took another dive into a black hole, she decided to wait.

She wondered if Julia had returned from India. *There's so much I want to tell her about Paris and Sam—mainly Sam.* She called her friend's parents' house, was told she'd moved to Everett, and was given the phone number.

As soon as Julia answered the phone, Maddie said, "I've missed you. When did you get back and when can we get together? Oh, and guess what? I'll be moving to Somerville. We'll be three miles apart."

Julia laughed. "You sound like me when I get overexcited. Not even a breath between sentences. I I got back a week ago and would have called, but between the move and jet lag I was in a coma for the last three days."

"How about dinner tonight?"

"Perfect. Where and what time?"

"Let's meet halfway. The Tappa Bar in Winchester around six."

Giggling like two teenagers, they strolled inside arm in arm. As soon as they sat, Maddie said, "I see you still have that hippie vibe going on."

"Not for long. I'm applying to the doctorate program at Boston University."

"Your parents must be thrilled."

"Yeah, they are, but I still intend to dress in boho style when I'm not doing my clinical rotations."

"Wait till you see the outfits I wore in Paris."

"No way. Not Miss Prim and Proper. Any other major changes you made while you were there?"

"I, well, I . . . I met someone."

"So that's the reason you can't stop grinning like a Cheshire cat."

She gushed, "He's amazing. Thoughtful, supportive, and so good-looking."

"He sounds nice. How did you meet him?"

"We took the same class."

"Not to sound corny, but did he sweep you off your feet?"

"No. I mean he tried, like for weeks, but I kept putting him off. A few times, I was rude and acted like an idiot, but he pursued me until I agreed to go out with him."

"Does he live in Paris?"

"No. He lives in Massachusetts. He's starting a design company with his partner in the Boston area."

"It's about time you dated. But take it slow."

She played with the menu. "It's serious, Julia. He told me he loves me."

"Don't you think that's rushing it? How much do you know about him?"

"Enough to feel the same way." She sighed. "Please don't look at me that way. This is not a mistake. You'll see once you spend time with him."

"I'll take your word. But when I meet him, I'm warning him if he ever hurts you, he'll have to deal with me."

She raised her eyebrows and laughed. "That's what I call a real threat. Now fill me in about India, and I'll tell you how fabulous Paris was."

15

SAM

THE CAB DRIVER dropped Sam off in front of the house. The manicured landscape had always been his dad's terrain. He pampered it like a newborn baby. With a tinge of coated irony, he thought, *Better than how he treated me.* He planned to stay for a few days—enough time to spend with his mom, tell her about Maddie, and have it out with his father. As he walked toward the kitchen, he halted at the heated sound of his dad's voice. He cracked open the door and watched his father pacing the floor.

"Now that the evil bastard is dead, his next move should be to rot in the city dump."

His mother's face reddened. "Your father was a terrible man and what he did to his family was unconscionable."

Christ, they're talking about my grandfather. They told me he died before I was born. Why would they lie, and what did he do that was so horrendous?

She pointed to the cardboard box. "What's this?"

"Everything he owns."

"Do you know what's in there?"

"Not a clue. The idea of handling his stuff made my skin crawl, so I had the attendant pack it."

"Do you mind if I open it to see if anything is good enough to donate?"

"Go ahead, but I guarantee you won't find anything of value."

She rummaged through the clothes. "You're right. Nothing worth keeping." She took out an oversize shoebox, opened it, and saw several photographs. "Have you seen these before?"

"I'm not interested in looking at anything he saved."

She held up a manila envelope. "This was at the bottom. You sure you don't want to see what's in it?"

He scowled. "Positive."

"It could be a will."

"The only thing he left me are the scars on my back."

"I'm going to check just to make sure." A hand went to her throat. "Oh God, Martin. These have to be destroyed. What if . . ." She grabbed his arm. "What if Sam finds out?"

His father's face turned a deep shade of purple when he looked at what she was holding. Sam thought, *What in God's name is going on with them?*

"What the hell? That sick son of a bitch kept all this crap." He put everything back in the shoebox, sealed it with duct tape, and tossed it into the cardboard box. "I'll stick it in the basement and get rid of it tomorrow morning."

Primed to rush in and confront them, Sam reconsidered. *I can't risk them lying to me again.* He waited until his father returned and coughed to warn them he was home. "Hi, Mom, Dad."

He caught the alarmed expression on his mother's face, followed by an anxious smile.

"You weren't supposed to get home until late this afternoon."

"Are you disappointed?"

"No, of course not."

She lifted her arms to hug him. "I've missed you."

"Same here." Despite the nagging questions about what they were hiding, he said, "I have so much to tell you."

"If I had known, I wouldn't have agreed to do an extra shift at the hospital."

"That's okay, I'm not going anywhere." He turned to his father, who wore the face of someone spooked. "Day off?"

"No, I'm going back to work, but I needed to take care of something."

So do I.

Sam brushed away the mummified insects captured in cobwebs that hung from the basement ceiling. He walked over to his father's tool bench. Two cardboard boxes were labeled *Church Donations* and *Goodwill.* One was unmarked. *This must be it.* He dug through the layers of old clothes until he found the shoebox. Across the top, in shaky handwriting, was *Luther J. Middleton.* He ripped off the tape and took out the black-and-white photographs.

A boy with a thick head of hair wore a loose white shirt and baggy pants held up by suspenders. Written on the back was his name and the date—*Angus Middleton, age fifteen, 1887.* An adrenaline spike raced through him. *It's my great-grandfather.* Another photograph showed a boy with the same crop of hair, wearing a dark shirt with rolled-up sleeves and a striped vest with a bowtie. Taken in 1910, it was eighteen-year-old Luther—his grandfather.

He studied a photo of a ramshackle house with three kids gathered on the steps of a failing porch. He couldn't decide who looked shoddier—the mangy dog lying on the ground or the kids. *Clara*, *Martin*, and *Marshall* were written above their heads. He could tell the boys were twins. *Why would they keep a secret about my aunt and an uncle.?* He unfolded two newspaper articles with creases so old they almost ripped. The headline in the first one read, "Angus Middleton, 32, Convicted of Rape and Murder of a Prostitute." *Jesus Christ, my great-grandfather was a goddamn monster and sentenced to life in prison. I'm done here. I don't need to read anymore.* About to place the other one back, he stopped. *I've come this far, I might as well finish what I started.*

The other one read, "Marshall Middleton, the sixteen-year-old son of Luther and Agnes Middleton, was found guilty of battering to death a twelve-year-old boy he dumped in the town cemetery. He was charged with voluntary manslaughter and sentenced to ten years in an upstate New York prison." His breath suspended, the dank and musty walls of the basement closed in. To find out he came from a generation of men who committed indescribable acts of violence made him want to vomit. *So, this is the fucked-up secret my parents didn't want me to know about.*

The discovery in the basement unnerved Sam even more when he headed upstairs and placed the photographs side by side, looked in the mirror, and compared the faces to his. He gripped the sides of the bathroom sink, his knuckles blending with the white porcelain. The resemblances, right down to what appeared as a mark on the left temple, shocked him.

He drifted from room to room. Unable to make sense of everything, he thought, *I need a drink to settle myself before Mom comes home.* He found the key to the locked cabinet and took out a bottle of wine. Exhausted by the find in the basement and jet lag, three drinks later, he fell into a restless sleep on the couch in the den. When he woke, disoriented and frantic, hands curled into fists and ready to defend himself, he blinked, looked around the room, and then realized where he was. Every detail of a hellish nightmare came back.

Paralyzed and naked, he stood amid a pitch-black, empty wasteland. A putrid smell filled his nostrils, burned his throat, and turned his stomach. The faces of his ancestors appeard with ghoulish grins as ripples of mocked laughter swirled around him. Backed against an invisible wall, damning forces confronted him.

He heard his mother come in and waited to call her until the stomping sensation in his chest lifted. "Mom, I'm in the den, can you come in here?"

She frowned when she saw the empty wineglass on the end table. "Is something wrong?"

Hands clasped between his knees, he said, "You better sit. I found out something disturbing."

"What? Are you sick?"

He reached behind him and showed her the envelope.

A hand cupped her mouth. "How did you get this?"

"I overheard your conversation with Dad, so I looked through the box in the basement."

"Sam, whatever you read doesn't affect you."

His nostrils flared. "Obviously it does, since you didn't want me to know about it. You both lied about my grandfather being alive. I never knew about dad's twin and my aunt. Or that I had a bunch of lunatic relatives who killed and raped innocent people."

Her voice thinned. "Your dad was so ashamed of his family, he never wanted you to find out."

"Too late." He pulled out the articles. "Tell me every sordid detail."

She shifted in her seat. "What more can I say that you haven't read?"

"How long have you known?"

"Three years after we were married, I found a letter from his brother mixed in with our mail. It shocked me to learn he had a twin in prison."

"Weren't you afraid he would show up on your doorstep when he got released?"

"Thank God, no. Your father made sure it would never happen. We sold our house and moved six months later."

"It's conceivable he's still alive. He'd be what, fifty-six? Plenty of time to attack and kill more people, if he hasn't already." The grim silence between them told him she had considered the same thing. "At least that low-life, murdering rapist Angus got what he deserved. What happened to my aunt?"

"She died of diphtheria when she was three. It started with a sore throat and a fever. By the time she got to the hospital, her heart failed."

"What about my grandmother and Luther?"

"Your grandfather, he . . ."

His eyes reduced to slits. "What? Did he murder her and get away with it?"

She stammered. "No, but what he did . . ."

He thought of Maddie. "It's important I know everything about my background."

"Why? All of this happened before you were born."

"It mattered enough for you to find about Dad's past."

She pinched the bridge of her nose and stared at the envelope. "I wish to God I hadn't. Your grandmother Agnes's entire life was a tragedy. She was an innocent sixteen-year-old when she married Luther. He turned out to be a tyrant who demeaned her, made her feel worthless, and repeatedly beat her. Drunk or sober, he'd wait for any chance to get angry. Almost everything she did sent him into a tirade. A speck of dust on the furniture. The way she did the laundry. How she fed the livestock. Or if his dinner wasn't on the table at the exact time he demanded. And if she missed a wrinkle in his overalls with the flatiron, he threatened to use it on her. Each time she tried to escape, he would grab her by the hair and drag her around the room. When he was done, he'd leave her cringing in a corner."

"Jesus Christ, don't tell me he hurt his kids, too."

"He never got to Clara and Marshall. If he was on the attack, your dad made them go up to the hayloft with strict orders not to move. He would run back to the house with a farm tool and try to protect his mother. Luther, at six five and built like an ox, was no match. All your dad could do was watch the violence unfold until he got caught."

Sam's voice, now laced with disgust and hatred, spoke the question he had to ask. "What did he do to him?"

"Haven't you heard enough?"

Sam saw how difficult this was for her, but he was done being left in the dark. He knelt in front of her and put his arms on her shoulders. "Please, no more secrets."

Her eyes widened with grief. "When Luther found out your dad witnessed the brutality, he beat him repeatedly with a whip. He still has the scars on his back."

"Why the hell weren't the police called?"

"Luther had an in with police."

"Then someone should have done away with that scumbag."

"Your father almost did."

When tears slipped from the corner of her eyes and slid down her cheeks, he wiped them with his thumbs. His voice softened. "Mom, what did he do?"

"Please, no more. I've said too much already."

"He's my father. I have a right to know."

"Promise you won't hold it against him."

Unsure if he could, he nodded.

16

MADDIE

AFTER SPENDING A delightful evening with Julia, Maddie wasn't looking forward to putting another damper on her spirits by sorting through her parents' room. She knew everything except her father's clothes would be the same as the day her mom died. He had repurposed the spare room into his bedroom and never returned to theirs.

Inside, she sat on the quilted comforter detailed with embroidered peacocks. For hours, she would curl up against the large fluffy pillows while she watched her mother dress for church, a party, or a night out with her father. Feeling the soft texture of fabric against her skin, she yearned for a hint of her scent. On top of the dresser was the mahogany jewelry box. Tempted to open it and try on the pearl necklace and earrings her father had bought for their first anniversary, she released a dismal sigh. *Not today.*

She bent down on the floor when she saw unwrapped boxes peeking out from underneath the bed. Inside, there several gifts for Annie— *Bedtime Stories, Playtime with Nancy, The Shaggy*

Dog, and a pink, hand-knit sweater trimmed in white angora with heart-shaped buttons and a matching hat. Her eyes glistened when she pressed them to her cheek. *I miss you so much, little one.*

When she opened hers, the corners of her mouth slid upward. One was the Supreme paint set with sixty-four blocks of paint and a color wheel—a budding artist's dream. Each time her mom had taken her to the Isabella Stewart Gardner Museum in Boston, they would spend the entire afternoon going from room to room or sitting in front of a painting with sketch pads and paint. She remembered how she would stand close to a particular piece and want to run her fingers over the texture and imagine what the artist felt.

She had to stretch an arm to reach the tiny box under the bed. Inside lay an expensive gold necklace and a pendant with a guardian angel attached—a gift from her mom who believed it would keep her safe, similar to the Saint Michael's pin she had worn every day. She thought, *There was never any protection for you and Annie.*

On the nightstand lay a journal with a heart-shaped lock. On the cover, *My Life's Journey by Katherine Lynette O'Dell* was embossed with gold lettering. She ran a finger across her mother's name. To read it now would drive her into another sea of darkness. Like the vacant spaces in the scrapbooks, there would be too many empty pages. She wondered if the day would come when she could read it with a different lens—one of joy, not sorrow.

With more to do, she put the journal aside and took out the clothes and hats from the closet. One dress stood out from the rest—a lovely blush-toned, satin sheath gown with short, puffed sleeves and a matching bolero jacket. The bodice formed a jeweled neckline, with six covered pearl buttons down the back. Holding it up to her neck, she gazed in the full-length mirror. She didn't have to imagine how radiant her mother must have looked in her wedding dress, or her dad's expression of love and devotion when she walked down the church aisle.

After her father's clothes had been boxed, with one last check, she caught the earthy aroma of the wooden cigar box with its white owl on the front. One cigar remained. The colored band removed, she placed it on her ring finger. Her dad used to say, "Someday, a wonderful boy will slip a real one on your finger, and it will be one of the happiest days of your life." Her heart soared at the thought of her future with Sam.

Done sorting what to give away, she reconsidered the pendant, kept the journal, the jewelry box, and the cigar box. When she tried to save the paper ring, it came unglued. It seemed oddly symbolic of what had transpired between her and her dad in the weeks after the deaths of her mom and sister. Along with his neglect and withdrawal, and her sick grandmother, the desolation she felt had been further fueled by having no one to confide in.

The tallest in her middle-grade class, and the only one with curly red hair, she had felt like an outcast. Forced to grapple with school-yard cliques, gross comments from boys, and the lunchroom hierarchy, her fears had heightened the first time she saw the girls, including two best friends, stroll out of the shower stalls naked. They didn't look like her. Her breasts were bigger, her hips wider, and a fuzz of hair had seemed to appear overnight under her arms and between her legs. Locked in a bathroom stall, she cried, thinking, *Oh God, what's happening to me? I'm turning into a freak.*

Life had gotten worse the day she woke up with cramps and tender breasts. When she noticed spots of blood on her underwear, she went to the school nurse, thinking she had a terrible disease. After a long, mortifying explanation of what it meant and being shown how to wear a bulky pad attached to a belt around her waist, the nurse gave her extra ones to take home. Awkward and uncomfortable, she had willed herself not to cry the rest of the school day and on the bus ride home. Once she realized she needed a bra, there was the dilemma of figuring out what size and kind to buy and having to go shopping with her father, as well as the added embarrassment of going to the store with him for another box of pads.

The insecurities and conflicting thoughts had created her inability to cope with the extreme mood swings. Crying spells, anxiety, and angry outbursts plagued her, especially toward her father, even after he learned the right way to wash the clothes and iron them.

One afternoon, she had stopped to watch him iron her school uniform.

He had held it up and grinned. "I got all the pleats straight and didn't ruin any. And I know now to separate the whites from the darks before I do the wash. So you don't have to worry about me spoiling your clothes."

That he looked so proud of himself had made her furious. She spit out the words with no thought of how they sounded. "If you're waiting for me to say something nice, like 'good job' or 'thank you,' forget it."

The coldness in her demeanor hadn't stopped him. Every morning, next to her book bag, he had set the table with three choices of cereals and juices. On weekends, when he made pancakes or French toast, she saw the pain cloud his features when she refused to eat. Nothing seemed to deter him. Instead of peanut butter, inside her lunch box were ham and cheese sandwiches on Wonder Bread. Plastic containers with fresh fruit and Hostess treats were included. Vindictively, she brought back everything except the snacks.

"I'm trying, Maddie."

"Well, stop. No matter what you make, it will never be like Mom's."

He had spent hours working on sprucing up the kitchen. The wallpaper—her mother's favorite seafoam-green pottery jars with a scattering of floral bouquets—had warped at the edges. Instead of stripping it, he carefully glued the seams that no longer held. He tightened the loose hinges on the cabinet doors and replaced the rusty knobs with shiny new fixtures. The house smelled of lemon and cleaning detergent, and the dust and cobwebs were swept away. He polished every piece of furniture until it glistened. The bathroom floor, sink, and tub were scrubbed, and the mirror received a Windex sparkle.

When he asked, "How about I freshen up the place with a new coat of paint?" She had thrown him a backward glance and said, "Whatever." She wanted to add, *You can wax and mop the floors and repaint, but it won't cover up the sadness.* A week later, he had painted all the rooms a soft ivory, except hers. Sample paint chips in greens and blues—her favorite colors—lay on her dresser.

One evening, she stopped and took in the new look of the house and realized, despite her wretched behavior, he had done all this hoping she'd forgive him. It had taken her weeks to understand why her mom's death hit him so hard. She had been his life's partner, his go-to person for companionship—things she and Annie couldn't give him. *Dad, we were both lost in our own grief. When you finally came around to comfort me, what did I do? I acted badly and downright mean. I made you feel like nothing you did mattered.*

She recalled an important lesson her mother had taught her. "If someone hurts you, remember you can't always know what's in their hearts, so be kind." Her eyes welled with shameful tears. *Mom, you would be so disappointed in me.*

The next morning, on her way out the door, she had said, "Hey, Dad. Thanks for making me breakfast and lunch."

His grin extended across his face. "You're welcome. See you when you get home."

"Oh yeah, I almost forgot to tell you. I'm the only one who got an A+ on my math test."

"That's terrific. It was my worse subject in school. Your mother . . . Maddie, I didn't mean to mention her."

She had grinned. "I got it from her. She was the math whiz."

Healing had begun that day.

17

SAM

SAM CLIMBED THE stairs a third time, carried boxes to the second floor, and entered the efficiency apartment Joe had rented for him in Cambridge. It had a multipurpose room, a fully equipped kitchen, a separate bathroom, and a bedroom. The furnishings were sparse, but it worked for the time being. After one more look before he left, and attempting to put aside what he learned about his ancestors, he thought, *Finally, the freedom and independence I've been dreaming about.*

He took the T to the office in a low-rent neighborhood. Outside the building hung the *Middleton and Rossi* shingle. Going up three flights, he had to push his shoulder against the door to open it. *Looks like we'll have some fixing up to do.* When Joe crossed the room, the grin nearly split his face.

"It's about time you got here. What do you think? Some of the furniture is from my parents. The rest I got at garage sales—enough to furnish two small—and I mean *small*—offices and a separate room to squeeze in a long folding table, which will be our first conference room. The landlord gave us a break on the rent if we paint the place."

Sam slapped him on the back and gave the room a once-over. "You've done a terrific job."

Joe chided, "Yeah, while you were three thousand miles away, I busted my butt to find it and get it ready for business. I took a few ads out in the local papers to create a buzz around town and notified our friends and family. And get this: we already have two new clients. There's still more we need to do for exposure, so I drafted a marketing plan we can go over."

"I knew I made a wise decision when I chose you to be my partner."

"Careful, pal. When you're not looking, I may decide to rearrange the names on our sign."

The back-and-forth needling reminded Sam of how they'd acted when they were kids. *Next to my mom, he is the most important person in my life. And there is—or was—Maddie.*

"Hey, you look like you're going to get emotional. The place isn't that great."

"Don't be stupid. What's in the crate?"

"Wait until you see. You can do the honors."

Joe fetched a crowbar off the windowsill and handed it to him. The nails squeaked, and the lid lifted. He dug out the packing material. "Wow." He ran his hand along the gleaming edge of a brand-new drafting table. "What a badass gift from your parents."

"No, bro. It's yours. When I called to check when you would be getting back, your dad brought it over. Mine's in my office. Except for a chair, it takes up the entire space."

For a second, he was dumbfounded to think his father would care enough to buy the one thing he needed. *No way. This has to be my mom's doing.* "How about we get started? Do you have the paint?"

"Whoa, not so fast. Tell me about Maddie. Your last postcard made it sound like you two were serious."

"It was, but I'm done with relationships."

"Aren't you a little young for monkhood?"

His face tightened. "I found out something disturbing that could affect me . . . and us."

"Like what?"

"Where's the paint?"

"Don't change the subject. The walls can wait."

He felt the blood pumping in his ears. "I don't know where to start."

"How about the beginning?"

The cadence in his voice was slow, but the more he spoke, the more the words gushed out as if a dam had broken. "My parents hid some pretty damning secrets about my dad's family." When he finished with the ugly details, Joe's expression looked as if he'd weathered the effects of a horror movie.

"That is beyond sick, but what has it got to do with you?"

"Everything. My life is in a fucking holding pattern, wondering if I'll do something awful—hurt somebody or . . ."

"Hold on. Just because you've got a few hideous nut jobs hanging off the family tree doesn't mean you'll turn into the devil incarnate. I've known you since we were kids. Remember how we were thick as thieves growing up? What about our four years in college? We lived in a space smaller than a prison cell. I would have known if you were that notorious killer Ed Gein. For Christ sake, you don't even have a temper."

His cheeks smarted. "I'm no saint, but I've work hard to control it—thanks to my father for demonstrating what happens when you don't."

"Geez, you must be like my mom's pressure cooker, ready to explode if the lid comes off."

A fixed grin formed Sam's mouth.

"Come on, it's a joke."

He made a face. "Hardly a joke."

"Have you seen her since you got back?"

Sam shook his head. "Not yet."

"Are you going to tell her why you're no longer interested?"

"Oh, sure. 'Maddie, I can't see you anymore because I might do something terrible, and don't forget my murdering uncle who might be on the loose and come after us.' I'm done talking about this. Go get the brushes."

He lumbered into his office, leaned against the wall, and felt the misery ripping through him. In Paris, he'd reassured her she could trust him. Part of that meant no secrets—like the awful ones her father kept from her. He finally understood the dilemma his dad faced. If he'd told his mother before they married, she might have run in the other direction.

18

MADDIE

IT TOOK THREE days before Maddie finished marking the boxes for Goodwill, the Salvation Army, and homeless shelters. She sent the kitchen table and chairs, her bedroom furniture, personal items, and a box of photographs to her apartment. After the move, she planned to hit local tag sales and flea markets. Emotions were interspersed with heartache and happier times as she made a final inspection of each room.

In a few weeks, the house would be ready to greet the new family. A young couple with four-year-old twin girls and a six-year-old boy had bought it. She envisioned them celebrating birthday parties with cake and gifts. And, the holidays. A turkey with all the trimmings. A tree decorated with bright-colored bubble lights, Disney character ornaments, and long strands of silver tinsel with red-and-gold beaded garland. They would tear into wrapped presents with stuck-on bows and yell, "Wow, look what Santa brought me. It's what I've always wanted," to the delight of their parents. The images made her smile, but so did the sadness of the last Thanksgiving and Christmas with her father. Close to being mired in sorrow, she muttered, "Enough of this," and reached into her jeans pocket to take out the letter that had arrived in the mail today postmarked Paris.

> *Dear Sweet Maddie,*
>
> *On my way to the airport and I already miss you. I hope you know how amazing you are and how happy I am you're in my life. There is so much more to say, but it will have to wait until I see you. You gave me your number and the day you're back. I love you, and I can't wait to see you.*
>
> *Sam*

She pressed it to her lips. Until now, her entire being had been uprooted because of all the losses. Like a force of nature, Sam had blown into her life and made her believe she deserved love and happiness. She wondered what life would be like with him. Besides the undeniable chemistry, she had so much to learn. His likes and dislikes. Early-morning person or night owl. Movies and TV shows—comedy or drama. Foods he liked, and those he didn't. The list could go on forever—a word that made her feel safe.

Eager for his call, she picked up the phone every hour to make sure it wasn't prematurely disconnected. But as the day turned to night, she became agitated. Fingernails bit to the quick, her mind overran with unwanted thoughts. *He changed his mind. Realized I carry too much baggage, or picked up with an old girlfriend. Worse, he never loved me.* It didn't surprise her. She had found out the harsh way to always expect the worst. *What a stupid, gullible fool. I should have never set myself up to be hurt again.*

After a tumultuous night, her eyes gritty with exhaustion, she squinted at the eight on the hour hand. The sound of the phone interrupted the need to blot out the world. *It must be the movers to say they're on their way.*

Dressed in a worn-out college shirt and shorts, she shoved her feet into flip-flops and said, "Hello."

"Hi, it's Sam."

The sound of his voice made her heartbeat skip like a stone across the water. She wanted to blurt out, *I was afraid you wouldn't call.* Instead, she kept an even tone. "Hi, how are you?"

"Doing okay. Busy getting the office ready and tracking down new clients."

"Sounds like you're off to a good start. I'll be moving into my new place today."

"Sorry to cut this short, but Joe's calling me. We're in the middle of discussing a new prospect. Have you been to Doyle's Café in Boston?"

"No, but if you give me the address, I'm sure I can find it."

"Can you meet me there on Saturday at seven?"

"Can't wait. Sam, I miss you." She waited for his response. Instead, what she got was the dial tone.

After the movers left, she had one last thing to do. On her mother's stationary, she wrote:

Dear Family,

May your home be filled with love, laugher, and good health. This is to record all your wonder-ful memories.

Sincerely,
Madelynn O'Dell

She taped the note onto a red suede journal engraved with a heart and a semiprecious stone closure—similar to the one she planned to purchase. *Maybe I should buy two. I already have so many things to write about since I met Sam.*

She stood on the new welcome doormat and ran a hand over the oak door with its three rectangular panes of glass. Twisting the bronze doorknob to make sure it locked, she gazed down the street. She'd never paid much attention to the rows of small, box-shaped houses. Hers was indistinguishable from the others, yet different inside. Not just the painted walls and everything in it, but the full range of emotions. Whatever sorrows her neighbors may have faced, or are facing, she prayed love found its way to heal them. She turned the house key over in her palm and thought, *Every door has an entrance and an exit—a transition from one place to the next.* She finally shut the door on uncertainty and hardship. Tonight, she would open a new one full of exciting pos-sibilities and a bright new future with Sam.

Maddie cut through the heavy-duty taped boxes in the new apart-ment and neatly arranged kitchen items in the cabinets. In the bedroom, she hung clothes in the small closet and placed the rest

in dresser drawers. Toiletries put away, she arranged and rear-
ranged what little furniture she'd brought, along with the framed
pictures her mother had taken. After she measured the windows
for curtains and the worn surfaces of the floor for rugs, she walked
to the market to stock the refrigerator.

Unable to eat, her stomach shifted. Time felt as if it had slowed
to a snail's pace. She drummed her fingers on the table and gave
another glance at the ticking cat clock—one of the few mementos
she'd kept.

On her bed lay a white box tied with a gold ribbon. Inside
was a silk, sleeveless, black dress—a couture knock-off found in
a secondhand shop on a side street in the Latin Quarter. She
smoothed out the wrinkles, set out a pair of opened-toed, black,
patent leather high heels, and slipped on the dress that hugged
every curve.

19

SAM

SAM ARRIVED AT Doyle's Café an hour early and took a seat at the bar. His nerves a hot, twisted mess, he stared at the beer taps. *What was I thinking? I shouldn't end it in a noisy, crowded place.* But he knew he would weaken if they were alone.

The bartender asked, "What can I get you?"

"Club soda with lime."

When his drink arrived, he jabbed at the ice cubes with a swizzle stick and said, "Damn it." *If only I had known about my family before I met her—or better yet, never found out.*

"Sure, you don't want something stronger?"

"No, thanks. What do I owe you?"

"This round is on me."

He swiveled off the stool, found a table in a dark corner, and waited. His legs jiggled as he folded and unfolded a cocktail napkin. Suddenly, a loud cry roared over the racket. Cat whistles followed.

"Hey, guys, check out the door."

A streetlight illuminated Maddie's silhouette in the entrance. Gone was the bohemian style. Sleek in a snug-fitting dress, her red hair rested in soft waves around her shoulders. Sam rose, stumbled over the chair, and waved. When she stood in front of him, her green eyes twinkled and the dimples in her cheeks deepened. He sucked in a breath. *How is it conceivable she could be any more stunning?*

"Sam, it's so good to see you."

He righted his chair and slid hers out. "You look amazing." He ached to kiss her, but what he had to say needed to be swift and to the point. Any conversation would defeat what he was about to do.

Focusing on the rising bubbles in his drink, he kept his tone pragmatic. "You're a terrific girl, and we had a great time in Paris. But once I got back, I realized my career has to come first, and I'm not ready for a serious commitment. It wouldn't be fair to you." The color went out of her face, and when she spoke, he caught the confusion in her voice.

"I don't understand. What about everything you said in Paris and the letter you sent?"

Keep going. Finish what you started. No offer of an explanation, he delivered the final blow. "I would still like to get together for drinks and share notes on how we're doing." The words sounded cruel, but he didn't want to leave room to change his mind. When she opened her mouth and said nothing, he wanted to say, *Scream at me. Hit me. Tell me you hate me. I deserve it and more.*

The air became thick with bitterness, and her expression hardened. She took out his letter, threw it at him, and walked out. Feeling like the biggest rat, he thought, *How long did it take to destroy two lives? Ten minutes?*

20

MADDIE

MADDIE COULD NOT escape the scene in Doyle's bar. Just like that, Sam had ended it. No lead-up, no softening of words. It was the type of breakup that threw everything you believed and hoped for into question. Besides all the lies, he had stolen something precious. Paris was the first time she gave herself willingly and unconditionally to someone who didn't deserve it.

The hurt in her heart escalated to a burning, glaring pain. She remembered how he had pulled her in. The effortless way she fit into the curve of his body. The way he filled the empty spaces in her heart, and how she felt when she heard his voice, deep and soft, when he whispered, "I love you."

Unable to dull the anguish, she didn't know if she had the strength to go through this alone. She thought of Julia. All she had to do was pick up the phone. Too ashamed, she thought, *I can't. Not after I fell for a guy who turned out to be so shallow and heartless.*

When the phone rang, it startled her. *Sam. He's calling to say he made a terrible mistake.* Anticipating his sorrowful apology, she said, "Sam."

"Nope," Julia said. "It's me. I figured I would give you a few days until you settled into your new place."

Afraid to speak, Maddie remained silent.

"Are you still there?" She paused. "Maddie, is something wrong?"

She held back an ugly sob. "Julia, he broke up with me, told me he loved me and wanted to spend the rest of his life with me. All this time, I let myself be fooled by his sweet talk and empty promises." This time the floodgates opened, and she bawled.

"Don't go anywhere. I'm coming over."

Her hand ran across the stove and the kitchen counter. She had dreamed of Sam coming over for weekend dinners. She would surprise him what a good cook she was. Over a glass of wine, they'd talk about their future. When he proposed, she didn't care if he had no money for a ring. His asking was all she needed. They'd never discussed children, but she knew she wanted a house full of noise. He might disagree on how many, but either way, he would be a great father.

Along with their busy work schedules, they would have an active social life. Double dates with Joe and his girlfriend. If Julia met someone and could take a break from her classes, it would be the six of them. Instead, he'd played with her emotions, made her feel small and insignificant and ache in places she didn't know she had.

On the couch, with knees clutched to her chest, she heard the knock on the door. "It's open."

Julia rushed in and sat beside her. "I still can't believe the way he spoke to me. So matter of fact, as if what we shared in Paris meant nothing. He said he wanted to be friends. Get together, have a drink, talk about our careers." Her gaze wandered. "Maybe I'm not worthy of being loved."

"You listen to me. It's not you. He's a brainless prick, and eventually he'll get what's coming to him."

"I hate him for what he's done, yet I can't stop these feelings I have for him."

"Your emotions are going to be all over the place, and it won't be easy to get over him. But I promise the day will come when you won't feel this way. No matter how difficult it seems in the beginning, the most important thing you can do is to move forward one step at a time and keep busy."

Despite how she felt, she laughed. "You already sound like a psychologist."

"It will take me years to become one. What about you? When does teaching start?"

"Summer session begins in a week."

"Good. Are you still planning to check out galleries?"

She lifted her shoulders. "At some point."

It was late by the time Julia left. As Maddie got ready for bed, she picked up the photograph of her father pointing to a butterfly that had landed on her shoulder. She recalled the last thing he wrote in the letter inside the journal he gave her. *There is still so much good in the world waiting to receive you.* She thought, *I'm not sure anymore if I believe that.*

After four weeks, when all Maddie could do was bury herself in teaching and feeling sorry for herself, she decided she'd had enough of the self-pity. She started to paint and check out galleries in Market Square in downtown Boston. Discouraged when they were not taking on new clients and ready to give up, the WJS gallery caught her eye. She went inside. Different from the other galleries, there was something about its simplicity. The stark white walls and well-placed lightning allowed the eyes to focus on each piece. She imagined showing her work here. People would be drawn in from the street to get a closer look. She pictured what she would say to admirers. *I painted this one in Paris when I was studying abroad. If you're interested, I have several more waiting to be hung.*

She was studying several canvases resting against a wall when a handsome, gray-haired man with gold-framed glasses and dressed in a gray plaid suit with a bright-red patterned ascot approached her.

"Which one takes your fancy, young lady?"

"I—" She gulped and rushed ahead. "I'm a fan of Impressionists. It's this one over here on the right. But that one"—she pointed to a tempera painting—"should be in the window. It's absolutely gorgeous. In every gallery I've been in, I haven't seen one like it."

"You seem to know a little about art. I'm preparing for a new installation. Where do you think I should place these?"

Her cheeks tinged a shade of pink. "Oh, I'd never assume to know."

He glanced at her paint-stained fingers. "I think you know more than you realize. Where did you study art?"

"Northeastern. And a semester at the Sorbonne, where I painted every day."

"I'd like to see your work, Miss . . ."

Her heart skipped several beats. "Madelynn . . . Maddie O'Dell."

"Can you come back at five? People are finished browsing and shopping by then."

"Yes. And thank you, Mister . . ."

"William Strathmore."

"I'll see you at five. And thank you again."

Instead of the T, she took a cab to her apartment, told the driver to wait, and charged up the stairs to grab her portfolio. Giddy with excitement, she thought she'd explode. *Was her dream finally coming true?*

As she opened the gallery door, doubts blurred her enthusiasm. *Prepare yourself. He may decide not to accept any of your work.* Before she announced herself, he strolled in from another room.

"You're right on time, Maddie. Select three of your paintings and place them on the empty easels."

He stood back, propped his elbow with his hand, and lifted the other to cradle his chin and cheek. When he stepped forward to get a closer look at the canvases, her hands turned clammy. *How embarrassing. He thinks they're not good enough for his gallery.* She readied herself for another rejection.

"I'm sure I'm not the first person to tell you what a skilled artist you are. Your paintings will do well here."

He smiled and extended his hand to shake hers. Aware she was pumping it, her face turned scarlet. "Mr. Strathmore, you don't know how much this means to me."

He chuckled. "The name is Bill, and I think I do. Leave the portfolio here. Stop by Saturday, and I'll show you what I've selected."

Outside the gallery, she squared her shoulders. The joy of someone viewing her work and liking it pushed aside her thoughts about Sam.

When Maddie returned to the gallery, the closed sign hung on the door and there were no lights or movement. *Did I get the date wrong?* Ready to leave, she heard a voice call out.

"Wait. The damn—sorry—the darn T at my stop wasn't running, so I had to take a cab." He pulled out a key and stuck it in the lock. "Come in."

A half grin parted her mouth as she watched him scurry to turn on lights and grumble about the subway system. *He looks like a younger, slimmer version of Bill. I wonder if he's related?*

"Are you looking for something special or browsing?"

"No. I'm here to meet Mr. Strathmore—Bill—about my artwork."

"Oh, right. I'm his son, Jason. He's sorry for the inconvenience and wants to know if you can stop by later today?"

"Please tell him I'd be happy to."

"I probably shouldn't tell you before he does, but he's pretty impressed with your work. In fact, if you're available, he's considering offering you a part-time job now that I'm too busy to help here. But don't let on. Act excited."

"I promise it won't be acting."

It didn't take long before Maddie's confidence grew with every customer and window-shopper who entered the gallery. Because of her extensive knowledge of art in a variety of mediums, the serious buyers developed a trust in her expertise. The first time she sold a painting for a significant sum of money, Bill, a broad smile on his face, placed his hands on her shoulders.

"Someday, Madelynn O'Dell, I predict you will be famous and the owner of your own gallery. You'll be missed when that happens."

"No need to worry about that. I'm happy right where I am."

Her connection to the Strathmores was immediate. When Bill learned she had no living relatives, he and his wife, Rita, embraced her like a daughter. Her relationship with Jason was just as strong—like having a brother. His unassuming nature and funny disposition were hard to resist. And when he came by the gallery during its lull, they discussed art and his acting career. The Strathmores were a constant reminder of what true happiness felt like.

After Julia met Jason, the three of them spent weekends going to dinner, movies, and seeing his theater performances. She looked forward to those evenings, until the dynamics changed. Jason's relationship with the girl he was dating turned serious, and Julia met someone. They still got together for lunch, but whenever she was invited out with their significant others, she refused. It made her feel too much like an outsider. Concerned, Jason pestered her about her social life.

"I don't mean to pry, but I haven't heard you talk about dating."

She stammered, "I've never been comfortable, and I'm terrible with small talk."

"Well, it's time to change that. I'd like you to meet Rich, a graphic designer. He's easy to be with, and I know you'll enjoy his company."

Could it be any worse than watching another episode of Gilligans's Island *or* Get Smart? She delayed a response before she said, "Only if you join us."

"Will do. I already talked to him. He's free tonight. I made a six o'clock reservation at the Italian place across the street."

"Are you crazy? You already planned this without checking with me first?"

"If I had, what would you have said?"

"What do you think?"

"Exactly. You can't back out. The guy is interested in meeting you."

She looked down at what she was wearing. "I won't have time to go home and change."

"Girl, you could dress in a potato sack and still look gorgeous. I gotta go. Don't be late."

The view of the restaurant entrance in sight, she kept repositioning her arms and legs. *This is a mistake. If I'm lucky, he's changed his mind.* She released a drawn-out sigh when a guy with brown eyes and streaked blond hair dressed in a tailored suit walked toward her.

"You must be Maddie."

It was obvious Jason had mentioned the red hair.

He extended his hand. "I'm Rich. I hope you weren't waiting long."

"No." When he waved to the server and asked for the wine list, she said, "Shouldn't we wait for Jason?"

"He got a call from the producer to fill in for tonight's performance."

Without a buffer, she did her best to hide the discomfort that sat below her smile. It was a relief when he carried the conversation to cover the silences. When she declined dessert and another drink, his face read, *Let's call it a night.*

Putting on her coat, she couldn't remember a word he'd said. She'd spent the entire evening comparing him to Sam. The gentle way he laced his fingers through hers. Taking a lock of her hair and placing it behind her ear. The sound of his voice, his laugh, and his smile. As the hidden knots of memories unraveled, she struggled to blink back the tears. *I'm done with the dating scene. Being alone may be difficult, but evenings like this are worse.*

21

SAM

SAM SAT ACROSS from Joe in a Chinese restaurant, talking about how fast the business had grown. "It's hard to believe how well we've done since we opened our doors."

Joe said, "Oh, I can. I had to loosen my belt three notches because of the pounds I put on wining and dining clients."

Sam noticed his untouched plate. "Don't you like what you ordered?" He slid his sizzling dish toward him. "Here, try mine."

Joe pushed it back and said, "There's nothing's wrong with the food."

"Normally, you would have devoured your entire meal before my first bite." Sam lifted an eyebrow. "Now that you're engaged, did Cindy put you on a diet before the wedding?"

"No."

"So?"

"I'm concerned about you."

Sam gave him a quizzical look. "Why?"

"I've stopped counting the times you sit, stare at the wall, or pace in your office. Even after you outbid the big guys for that five-year contract, you didn't seem happy or excited."

He fiddled with the chopsticks. "It has nothing to do with work."

"Then what's the problem?"

Through a cheerless twist to his mouth, he said, "Maddie."

"What's it been? Seven months since you broke it off?"

"Doesn't matter. I still love her."

"Ever consider telling her?"

"Not after the way I treated her."

Sam stepped into his office and looked at the three bids strewn across his desk. If one got signed, they could get closer to renting an upscale space. Despite the long hours and the seven-day routine, the job didn't anesthetize him to what remained absent in his life.

When banging struck their shared wall, Sam walked into Joe's office. Above the bookshelves hung a canvas of vibrant colored blooms. He recognized the flower market with the bright-orange pavilions. His voice cracked. "Where did you buy that?"

"Faneuil Market. After my meeting yesterday, I heard early Christmas music playing inside a small gallery. I wandered in, loved the painting on the wall, selected the print, and never bothered to look who did it. When the salesperson came out from the office, I asked who the artist was. She told me she was and painted it in Paris. I immediately knew it was Maddie. I didn't have the heart to tell her I no longer wanted it."

"Did you say anything about me?"

"Should I have?"

"Hell no. She hates me. I convinced her I loved her, slept with her, and then, with a flick of a hand, dumped her like she was a nobody."

"I'll take it down."

"No. This is one of her best pieces."

"You sure?"

"Yeah. Time to get back to work. It's the one thing I know I won't mess up."

"Sam, go see her. Tell her you were an idiot for breaking up with her and beg for a second chance. What have you got to lose?"

When Joe handed him the receipt with the address, he balled it up and tossed it in the trash. Ten minutes later, he retrieved it, smoothed the creases, and left.

Sam pulled up his coat collar, tightened the wool scarf, and watched families stand along the cobbled promenade of Faneuil Hall Square. Despite the cold front, the jugglers, magicians, and the mime street performers continued to display their skills. Though he passed several cafes—Italian to German cuisine—food was the last thing on his mind.

Focused on storefront numbers, he measured each step until he reached fifty-seven. The air was knocked out of him when he saw Maddie laughing with a guy's arm around her waist. *This is a dumb idea. Leave before she sees you.* Too late. Released from the hold, she turned, and her eyes fixed on his. He tried to take off, but stopped when she came out and spoke.

"What are you doing here?"

A hot flush burned his cheeks. "Ahh . . . when I passed by, I saw you. My partner bought the flower market painting. Remember we were together when you painted it?" He wanted to slap the side of his head. *What a moron. Why would she want to remember anything to do with you? Say something.* "Maddie, I . . ." If her eyes were darts, he would have been the perfect target.

She raised her voice. "Don't come around here again."

Before he turned to go, the boyfriend walked outside. "Hey, is this guy bothering you?"

"Not anymore. He's leaving."

As the hustle of sidewalk shoppers pushed him forward, he thought, *I gained nothing by going there, except to find out how she has erased me from her life with someone else.*

Back in the office, he slumped into the chair and buried his hands in his hair. He couldn't get rid of the image of the guy's arm around her and how cheerful she looked. *I should be happy she's found someone who will treat her right.* He tried to work through a contract that needed immediate attention but never got past the first page. He looked up when Joe waltzed in.

"Christ, you look like hell."

"I saw her."

"What happened?"

"She has a boyfriend and told me to get lost—permanently."

"That must have been tough to hear. But at least you know it's over and you can move on."

Sam's shrug was heavy. "Whether it will mean anything to her or not, there's something I need to say before I can even consider letting go."

Sam entered Market Square to a burst of Christmas spirit. Illuminated by blinking white lights, the stores and restaurants bustled with shoppers. People swarmed in and out of decorated wooden stalls owned by local artisans selling unique handmade items. Laughter, blending with the holiday music, added to the lively atmosphere. He felt none of it.

Next to a kiosk with a direct view of the gallery, Sam's insides churned when the same guy planted a kiss on Maddie's cheek and hugged her. *If only I hadn't pursued the search for that bloody shoebox, it would be me in there.* Once the guy left, Sam stood on the sidewalk in front of the gallery. Maddie's back was to him. *I wonder how long I have before she pushes me out the door.* Three large silver bells on a red ribbon jingled when he opened the door.

"Sorry, I'm closing early."

His voice barely audible, he said, "Maddie." When she spun around, her eyes flared.

Before she opened her mouth to speak, he said, "Please hear me out. I promise I won't bother you again." Unfortunate timing, bad luck, fate—the boyfriend came back. *I can't stand and watch another display of affection.* If his feet didn't feel like they were mired in quicksand, he would have mumbled something stupid and bolted.

"Everyone at the restaurant is three drinks ahead. They want to hear all about our wedding plans, except Angie. She refuses to start without the maid of honor."

The guy looked at him and back at Maddie. "Everything okay here. Should I hang around and wait for you?"

"Go on. I can handle this."

"Okay," he said, and hurried out humming a tune.

Sam sputtered, "He's not your boyfriend?"

Her eyes drilled into his. "It's none of your business. Now get out so I can lock up and enjoy the rest of my evening."

When she returned with a set of keys, he saw tears clinging to her bottom lashes.

"Have you lost your mind or your hearing? I said go!"

He felt the magnitude of her anger but kept talking. "Not until you know how much I regret hurting you the way I did."

"I don't care what you have to say. Not today, not ever."

That evening, over drinks, Sam told Joe, "I saw her again. She came down hard when I tried to apologize."

Joe's eyes shifted skyward. "Did your brain short-circuit? Remember, she's involved with someone else."

"That guy in the gallery? He's a friend, and he's engaged." The heel of his hand pressed against his forehead. "When she got teary-eyed, it reminded me of how much I humiliated her."

"If it looked like she was going to cry, maybe a part of her still cares, but she's afraid to give you another chance."

"Even if she did, it won't change the goddamn family I was born into and how it could affect me." He startled when Joe's hand slammed the table.

"Man, you are so fucked-up. These irrational fears are messing with your head. Did you ever discuss this with your dad? Get his take on it?"

"No point. I got all the sick details from my mom. The only thing I wish I had done was tell him what a shitty father he turned out to be."

"You're way overdue in that category."

A week later, he got a late-night phone call. His father had died.

Sam found his mother in the kitchen, staring out the window. When she turned, her face was drawn and absent of color. His arms around her, she leaned into him and wept. "Come sit and tell me what happened."

She pulled a tissue from the sleeve of her sweater and dabbed her eyes. "They rushed him to the hospital last night. After two hours in the ICU, his heart finally gave out. A nurse said he told her he had been having tightness in his chest and tingling down his left arm on and off. For days, he didn't act or look right. I tried to get him to see his doctor, but he refused." She started to cry again. "It's my fault. I should have made him go."

He took her hand in his. "You're not to blame. We both knew how stubborn he could be when his mind was made up. What about the arrangements?"

"I took care of everything this morning. Knowing your dad, all he would want is a few friends and a priest to speak at the cemetery. Tuesday is the soonest I could schedule it."

"I'll stay as long as you need me." He looked around the kitchen. "This may not be the right time to discuss this, but with Dad gone, I'm concerned how you're going to manage living here alone?"

"Last year, we discussed selling the house and moving into a smaller place with little or no upkeep outside."

He was glad she was thinking about selling. Growing up here, his father's erratic temper had made her life and his miserable. "The move will be good for you."

"Are you hungry? Several women from the church came by and brought a couple of casseroles."

"Unless you're not up to it, why don't we go out for a bite to eat?"

She stood and hugged him. "I'm so glad you're here, Sam. It means so much to me."

He got why she said this. He spoke to her often and met for lunch or dinner but made excuses to go back home. When he left seven months ago, he'd vowed never to be in his father's presence after she'd finally told him what he'd done to his grandfather.

His dad had been in the fields, preparing them for planting when Luther had walked up to him, cracking the whip on the ground. An all too familiar scenario had made something snap inside him. He swung the pitchfork and struck him in the head. Once Luther fell, he kept hitting him until he stopped moving.

His mother had clutched his arm and said, "Sam, I don't condone your father's behavior, but it pales in comparison to what your grandfather did to him and his family."

He had insisted on knowing what happened after the beating. She told him the head trauma left Luther incapacitated and in a wheelchair. Afraid to get his dad in trouble, his grandmother, Agnes, refused to take him to the hospital. A doctor, who made house calls, had done what he could to mend and stabilize him. Agnes took care of him with the help of his dad and his brother. After Marshall went to jail and Agnes died, he sold the farm and sent his grandfather to the nursing home.

He understood his grandfather was rotten to the core. But he needed to know how his mom could forget all the times his dad had threatened to hit him, and the night he came close to slamming his fist into his face. She had said he was terrified because he was brought up with so much physical and emotional abuse, and he didn't know how to relate to him. Too often, he had witnessed what happened when someone lost control, and his own acting out had scared him. Afraid he would turn out like Luther, he never trusted himself to be a good father. Sam wanted to know why she had stayed and if she'd ever been afraid he would hurt them.

She said, "Never."

He'd told her, "They're in my DNA—Angus, Luther, Marshall, Dad." Pushing back his hair, he had pointed to the strange-looking birthmark. He'd read somewhere certain societies viewed it as a sign of being possessed by demons. It had sounded crazy, but maybe evil ran through his blood. But his mother had reassured him that he and his father were not cursed and the mark didn't represent anything wicked. He had searched her face and asked, "If you had known, would you still have married him?"

Recalling all the secrets his parents kept hidden about his family, he thought about Paris and the night of that out-of-control party. On his way home, it had creeped him out when he felt a black cloud hovering over his future. Had this been another premonition that more was yet to come?

"Sam are you okay? You were staring out the window and didn't answer me when I said I found a letter in your dad's suit pocket. I'm not sure when he planned to give it to you." She handed it to him and said, "I'm going to freshen up before we go out."

"I'm fine," taking the letter. Smudged fingerprints surrounded the edges, as if it'd been handled repeatedly. *Is this his way of making me feel like shit again?* At first he decided not to read it, but then reconsidered. *Whatever he had to say can't affect me anymore.*

> *Sam,*
>
> *I'm not good with words, but I want you to know how miserable I feel about the terrible way I treated you and the things I said. You never deserved that or to think you could turn out like my family. I'm so proud of the fine young man you are, and maybe someday you'll give me the chance to show you before it's too late. I love you, son. I always have. I just have trouble showing you.*
>
> *Dad*

The date it had been written was after he moved out of the house. He had plenty of opportunities to mail it or give it to his mother. *So why did he wait? Did he have second thoughts?* He was tearing the letter in two when his mother came back.

"Did he write something that upset you?"

"Yes. His lame attempt to make amends. He said I could never turn out like his side of the family. Like that was supposed to absolve him for the way he treated me and made me think there was something wrong with me." He waved the torn letter. "This doesn't change anything. It's too late. The harm was done over twenty years ago."

"I wish . . ."

"You know what I wish? I wish I didn't have to break up with a fantastic girl because . . ."

"You have a girlfriend?"

His shoulders drooped. "Had."

"Tell me about her."

He told her how they met in Paris and what she had been through. How he realized there was something special about her. "Mom, she's like nobody I've ever met. I'm in love with her, and she felt the same way."

"She sounds wonderful. What happened?"

"When I found out about Dad's relatives, and what he did to Luther, it petrified me. I was scared I might do something unforgivable one day."

"Oh, Sam, I thought I made it clear you aren't capable of anything like that." Her hands gently pressed against his chest. "It's not in your nature to be anything but a good, loving, caring person."

"Even if that were true, none of it matters now. The way I broke up with her was indefensible. Now she wants nothing to do with me."

"You listen to me. Go back and fight for her. Make her see what I've known all along."

Sam sat in his office, staring at the blinking lights on the answering machine, when Joe came in and dropped into a chair.

"You're back already?" Joe asked. "I would have been there if we didn't have those two deadlines to meet. How's your mom?"

"She has her work and her friends. She's thinking about selling the house and moving."

"What about you?"

"I'm okay. Catch me up on what needs to be worked on." His attention on Maddie, he drifted in and out of Joe's update. Somewhere in the pile of hurt, he prayed there would be a part of her that still had feelings for him. How to make her see that was the burning question. He felt a pencil hit his chest. "Hey, what was that for?"

"Have you listened to a word I said?"

"Yes."

"If you did, you would smile about the closing of one of our recent deals. Instead, you've got this dogged look on your face, like you're trying to figure out something."

"It's Maddie. I'm going to try to get her back."

"I don't get why you would put yourself through more rejections."

He toyed with the pencil. "It's a harebrain idea, but I need to try."

"How do you plan on doing that when she's made it pretty clear it's over?"

His shoulders fell. "Still trying to figure that out."

Sam leaned against the same Market Square kiosk and watched, for the fourth time, the flowers and notes he sent to Maddie trashed along with his efforts. Each time, the owner had asked, "Can I interest you in today's special?" Feeling guilty, he purchased a leather wallet with plastic inserts for photographs. He shoved it in his pocket and thought, *Any more rebuffs and it will stay empty.* When Joe found out what he was doing, he laid into him.

"You've gone completely batshit, and your workload has taken a hit. Haven't you groveled enough? Besides me covering for you, tell me what the hell is motivating you to keep up this worthless pursuit?"

"She hasn't tried to get me arrested for harassment."

"Well, I guess that's something."

"I get how absurd it looks, but I can't give up, at least not yet. Maybe she has to clobber me over the head to get the message across."

Joe raised a fist over his head. "If she doesn't, I will."

22

MADDIE

MADDIE REMEMBERED THE first time she'd received one of Sam's floral arrangements. Jason had walked into the gallery, placed them on the counter, and said, "I've got your coffee and flowers."

"They're gorgeous. Peonies were my mom's favorite."

"Someone went to a lot of trouble to buy these in the middle of winter."

"I bet it's from the new artist your dad signed on three weeks ago."

"Nope. A card and an envelope have your name on them. Do you have a secret admirer you're not telling me about?"

"Hardly. Let me see."

The color ebbed from her face when she recognized the writing. She snapped the flowers in two, dumped them in the trash, along with the card and the unread note. Rushing outside without a coat, the frigid air whirled around her. He was nowhere in sight. She ran back in, slammed the door, making it rattle on its hinges.

"Are you being stalked?"

"That's an understatement."

"If it's that guy who's been here before, we should notify the authorities."

"He's a nobody." *Who thinks he can do something to make up for how much he hurt me.*

The following Saturday, when the gallery door chimed, Maddie lifted her head from a stack of receipts. Sam was standing there, holding a glossy white bag.

She crossed her arms and gave him an exasperated look. "What you're doing isn't working. It's a waste of time and money on someone who doesn't care or appreciate the effort."

With a slight smile, he handed her the bag. "I can't imagine a nicer way to spend my hard-earned dollars," he said, and walked out.

He had decorated the front of the bag with places they visited—the Eiffel Tower, the Louvre, and the Champ de Mars Gardens where they'd ridden bicycles and picnicked. As if a child had done it, they were pictures cut and pasted from a travel guide. Ready to throw it out, her curiosity overruled the anger. An involuntary reflex caused her mouth to curl into a grin when she took out the box from the famous sweetshop, Ladurée—a tea salon in Paris.

As she removed the cover, a rainbow of colors leaped out. The American version was no comparison to French macarons. Their crunchy outer layers tasted like meringue with a creamy filling. She remembered the afternoon he'd taken her there. The server had presented an arrangement of delicate cookies on a tier of patterned ceramic dishes. To her, it had been an edible work of art.

Unable to resist, she bit into a pink one. Thoughts of Sam slipped in as easily as the raspberry filling melted on her tongue. It startled her when a sudden warmth flowed through her body. *Why now? Why this gift?* She opened the bottom drawer, took out the notes bound with a rubber band, and kneaded her forehead. *What compelled me to keep taking them out of the trash?* On an impulse, she decided to read them. Every word he wrote hit her like a steel fist—"I never stopped loving you. I'm so sorry I hurt you. Please forgive me and give me another chance." As repressed memories stirred, she stumbled around an unimaginable thought. *Do I still have feelings for him after what he did?*

A week later, while she was busy rearranging paintings, her back stiffened when she heard her name.

"Hello, Maddie."

She turned, an indignant expression on her face.

"I know you haven't read my notes, but I need to tell you how I feel before you show me the door. I never stopped loving you. You mean everything to me. Nothing in my life matters, not even my career, if you aren't part of it. I want to make it up to you."

She thrust her chin at him. "After all the lies and promises, not to mention the rotten way you treated me, you expect me to believe you?"

He closed the gap between them. "The only lie is the hateful excuse I gave you. Here's the truth. I never told you how afraid I was that I would turn out like my dad. The doubts kept messing with my head, and I figured you'd be better off without me."

"And, what's so different now?"

"When I went home after my father died, my mom found a letter he wrote to me. He blamed himself for the way he treated me and said it was because of the way his father treated him. When I finally told her about you, she was thrilled, until I said why I ended it. She reassured me I would never turn out like him. I should have never lied, and I've regretted it every day since I broke it off. Please, Maddie, I just want another chance."

"You should have trusted me to understand. Without that, whatever existed between us was built on false promises."

"I . . ."

She put up her palm. "No more, Sam. I want you out of my life." When he left, she called Julia. "If you're free, let's meet for dinner."

"Sure."

"There's a Mexican place around the corner from the gallery. I'll meet you there at six."

When she arrived, Julie was already seated. She placed the decorated bag on the table.

"What's the occasion? It's not my birthday."

"Look inside. It's Sam's latest gift."

"Are you kidding me? Did these really come from Paris?"

"All the way." She relayed their entire conversation and what was in his notes.

"Seems like something may have changed."

"With him?"

"Sounds like it, but maybe you have too. You've hung onto those notes and didn't trash the macaroons. Tell me, what's going on in your head?"

She ran her fingers over the Paris cutouts on the bag. "I thought I was over him and there wouldn't be a chance in hell I'd ever take him back, but . . ."

"Do you still love him?"

Her shoulders wilted. "I don't know how I feel anymore. So where do I go from here?"

"Only one way to find out. If you're willing to take the risk, go out with him. But take it slow. See if you can trust him again."

The possibility of love and mistrust jockeyed for the same spot in her heart. She felt torn between a future with him and the fear of being hurt again.

23

SAM

THREE WEEKS LATER, Sam got the call. Maddie agreed to spend time with him under one condition. Lunch near Faneuil Hall Marketplace and an occasional dinner. Anything construed as intimate or romantic remained off-limits.

Their first few dates weren't easy. He knew she was nervous by the way she played with a piece of jewelry, her clothes, and her hair. Careful not to say anything that could be misconstrued, he kept the conversation on topics she seemed comfortable with— teaching, painting, the gallery, and his job. Only once, he forgot and mentioned their time in Paris. Her face blanched, and her body tensed. A hard knot formed in his gut as he waited to hear the same words she'd said in Paris. "I'd like to go now." He told her he was sorry and would never bring up Paris again.

When Joe asked how it was going, he told him, "We've been seeing each for weeks, and it's driving me nuts."

"I know. The day after you're with her, you're flying high or down in the dumps."

"I want more than a casual relationship."

"What if it's all she wants? Can you live with that?"

"To be with her and accept it will never turn serious again—I doubt it."

"Don't blow it by moving too fast. Give her more time. I think she's waiting to see if you'll let her down again."

"Always the voice of reason."

"What did she say when you told her you called it quits because of the idiotic notion you inherited shit from your whacked-out relatives?"

He looked down at his hands and didn't answer.

"What? You didn't tell her?"

"I did. What I said was partly true."

"But not everything? Christ, secrets like this have a way of blowing up in your face."

He saw the concerned look on Joe's face. "It has to be this way, or I'll risk losing her again."

Sam saw a slow change in Maddie. She didn't rush off after lunch or dinner, lingered over coffee or drinks, and seemed to enjoy herself. Their exchanges turned more personal when she mentioned her relationship with the Strathmores.

"Jason and I clicked immediately. It wasn't long before I realized how much he means to me. And Bill and Rita? Honest to God, I don't know how I would have managed if they weren't in my life."

"They sound wonderful."

"Would you like to come to my first exhibit at the gallery? You could meet them."

Stunned by her invite, he said, "Do you mind if I bring Joe and his girlfriend?"

"That would be great. Invite as many people as you want. I'll need all the moral support I can get. I wish Julia could come, but she's swamped studying for exams."

He remembered his initial encounter with Julia. It had happened the afternoon she came into the gallery. When Maddie introduced him and he extended his hand, she kept her grip tight, and not in a friendly way. It sent a clear message he had better not hurt her best friend again.

By the time Sam, Joe, and his girlfriend arrived at the gallery, it was teeming with attendees. He introduced Maddie before a group of people surrounded her. As the three of them moved from room to room, it amazed him to see her entire collection of work. He did his best to explain to Joe and his girlfriend what he'd learned from her. "Each one is a Paris painting, where people gathered at churches, buildings, and different monuments—like the one you bought for your office."

"Who knows?" Joe said. "Maybe when I'm rich and famous, I can buy the original."

Maddie approached them. "I'm so sorry I didn't get a chance to spend more time with you. Whenever I thought I had a free moment, Bill took my arm and introduced me to some interested buyers. I hope you're enjoying yourselves."

Joe smiled. "Cindy and I are having a great time. I'm sure you don't remember I bought one of your prints."

"I never forget the face of anyone who appreciates my work enough to pay for it. There're still appetizers, champagne, and wine left."

"No, thanks. We're going to take off. I look forward to following your career and saying I knew you when."

She laughed. "Thank you both for coming."

Sam said, "I'll take you up on that wine."

She took his hand. "First, let me introduce you to Bill and Rita. Jason couldn't make it, but is eager to meet you."

Warmly greeted by both of them, it encouraged him to take the next step when Bill mentioned Maddie never stopped talking about him.

Sam wanted to take her to a ritzy restaurant overlooking Boston Harbor but decided to play it safe and keep to their regular dinner dates. He chose a pizza place within walking distance of her apartment. Wired as if someone had zapped his chest with electric paddles, everything depended on how and what he would say. Preoccupied with screwing things up, he left a half-eaten pie on the wooden serving platter.

Maddie smiled. "Not hungry? Any other time, you would have devoured it and ordered a second."

He peeked at his watch. The place would be closing in thirty minutes. "Maddie, I've had a great time with you and . . ." His throat felt like he'd swallowed a jar of cotton balls. When he saw her eyes cloud over and her jaw tense, he thought, *Shit, that didn't come out right.* "I meant to say . . ."

She put her hands on the table, scraped back the chair, and stood. "No need to make another excuse."

When she picked up her purse and turned to leave, he stood and grabbed her arm. "Wait," he said, and dug into his pocket and opened the black velvet box. A sheen of sweat broke out across his forehead. His voice low and soft, he said, "I love you, Maddie, and I want to marry you." The heart-shaped diamond remained in its velvet crease. *This is not good. I should have given her more time.*

Maddie glanced at him and back at the ring. He was about to tell her it was okay if she didn't want to accept his proposal when she sat down, extended her left hand, and said, "Yes, Sam, I'll marry you."

24

MADDIE
1966

MADDIE LOVED THE way the white lace bohemian empire dress with the square neck and billowy sleeves made her feel beautiful. Admiring the bouquet of pale-pink peonies and wildflowers, she touched the vine-leaf, rose-gold headband that rested on the crown of her head. She looked at Julia. "I wanted to surprise Sam and wear something that reminded him of our time in Paris. Do you think he'll like it over something more traditional?"

"You're breathtaking. He might faint before he says 'I do.'"

She was relieved and happy Julia had finally come around to trusting Sam. It took some convincing, but he finally won her over.

"If you don't want to be seen at the church entrance, we should leave."

Maddie hadn't been inside a church since her father died. She would have preferred a civil ceremony but decided to do it for her mother. "Wait for me in the limo. I need a little time to myself." After a search through a box of old photographs, she'd found a wedding picture of her parents. She'd done her best to navigate life without their presence for important celebrations—birthdays, graduation, becoming an accomplished artist. Today was different. It carried a stark reminder of what she had lost. *I will never witness your reactions when I walk down the aisle in my wedding dress. You will never meet the love of my life, know our children, and your grandchildren. I miss you both so much, but the only way to honor your absence is to be happy, and I am—happier than I've been in a long time.*

June tenth was a perfect day. The sky, an unbroken backdrop of blue, allowed the sun to cast its rays on Maddie as she ascended the church steps. To keep it intimate, only Sam's mother, Joe and his girlfriend, Jason and his wife, and the Strathmores were invited. Her arm tucked in Bill's, they followed Julia down the aisle. When Sam released a gasp, she gripped the bouquet. *I should have bought a trendier dress.* But as she approached him, a broad grin extended across his face.

"You're gorgeous," he whispered. Reciting his vows, he said, "Maddie, I'll never be able to describe the happiness you've brought into my life. Your love and trust have made me a better person. I promise to cherish and protect you and never stop showing you how much I love you."

Her words rested behind her lips as they worked to break free when her turn came. "I can't wait to start our life together. You are my everything and all that I am and have, I offer to you in love and joy." Once they exchanged rings, the priest announced them man and wife. With tenderness, Sam lifted her chin and kissed her.

Compliments of the Strathmore's, the reception was at an expensive restaurant, followed by a sumptuous dinner. Seated next to Bill, Maddie turned to him. "Thank you for everything. I wish I could repay your kindness."

He folded his hands over hers. "You did the moment you stepped into our lives and let us embrace you as our daughter."

She dabbed a tear from the corner of her eye and looked around the room. Married to the love of her life and being surrounded by all the people who mattered made her heart swell. This was the door she had been waiting to walk through. No longer doubtful of Sam's love or a future with him, she knew it would never close behind her.

The ink wasn't dry on the on the marriage certificate when Maddie wanted to talk about having a baby. "We never discussed having a baby and when to start a family, but I don't want to wait."

Sam skirted the issue with excuses. "You've been so busy at the gallery and looking for places to open your own. Joe and I are working our butts off so we can move into a bigger building. Neither one of us has time to breathe or spend together, let alone care for a baby."

As the weeks turned into months, the longing for a baby grew stronger and a bottomless sadness set in. But it wasn't only the desire for a baby that dragged her down. In two weeks, she and Sam would celebrate their first Thanksgiving, followed by Christmas. Thoughts of her dad heightened the ache in her heart.

Maddie had stood in the kitchen doorway and watched her father preparing the Thanksgiving dinner. "Hi, Dad."

The dishtowel fell to the floor. "What a surprise. I didn't expect you until later."

He stretched his arms wide. "Come, give me a hug."

A grayish hue had settled above his cheekbones, and his bulky frame had thinned. *Last month, he didn't look this way.* Her voice shook. "Are you feeling okay?"

"I'm fine, except for the occasional bouts of heartburn. I need to be careful what I eat." He had rubbed his stomach. "I also need to lose weight."

"No way. You could stand to put on a few more pounds." Her eyebrows lowered into a quizzical frown at the size of the bird on the stove. "That turkey could feed the entire neighborhood."

He lifted his shoulders. "Ever since I misplaced your mom's note card on how to calculate the number of pounds for each person, I figured it was safer to go bigger."

She snickered. "We'll be cackling the entire weekend." Concerned he would have trouble lifting it, she had said, "I'll put it in the pan."

He flexed a pencil-thin arm into a biceps curl. "I can handle it."

The dishes done and leftovers sealed in Tupperware containers, she carried the dessert into the living room. When she had handed him a slice of pumpkin pie, he jiggled his belt.

"No thanks. One more bite and these pants won't fit."

Her eyes narrowed. *He ate next to nothing at dinner and pushed the food around the plate like a three-year-old. Before I go back to school, I'm going to insist he get a complete checkup.*

When he had leaned back in the chair and closed his eyes, she gave him a gentle shake. "Go to bed. It's been a long day."

He kissed the top of her head and lifted a hand in a military salute. "A big breakfast will be on the table before you go back to school."

She noticed him slowly drag his feet out of the room and whispered, "Please be all right."

Packed and ready to leave the next morning, Maddie had said, "During semester break, let's go to Boston's Theater District, see a play, and stuff our faces at Caffe Vittoria."

"Sounds great. I'm looking forward to another Christmas with my special girl."

Her eyes had misted over. "I love you, Dad. Promise me you'll see the doctor."

"I'll call for an appointment on Monday."

She thought about the fake tree hidden in an unused part of the shed. A grin flashed across her face when she remembered her parents' exchange the weekend he'd brought it home.

"John Patrick O'Dell, take that fake tree out of here. It's bad enough you stuck me with that ridiculous red, tail-wagging cat clock hanging above the kitchen window."

"Kate, it's the hottest item in all the stores."

Sarcasm had leaped from her lips. "I've stopped counting the number of times I've heard you say that."

"You'll appreciate this. According to the manufacturer's warranty, the tree will never catch on fire."

"After all these years, you're suddenly worried about a fire?"

"That's not all." He shook the branches. "We'll never have to water the tree or vacuum up dry pine needles."

"You mean, *you* won't. We've always had gorgeous ten-foot trees, and none smelled like they came off an assembly line." She had rubbed her face in exasperation. "This thing you call a tree will topple over the second it's decorated."

"There is a perfect solution. I can buy a bigger one or to make sure this one stays upright, I'll tie a rope around it and hook it to the wall."

She had put him on notice. "No, to both ideas."

From the Sears bag, he handed her an angel with spun-glass hair and gold-foil wings. "I know how much you love them."

"I appreciate the lovely bribe, but next year, we get an actual tree."

Her mother never had a next year.

Maddie had planned a surprise for her father. She got home early for Christmas break and dragged the fake tree and ornaments into the living room. Stationed in its rightful place, she had decorated nonstop for two hours. One by one, she hung the ornaments. Glass-colored balls and bells. Red-and-white-striped candy canes. Handmade cookie ornaments and paper garlands cut into small colored strips of paper stuck together with glue. Weighted down with four strands of red, blue, and white lights, grateful it hadn't moved sideways, she had plugged the cord into the wall socket. With the tree lit up in all its glory, she sprinted to the door when she heard the car.

"Hi, Dad. Let me take your hat and coat."

"Can I come inside before I freeze out here?"

"Sorry. I'm excited to see you." She had kissed him on the cheek and snuggled into his arms. His usual robust hug was missing. A sinking feeling had alerted her something wasn't right. "I have a surprise for you. Close your eyes and promise not to peek."

He made an *X* across his chest. "Cross my heart and hope to die."

How she hated that phrase. When they had stood in front of the tree, she said, "You can open them." His face was a wash of confusion, and his silence stretched thin. The only sound came from the steam of the radiator as the heat flowed through the pipes. She pressed her locked fingers against her mouth and waited. When he beamed and his eyes crinkled, she exhaled.

He said, "There's something about it, but I can't find the right words to describe it."

"The French have a saying, *Il a un certain attrait.* It has a certain appeal to it."

"I'm going to let you in on a well-kept secret I never told your mother. The brush company, Addis, one of the first to make toilet bowl brushes, used the same method for constructing artificial trees."

She had burst into a fit of laughter. Fat tears streamed down her cheeks as she grabbed her side. "Oh my god. I can't remember when I laughed so hard."

He followed with a loud, throaty roar that burst from his mouth. "Imagine what your mom's response would have been."

"She'd say, 'You've got ten seconds to decide which one of you will be out the door first.'" When he coughed, she had watched him gradually lower into a chair and flinch. Seeing his lack of strength, dramatic weight loss, and distress, an iron vice of fear coiled around her stomach. She had pulled up a chair to face him, their knees touching. "This is more serious than heartburn. What aren't you telling me?"

Maddie and Sam spent their first Thanksgiving with the Strathmores and their extended family and friends. When dinner was ready, Bill suggested everyone say what they were thankful for.

At Sam's turn, she saw the undeniable love in his eyes. "I'm grateful to my beautiful wife, who continues to make me a better person." He raised his glass. "To you, Maddie. I feel—no, I *am*—the luckiest guy in the world."

When it was her turn, she squeezed his hand and said, "I am grateful for all the joy and happiness you have brought into my life." Throughout the day, she tried not to dwell on the last Thanksgiving with her father or how she would deal with Christmas around the corner.

The next day, Maddie turned the sign on the gallery door to *Closed* and stepped outside. The twinkling lights strung along the streets of the marketplace and the holiday cheer among the Christmas rush of shoppers made her heart sink even further than it had over Thanksgiving.

By the time she unlocked the door to their apartment, all she wanted was to kick off her shoes and fall into bed. But when she walked in, boxes of ornaments surrounded Sam, who was grinning like a kid.

"I took off early to get everything ready. Now all we have to do is get the tree, so we can decorate this weekend."

She dreaded the effort and stalled for time. "With all the hours I'm putting in at the gallery, can't it wait until the madness lets up?"

"I'll do it. Joe told me where I can buy a nice tree that won't be too expensive. Leave the decorating to me. Thanks to my mom, I've learned to be a master at it. Her motto: 'A tree can never have too much.'"

Her cheerlessness made her feel guilty. "Leave it to me. I don't want you going crazy."

A week later, and Maddie still hadn't decorated the tree, she walked into the apartment and gasped. In the corner stood a tree overdone with an explosion of color and an overabundance of blinking lights. Sam was busy throwing mounds of tinsel on it. When he turned around, his face looked apologetic. "I know it's pathetic, but there wasn't much to choose from. The good news—the guy gave it to me for nothing when I told him we were celebrating our first Christmas."

Hot, wet tears clouded her eyes.

He grabbed his jacket and keys. "Please don't cry. Whatever it costs, I'll find a nicer one."

Before she could explain why she was upset, he ran out the door. She picked up a handful of tinsel scattered on the floor. Twisting them into knots, she couldn't help but think about the last time she saw her father.

Maddie was glad she had taken the fake tree out of retirement. The unattended heartburn had turned out to be stomach cancer that spread. Her father had been admitted to the hospital two days after Christmas, and the doctor started an aggressive chemotherapy drug.

Except for a shower and a change of clothes, she had stayed at his bedside. As she stroked the roadmap of veins along his gaunt arms, her eyes had taken on an intense bloodshot look that came from hours of weeping. His sturdy physique looked emaciated, and his color looked like bleached bone. Consumed by pain, he was unreachable until the medication kicked in.

Each time he tried to speak, his voice was a gravelly whisper. "Maddie, I'm sorry for letting you down and for not being the father you deserved after your mom and sister died."

She reached for a tissue and wiped the tears on his cheeks. "There's nothing to forgive or regret. You were . . . you are the kindest, gentlest, loving man I know."

"I need to tell you one more thing before I . . . before it's too late." When his voice faded, he beckoned her closer. "Promise me you will go to Paris. It's what your mother would have wanted."

As she listened to his labored breathing, she realized he wouldn't be with her much longer. She held his hand and pressed it to her lips. The birdlike bones felt fragile beneath her fingers. "I promise."

"I love you, Maddie."

"I love you too." She had let out a deep, agonizing sound when he closed his eyes for the last time. Once again, another darkness had drifted over her.

25

SAM
1976

SAM LACED HIS hands behind his head, rocked back in his chair, and looked out the massive windows. The soft reflections of the skyline on the Charles River displayed a romantic quality. The allure of the twinkling city lights made him think of Maddie—fingers interlaced, standing on the Pont Neuf bridge, gazing at the Seine.

Joe strolled in. "What's with the big grin on your face? Did you close the deal?"

Rubbing his hands together, he said, "You know what tonight is?"

"Better remind me."

"It's our tenth anniversary."

"I would have never guessed. Your face glows like a hundred-watt bulb every time you mention it."

His ears turned red. "You would think it was our first." He looked at his watch. "I've got some cleanup work on my desk. Then I'm out of here. My girl has a big surprise waiting for me."

"I bet it's a new car. Maybe a BMW to replace that apple-red Mustang."

"I've left enough hints."

Life had been good to them. Five years ago, the firm did well enough to move to a suite of offices in the Prudential Building, along with hiring two junior architects. Maddie's gallery on Newbury Street in Boston had a slow start, but over time, it flourished with the influx of prominent artists. Their paintings, hers included, brought in a significant amount of money and recognition.

Everything had worked according to plan, until Joe's and Jason's wives were pregnant for the second time. Maddie had told him his excuses no longer carried any weight.

"We're established and secure enough to start a family."

Her no-nonsense tone made it difficult to disagree. Fear had plagued him the first time she mentioned wanting a baby. What if it turned out to be a boy and somewhere in his DNA a source of evil existed?

He didn't have to worry. Maddie's difficulty wasn't getting pregnant but carrying a baby to term. Every miscarriage brought a fresh veil of grief that ripped her raw. Each month, Sam found her in the bathroom, sobbing.

"There's something wrong with me. You never should have married me."

Her devastation tormented him, and so did his guilt over feeling relieved. He tried and failed to convince her they could be happy as long as they had each other. But when he overheard her tell Julia, "My life is meaningless without a child," the words had sliced through him.

Sam pulled into the paved circular driveway and admired the turn-of-the-century, gated Victorian estate. With a steeple-pitched roof, tall windows, wrapped porches, intricate trim, and vibrant colors, it had a dollhouse-like exterior. Three years ago, he'd surprised Maddie with the keys. After looking at dozens of houses, she'd fallen in love with this one. The need for a complete inside renovation meant a lot of time and work. Knowing she never completely got over the losses, he hoped it would be a healthy diversion.

In the dining room, Frank Sinatra's silky voice floated through the air.

> *And I'm in love to stay*
> *As we go through the years*
> *Day by day.*

A perfect song for the occasion. He look around the room. An enormous crystal chandelier sparkled from the glow of lit candles on every flat surface. The expensive furniture, antiques, and Oriental rugs were additional signs of their success and good fortune. An arrangement of pink peonies and white roses towering in a Waterford vase, were on a table set with their best china. A bottle of champagne chilled on the buffet. Savoring the fragrances wafting from the kitchen, he crept up behind her and put his arms around her waist.

She yelped. "You scared me."

"Were you expecting someone else?" He kissed the back of her neck. "Happy anniversary."

Her eyes held a mischievous gleam when she turned. "Let's go into the other room. Dinner can wait." She took his hand. "I want to give you your gifts."

As soon as he sat, she placed two tiny boxes in front of him. *I guess I'm not getting that BMW.*

"Hurry. Open the one wrapped in silver."

He chuckled at her eagerness. "First, a toast to my gorgeous wife." He raised a glass. "Here with you, I have everything I ever wanted. I love you."

She kissed his cheek. "I love you too. Now open it."

To tease her, he brought it to his ear and shook. When she pouted, he thought, *I better do as I'm told.* He ripped the paper and lifted the lid. On top of the blue velvet interior was a set of keys and a picture of a station wagon. It was the last thing he dreamed of owning.

He fumbled a halfhearted thank-you and studied the second box. *Please let it be something I can be excited about.*

She tapped her foot on the floor. "What are you waiting for?"

When he pulled back the tissue paper, his body went taut like the strings on a guitar. A tiny object lay nestled on a pillow of white. Blood drained from his face—a baby pacifier. He stared at her explosive grin.

"It's a miracle, Sam. After all this time, I'm . . . we're going to have a baby. The nurse had to keep reassuring me it was true." She giggled. "You look like you're ready to pass out. I know it's a shock, but imagine how amazing our lives will be. We're finally going to be a real family, something we've always wanted."

Experiencing a sudden tightness in his chest, if he didn't know better, he would've thought it was a heart attack. The Paris tickets stayed in his pocket.

Sam tried to deny the pregnancy. *The nausea is a lingering flu. The doctor will call and tell us they made a regrettable mistake.* But reality set in when he found her caressing the slight bump underneath her nightgown. The last time he'd seen her this blissful was their wedding day. It triggered the priest's parting words when they'd sat down to discuss the wedding ceremony. "What's most important in a marriage is honesty. This builds the trust necessary for a relationship to be strong and weather any challenges." As if someone had wielded a knife, guilt slashed through him. *From the beginning, I should have risked telling her I never wanted kids and why.*

During every conversation, Maddie burst into endless chatter of how wonderful it would be to celebrate the baby's first tooth, first steps, first birthday, first day of school, and the day he would become a famous architect or artist. By the time she finished planning their child's future, they were grandparents three times over. Any enthusiasm he tried to have about becoming a father waned each time she implied it was a boy. When she wanted to discuss a list of boy's names, he said, "What, no girl's names?"

"I'm partial to Gracie, but I'm positive . . ." She grasped his hand. "Do you feel him moving?"

He shook his head. "I guess it doesn't like my touch."

"Don't be silly. Keep your hand there."

A ripple ran across her belly and then another. He thought, *Please let this baby be a girl.*

Each month, he marveled at the physical changes. The rounding of her body, the swell of her breasts, the widening of her hips—all telltale signs of a growing pregnancy. Once the morning sickness subsided, day or night, she had irresistible cravings. Dill pickles dipped in chunky peanut butter and any kind of greasy fast food. Despite her happiness, he recognized the underlying fear, anxiety, and dread of another miscarriage. Outside the nursery, he listened to her break into spontaneous bouts of crying. "I can't bear it if I lose you." It was during those moments he prayed, *Please don't let her lose this baby. I don't care if it's a boy.*

Every doctor's appointment was fraught with a nerve-racking silence until he declared, "You're doing fine. Right on schedule." She'd finally relax when he said, "Would you like to listen to your baby's heartbeat?"

At the first sight of dawn, Maddie's sudden outburst woke Sam from an exhausted stupor. Frantic, she let out a wail. "Oh God, this can't be happening." He kept his voice calm, knowing the baby wasn't due for another three weeks. "Are you sure? Maybe it's false labor."

She screamed, "What is wrong with you. These are real. If you don't get me to the hospital, I'll have this baby on the bedroom floor."

Rather than drive at manic speed, he called a taxi. The pain dominated her and seemed to reach into infinity. Beaded perspiration clung to her forehead, and her face changed to garish hues of red with each contraction. She turned hysterical when a gush of water spilled out and puddled at her feet. Helplessness washed over him. *Jesus Christ, I'm not made for this. Neither is she. We never should have become parents.*

When he'd asked Joe about his experiences in the delivery room, he told him, "You'll hear sounds come out of your wife's mouth you never thought possible. The shrieking and screaming will sound like an exorcism."

Self-assured, Sam said, "No way she's going to act like that. We took those Lamaze classes, so everything will go smoothly."

Joe chuckled, "Glad you're so confident."

By the time they reached the hospital, Sam was in the throes of delivery-room anxiety. He looked at Maddie. "Maybe it's better if I sit it out in the waiting room." When another contraction barreled through her, she squeezed his hand so tight the bones felt like they were ready to snap. He tried to pull away but stopped when she spoke through gritted teeth.

"Go put on those surgical scrubs. I didn't get pregnant on my own."

Struck by how she said it, he wondered, *What the hell am I in for?* As she writhed in pain and the ligaments protruded in her neck, it was as if she was sucked into a powerful vortex. Never using foul language before, he listened in disbelief to her string of unbridled expletives in between the yelling. He turned to the nurse. "Can't you give her something?" *Or me.*

"She's past the point of medication."

He wrung his hands. "What can I do?"

"Did you take the lamaze classes?"

What an idiot. How could I forget? "Maddie, remember you need to focus on your breathing to deal with the pain." Once the contractions passed, he massaged her temples and spoke words of encouragement. "You're doing great. It'll be over soon. Then you'll be holding our baby." When the contractions came at record speed and the fetal printout showed crests the size of an 8.0 earthquake, he quickly learned anything he said or did wouldn't make a difference except to rile her.

Despite the coolness of the room, a prickly sensation seized him. Heat inched up the back of his neck and into his face. Everything turned fuzzy. *Oh shit, I'm going to pass out.* He grabbed the metal bed rail, closed his eyes, took slow, deep breaths, and counted backward from one hundred. Less anxious, he thought, *At least the class instructions weren't a waste of time.*

His eyes snapped open when the obstetrician said, "This is it, Maddie. Give us one big push." Her shriek made it sound as if her insides were being ripped out with a blunt instrument. Seconds later, a wail split the air.

"Congratulations. You are the proud parents of a baby girl."

Several tense moments passed while the nurse performed the evaluation. When the baby was swaddled and given to Maddie, Sam was drunk with relief and happiness. He brushed away Maddie's sweat and tears and said, "You're amazing. I can't believe you brought this tiny life into the world."

"Sam, isn't she the most beautiful baby you've ever seen?"

He pressed his head against hers and stared at his daughter. "Yes, she is. What do you want to name her?"

"Gracie. It means proof of God's grace."

"It's a perfect name."

The bliss shattered when she released a loud grunt. "Oh no, it feels like another contraction."

His knees buckled. "Another baby?"

The doctor said, "Hold your daughter while I recheck your wife."

He kissed her soft pink cheek and watched her tiny fingers wrap around his. Tears blossomed as an immeasurable love swept over him. Because of this precious miracle, he cast aside any doubts about the father he would be.

The doctor announced, "We're about to have another arrival."

Sam clutched the baby to his chest. *No one ever said anything about twins.* A sharp, angry cry vaulted off the walls.

"You have a spirited boy. He's a sneaky one, hiding behind his sister."

Like being underwater, every movement and noise in the room sounded slow and muffled. His brain couldn't comprehend anything except to register shock.

Sam sat on the bed next to Maddie when the nurse brought the twins into the room. He saw the pure joy of maternal love spread across her face when Gracie was placed in her arms. When he looked closer, the fuzz of red hair peeked out from the knit hat. "Looks like there's another redhead in the family. What about her eyes? Are they a gorgeous green like yours?"

"Right now, they're gray. I read it could be six to nine months before we know the true color. I'm hoping our son will have your blue color and blond hair."

Sam turned to the sound from the other crib. *Please let him take after Maddie.*

"Our son is asking for you."

He stood there.

Maddie teased, "Go on, pick him up. He won't break. We need to give him a name. Since you're not in favor of Sam Junior, what about Brian? It means strong, virtuous, and honorable."

He slowly moved the blue hat from his son's left temple. Weightlessness surged through his body. No birthmark. No stamp of evil on his son. A thankful smile split his face. "Brian it is."

When the nurse came back for the twins, Maddie asked how soon they could go home. She explained that they needed to stay in the special care nursery because of their weight. Stroking the pink-and-blue knitted homecoming baby sets she said, "Sam, what if something awful happens when we're not here?"

He saw the flash of apprehension in her eyes. "Nothing is going to happen. They'll be well taken care of and home as soon as they put on a few more pounds."

"It's not supposed to be this way. They need to go home with us, so we can bond as a family."

He placed both hands on her cheeks. "I know little about being a father, but I'm certain your connection is already strong. Before they were born, I watched every time you caressed your stomach, talked and sang to them. And right after they were born, they heard your voice and felt your touch. The best part—you will have a lifetime to show it."

Sam sat in the kitchen, his nerves singed and patience doused. It had been another horrific night with Brian's nonstop howling. More milk, more rocking, more pacing—nothing he did worked. At the start, it had been a challenge to get the twins into a routine. By the fourth week, Gracie settled in and only cried when she was hungry or needed to be changed—unlike her brother, who rarely slept or napped. In between feedings, his cries escalated into mind-bending screeches that lasted for hours. More than once, an eerie feeling rippled from the pit of his stomach. Something wasn't right with their son.

What happened last night scared him. He had gotten so angry his hands coiled into fists, and he had to walk out of the room to cool off. Stunned by his reaction, he had wondered if it meant he would turn out like his father—an unfit parent or something worse. If only he could talk to his mother. She was the one person who would tell him, again, to stop this foolish thinking. But she was gone. He'd never gotten over the heartrending loss of three years ago, when she'd suffered a brain bleed and died.

Sam looked at the clock. Maddie must be up with Gracie. He stopped and peeked into Brian's room. The only sound was a slight snore. Grateful for the reprieve, he went to the spare bedroom, where Maddie was feeding Gracie. They decided to separate them because of Brian's continuous eruptions. "How's our sweet girl and her mama doing?"

"Perfect. Her tummy is full, and she's ready for a nap. You look like you need one too."

He released a long, audible sigh. "I need more than a nap. How about a week in a coma? I'm ashamed to admit I can't handle it when Brian acts as if . . ." *Something is torturing him.* "How do you stay so calm?"

"Trust me, I have my breaking point, but I remind myself he'll eventually grow out of it."

When the pediatrician put him on medication for colic, he'd assured them the symptoms would disappear in three to four months. Sam remembered thinking, *I'm not sure I'll survive that long.* "I need to talk to you about the office. Joe and the other architects are stretched thin. I've tried to focus on work, but with Brian, it's been difficult."

"Why don't we hire a full-time nurse? She can help with Gracie."

The pent-up tension released, he said, "You'll be okay with this?" Before she was able to answer, earsplitting sounds vibrated from the nursery. "Stay, I'll go." He squared his shoulders and entered the room. Red-faced and squealing, his arms and legs flailing, Brian freed himself from the tightly wrapped blanket. Sam uttered a soft curse and waited until Brian's body went limp. His stomach grew tight when he smoothed back his son's wet hair. In the dim light, he spotted a faint pink spot on his left temple. He blinked twice, hoping what he saw wasn't what he was thinking. Tucking him in the crook of his arm, he questioned Maddie. "I never noticed the mark on Brian's face." *Probably because I try to avoid handling him whenever I can.*

"The pediatrician said some marks don't appear at birth. To me, it looks a little like yours. I'm going to put Gracie down for a nap. I'll call the nursing agency and set up interviews for next week. Let Joe know you're going back to the office."

He carried Brian to the large bay window in the living room and pulled aside the drapes. In the brighter light, he made out the shape that resembled his. Talking to himself he said, "No, damn it. It's just a mark and doesn't mean anything sinister."

Until . . .

Sam watched Brian fight through the toddler stage like someone possessed. With no windup period or warning, his temper was immediate and violent. Anything could trigger it. The raw and unfettered shrieking made Sam's blood curdle. Anyone walking by the house would think a child's legs and arms were being torn from the sockets. Whenever the doorbell rang, he feared someone from child protective services would be standing on the steps.

If Brian didn't get his way, he sustained his anger for hours by kicking and thrashing on the floor. Months of toilet training ended in a battle of wills. Nothing was safe when he was around. To vent his fury, twice he smashed the toilet seat cover with a hammer he found underneath the kitchen sink. He broke his toys, tore apart stuffed animals, ripped his books, and ruined clothes with permanent magic markers.

A mounting rage besieged Sam and found its way through the cracks in his demeanor.

Instinctively, he wanted to deliver a memorable lashing, but two things handcuffed him—the image of his father ready to strike him, and the fear of alienating Maddie. As the only means of punishment, he would stick Brian in his room or lay down threats. "If you don't cut this out, you're going to regret it." Both proved ineffective.

The clashes, over time, had fostered a potent division between Maddie and him, which led to multiple heated discussions about their son's behavior. "He's like a ticking time bomb ready to explode," argued Sam. "His anger and aggression are symptoms of a serious problem. We need to talk to the pediatrician and see what kind of help he should get."

Maddie's response was always the same. "He's testing his boundaries like all children do. When he gets a little ill-tempered, it's because he hasn't had time to learn the proper way to communicate. Your relationship with him would be healthier if you didn't overreact to everything he says and does."

Sam wondered what mumbo jumbo child-rearing books she had been reading. He set his mouth in a hard line. "Compared to his, Gracie's tantrums were docile and ended when she turned three."

"Give him space. He's more sensitive about things."

Christ almighty, she believes what she's saying. "There's something else. Doesn't it worry you how he resists being touched or backs away from any kind of affection? If you try to hug him, it's like putting your arms around a stone-cold statue."

She knitted her eyebrows. "Stop creating something that's not there."

Brian's dreadful behavior continued to escalate. By the age of six, rarely did a day go by when he didn't take every opportunity to torture Sam.

One Saturday morning was no different. An altercation started before Sam had his first cup of coffee. Brian marched into the kitchen waving a Patriot's T-shirt.

"Let me remove the tags before you wear it," Sam said.

"No, I hate it. You were supposed to buy me a Bruins shirt."

"That's not what you asked for."

Brian threw it on the floor. "That's not what I told you."

The belligerent tone made Sam's blood pressure skyrocket. In no mood to invest energy into another dispute, his thoughts were on Gracie. She was at the doctor because she didn't feel well. "You have ten minutes to eat what's in front of you. Otherwise, nothing until dinner."

"I hate this cereal. I want another kind."

"Since when?"

"Since right now."

The time for patience and calm was over. He knelt in front of him and pinched both cheeks until Brian yelped. "Keep up the nastiness and it won't be only your face that'll hurt. Get dressed. We have to go to the grocery store for your mother."

He stamped his feet. "I don't want to go to the stupid store. I want to be with my sister."

"You're coming with me. GO. GET. DRESSED."

Five minutes into shopping, Sam got frantic when he realized Brian was no longer behind him. *Oh God. What if a stranger has taken him?* He raced around the store, calling his name, until he heard an irate voice followed by his son's.

"Stop making that mess. Where are your parents?"

"I'm hungry. My dad refused to feed me this morning and told me I couldn't eat until dinner."

Two aisled down Sam found him surrounded by boxes of spilled cereal, shoveling a handful of Cocoa Puffs into his mouth. Anger replaced his fear. "What the heck are you doing?"

"You said I couldn't eat anything until supper, and I couldn't wait."

A glob of Cocoa Puffs mixed with saliva spewed from his mouth. Pieces landed on Sam's shirt. Unable to avoid the appalled looks of the staff and shoppers, he said through clamped teeth, "You'll pay for this when we get home."

"You better not beat me again."

Sam didn't stop to see the shocked expressions on anyone's face when he lifted Brian by one arm, feet hardly touching the ground. He dragged him to the car and tossed him into the back seat. When he saw the sneer on his face in the rearview mirror, his hands seized the steering wheel so tight his forearms cramped.

He pulled this stunt on purpose—like everything else he does. Scratches had mysteriously appeared on the passenger side of his new car. His keys and wallet had gone missing. An expensive vase had been shattered. Brian's explanations rolled off his tongue like sugarcoated candy.

"I bet your keys and wallet dropped out of your pockets. Someone must have damaged the door in a parking lot. The dog broke the vase."

All calculated lies. He'd detected tiny, smudged handprints on the door. The keys were found stuffed between the cushions of his leather recliner. The wallet miraculously turned up on the garage floor. And there was no way the dog could have reached the vase. It had been a jolt to realize how skilled a liar Brian had become, always prepared with a rational explanation—which Maddie continued to believe.

When they returned from the market, Sam ordered Brian to his room. "Get in there and don't come out until I tell you."

Brian drew back his lips. "Try to make me."

Sam raised his hand. "If I use this, you won't be sitting down for a month."

Brian puffed out his chest. "Don't make a promise you can't keep."

His fists clenched. *Leave before you do something you'll regret.*

As soon as he heard Maddie's voice coming from Gracie's room, he went in, sat on the bed, and said, "How's my little princess doing?"

"Just tired, Daddy."

He planted a kiss on the top of her head. "I'll come in later, and if you feel up to it, I can finish reading the book we started last night." He left her curled up on her side with her eyes closed. In the hallway, he asked Maddie, "What did the pediatrician say?"

"Nothing to worry about. Probably a virus like mono. He's seen several children with fatigue, fevers, and bruising. It should go away on its own in four to six weeks."

He let out a sigh of relief. "I expected it to be serious."

"Me too. How was your day with Brian?"

As if on cue, an ear-piercing sound from Brian's room bounced off the walls. No interest in investigating another hissy fit, he let her handle it.

When he heard Maddie yell, "Sam, get in here," he raced into the room and saw her pressing the blood-splattered Patriots T-shirt to Brian's forehead.

"Jesus, what happened?"

"I can't stop the bleeding. Call Mary across the street. She can drive us to the hospital."

He picked up the shirt. *Christ, there's so much blood.* Any harsh thoughts of the day's events dissolved when he visualized his son on a stretcher waiting for a doctor to arrive with a needle and thread to suture the cut.

Three hours later, he heard the car pull into the garage and rushed to open the door. When Maddie tried to move past him, he reached for her arm. "I wish I could have been there. How many stitches did he need?"

Her response was brusque. "None. Only a butterfly bandage. Once I get him comfortable, we need to talk."

Led by her, Brian turned and ogled him as if his bullshit meter was ticking in the black zone. An angry frown creased Sam's forehead. *That is not the face of a traumatized child.*

"Brian told me what happened in the store."

Sam didn't miss the crossness in her tone. He realized his version wouldn't match his son's. "His behavior, from the moment you left, was disgraceful. I'm sure he didn't mention the mess he made in the store. How he deliberately spit chewed cereal at me. Or embarrassed me by telling everyone who watched how he was starving because I refused to give him breakfast and wouldn't feed him until supper. The sickest comment he made: 'You better not beat me again.'"

"I don't know what to say except he's never that way with me, and he doesn't act mean to Gracie."

"So what are you saying?"

"None of this would have happened if you didn't go off on him every chance you get. I don't condone what he did, but a reprimand would have been sufficient. Instead, you yanked his arm and left a bruise. And when you shoved him into his room, he tripped and fell on the corner of the desk."

"God damnit, Maddie, none of it's true." As crazed as it sounded, he believed Brian deliberately hurt himself. He hesitated before he said, "What if I said he did it to himself to get back at me?"

Her eyes locked on his like magnets. "If you believe that, *you're* the one who needs serious help."

"It's Brian who needs the help, and it's high time you see that."

Two days later, the principal called and requested a meeting. "Mr. and Mrs. Middleton, please have a seat. I want to discuss what's been happening during recess. Yesterday, while the children were playing Freeze Tag, a little boy was pushed into the metal basketball stand, hard enough to make a deep gash on his cheek, which needed stitches. Today, during Red Light, Green Light, a girl fell and fractured her elbow. Three children implicated your son in both incidents."

Sam watched Maddie's glare deepen as she moved to the end of the chair.

"My son already explained what happened. The boy didn't look where he was going, and the girl stumbled over her feet. He knew they would blame him because he gets picked on and bullied in the schoolyard. Now that I'm here, what are *you* going to do about *that*?"

Sam found it disturbing how angry and indignant she got when she defended him. He wanted to point out it was the other way around with the bullying.

"If this were the case," the principal said, "one of our teachers would've addressed the situation. We don't believe they were accidents. Children at this age don't always have an off switch for raw emotions. You might want to consider counseling. There could be something deeply bothering him, which he is unable to talk about. Here are a couple of names our parents have used in the past."

Sam reached for it. "Thank you, we'll—"

Before he could finish, Maddie interrupted him. "That won't be necessary."

Her mouth tightened into a thin line when she looked at him. As they left the office, ominous thoughts pulsed through his head. *What if Brian's temperament has nothing to do with age and everything to do with something perverse? And what terrible things might he do next?*

26

BRIAN
1982

DURING THE THIRD week of first grade, Brian stood in the doorway of his sister's room with their lunch boxes. "Come on, lazybones. We'll be late for the bus." His breath quickened when she grabbed her belly and drew her knees up to her chest.

"I don't feel so good. Can you get Mom? Maybe she can give me that pink medicine. It tastes yucky, but it helps."

He knew she was in a bad way when her face matched the color of her favorite stuffed animal—a teddy bear turned gray from too many spins in the washing machine. It was not the first time she had tiny black and blue marks dotting her skinny arms and legs from banging into things, but she'd never had this many. His voice shook. "Mom, something is wrong with Gracie!"

Sitting on a green plastic chair across from Gracie's hospital bed, Brian winced when a bald, overweight doctor with a beak nose prodded every inch of her body. After he finished with the exam, a woman walked in with a cart filled with glass tubes. She stretched a flat rubber strap above his sister's elbow, tied it tight, and inserted a needle into her flesh. But she kept on sticking her until she got it right. Listening to her cry out with each prick, he yelled, "Stop it, you stupid jerk! You're hurting her! Get someone who knows what they're doing."

His parents, with tear-stained faces, stood in the doorway and motioned for him to step into the hallway. "What's wrong with Gracie?" His mother knelt and tried to fold her arms around him, but he wriggled away.

"Sweetheart, your sister is sick."

"How long before she can come home?"

"I'm not sure. She needs a special medicine that has to be put in a bag and given in her arm."

He snapped, "This place is awful. They make her even worse with all the sticking and poking. What's making her so sick?"

"It's difficult to explain."

"I want to know."

"It's an illness of the blood."

"What's it called?"

"Leukemia."

The word twisted around his tongue when he tried to pronounce it. "The medicine will make it go away, right?"

"We hope so. I'm going to stay with her. Dad will take you home to get your things for school and bring you back later."

He crossed his arms over his chest. "I'm not going. She needs me here."

The moment he'd discovered they'd shared the same space inside his mom's belly, he never thought of *her* or *me* but *us*. His mother used to say, "The longest time the two of you have been apart was the day you were born." Over time, they finished each other's sentences and communicated in a language unintelligible to everyone else. Neither felt complete without the other. Their inseparable bond had existed long before they could speak, and he vowed to never let it break.

It took only a week for Brian's principal to notify his parents. Told he acted out in class and refused to do his work, his mother agreed to have him tutored.

On the days chemotherapy played havoc with Gracie, Brian stayed by her side when each wave of nausea tossed her insides like a wrathful surf. The kidney-shaped basin in his hand, he stroked her back each time she retched and vomited. Once the side effects subsided, he wiped the sweat and puke from her face and prayed for a longer reprieve before the next strike.

After a rough morning, he noticed the corners of her mouth turn down while she picked at the bandages covering needle-pricked arms. "What's wrong? Does something hurt? I can push the buzzer to get the nurse."

"It's Mom and Dad. They're always sad. I can hear them crying outside my door." Her voice quavered. "It's my fault because I'm sick all the time."

A flush of anger roared through him like a brush fire. Only ignorant, weak people were incapable of controlling their emotions. "It's not your fault. Forget them. They're clueless. You're going to whip this." He stood and started for the door.

"Where are you going?"

"To have it out with them for upsetting you and making you feel awful."

"Please, Brian, don't say anything. Dad will get mad, and I hate when you two fight."

He saw the look of distress on her face. "Okay."

"Pinkie promise?"

His finger hooked around hers and gave a gentle squeezed. "Pinkie promise."

"I love you."

"Love you more." He glanced at the monitor registering her heart rate and placed a hand over his heart. Each beat was in sync with hers.

27

MADDIE

WHEN MADDIE HEARD Gracie's cancer diagnosis, it delivered a warranted guilt to her gut. She should have known it had nothing to do with the virus. Frenzied thoughts of the future took off like a stampede of wild horses. *Would she be the same happy, carefree little girl after the chemotherapy treatments? What was the magical number for a cure, five years? If she makes it, what are the chances the disease will show up when she's a teenager, a young woman, or older?* Teetering on the fringes of a nightmarish precipice, the unknowns threatened her sanity.

She read medical journals, pored over the latest clinical trials, and spoke with oncologists across the country. She kept a journal documenting the test results, medications, and the good days against the bad. Frantic for a second opinion, as if they had made a mistake, the blow hit harder when the answer turned out to be the same.

While Brian spent time with the tutor and Sam went to work, Maddie cherished the alone time with her daughter. Cuddled in bed, they talked about the things she would like to do when she felt better.

"Brian and I have never gone to an amusement park. I've seen the one advertised on TV. There's all these cool rides—a musical carousel, a mini Ferris wheel, bumper cars, and a gigantic water slide."

When her eyes grew bigger with each ride mentioned, Maddie smiled. "That should be fun. Anything else you want to do?"

"Maybe you should make a list so we won't forget."

She took a pen and paper out of her purse. "Okay, I'm ready."

"Go to Disneyland. It would be the best thing ever."

"That's a long trip on a plane."

"Even better. It will be me and Brian's first plane ride."

Stroking the soft red curls that still framed her pixie face, she got nervous when Gracie felt the port implanted under her collarbone. The doctors had inserted it for the chemotherapy medication because her veins were no longer suitable for IV sites. "Is it hurting you?"

"No, but there's something I've been afraid to talk about because I don't want to make anyone feel bad."

"Gracie, you could never do that." Anguish filled Maddie's heart when her daughter's tears rolled down her cheeks.

"I hate everything about this awful cancer. Being in this bed instead of my own. Constantly stuck with needles and taking medicine that makes me sick all the time. Mom, I'm not good at being brave anymore."

Maddie's expression tightened as if all her facial muscles were holding in her emotions. "Sweetie, you don't have to be brave with me or hide your feelings. I'm always here to listen." Gracie snuggled into the crevice of her arm and lay her head on her chest. Maddie kissed her forehead. "Now close your eyes and dream about all those special things we are going to do." A hand over her mouth to stop the sob from escaping, she thought, *What if the cancer takes her like it did my father?*

Surrounded by friends and their neighbors, Maddie had faced her dad's casket. Appearances hadn't changed since her mom and sister's funeral—black clothes, waxy faces, and the traces of too many wet tears. She had selected flowers made of lavender roses and deep-purple carnations. The florist explained they expressed gratitude for their time together. Inspecting the large spread on top of the casket, she thought it did nothing except be a gross reminder her father was dead and she was alone.

She had put together two bouquets from the spread of flowers and tied them with greenery. Buried three feet away lay her mother and sister. The inscription read:

Katherine Lynette O'Dell
October 10, 1918 ~ September 28th, 1955

"A mother holds her children's hands for a while, their hearts forever."

Grief had hollowed her out. *A while meant more than eleven years.* She knelt in front of her sister's headstone with a carved angel sitting on top.

Annie Grace O'Dell
August 13, 1950 ~ September 28th, 1955

"So Small, So Sweet, So Soon."

The tiny statue had done nothing to soften the brutal fact of what lay beneath it. At the time, her tears had fallen on the same ground, and the earth absorbed the same pain. She turned and looked at the endless rows of gravestones. There were those made of marble with new black lettering. Others had crumbled from years of weathering. *How can a place be so full and empty at the same time? What a cruel irony when lives are remembered by things so cold and immobile.*

After placing the flowers on her mother and sister's grave she folded her arms on her dad's smooth metallic casket and bent her head. Again, the world had shifted under her feet. *Dad, I should be home listening to your corny jokes and you telling me for the hundredth time how much you love me.* She had sworn never to return to a place that brought no solace. Trudging back to the car, the disquieting echo of "thanks for coming" had squeezed her brain—trivial words for what this day meant.

Brian's blistering stare startled Maddie when she saw him standing in the doorway of Gracie's room. "What's wrong?"

He whispered through gnashed teeth. "What if she wakes up and sees you all weepy? Haven't you figured out how it upsets her?"

She brushed the tears off her face. "Let's go to the cafeteria and talk while she's asleep."

"No, I'm staying here."

She quietly slid Gracie out of her arms. "I'm not asking."

In the cafeteria, Maddie watched him play with a plastic straw. A thumb over the top, he stuck it into the carton of chocolate milk and filled it. "Brian, when you're forced to deal with something so unimaginable, it's okay to express your feelings and talk about them." He pulled out the straw and made small circles of chocolate droplets on the table. She zeroed in on the off-putting silence and his impassive expression.

"I'm going back before she wakes up."

"Not until you tell me if you're scared, angry, or both." The circles kept widening. "If you're worried you might get sick, don't be." The doctor had assured her fraternal twins both rarely developed leukemia. Yet, it never quieted the fear it could happen. "Please, talk to me. I promise you'll feel better."

He stood and flicked the straw away. "I'm finished here."

At the elevator, he kept jabbing the button. When she placed a palm on his shoulder, he shirked it off. "If you change your mind . . ."

"I won't."

The toughness in his tone troubled her. She realized Gracie's illness had taken a huge toll on him. *If I can't help him, maybe he needs to meet with someone who can.*

She never had a chance to make the call.

28

SAM

WHEN SAM HEARD the word leukemia and saw Gracie's tiny body attached to an IV, thoughts pummeled his head. *What kind of world allows such a merciless injustice to a sweet, innocent child? She's only six years old. If she doesn't survive, the loss will shatter our family like a broken vase, and no one will be strong enough to mend the pieces.* Rage boiled inside him. He wanted to lash out. *At whom? God? The doctors?*

After the initial chemotherapy treatment, Maddie had asked if he believed she was going to make it.

"The doctors try to be encouraging, but when I see how sickly she looks, it petrifies me."

It frightened him too, but after the traumas she'd dealt with in the past, he needed to sound positive. "We have the top pediatric oncologist in the state and a drug with a proven track record. If I had any doubts, I would tell you." The one person he could be honest with was Joe.

Hunched over his desk, Sam's face twisted in grief. "She was supposed to have this beautiful life. Instead, she's subjected to a cycle of cancer drugs, horrendous side effects, and the excruciating wait for a remission. No remission means rounds of more potent drugs, and she might die anyway. Every day, I wake up and wonder if this is the day we're told there's nothing more anyone can do."

Joe put a hand on his back. "It breaks my heart to see you suffer. But she could still beat this."

His breath ragged, he tried to stifle the fear. "Remember our client Frank Sullivan?"

"Yes. Two years ago, we built that big spec house for him."

"His son had the same type of cancer. After he suffered through all the treatments, he died two years later." He pounded his fist on the table. "I should have spent more time with her and not gotten so wrapped up in Brian's insufferable behavior. The older he gets, the more he acts out. I wish it was him instead of my little girl." Stunned by his admission, his voice cracked. "Christ, Joe, I didn't mean it."

"I know you didn't. You've said he's always been kind and loving with Gracie. Has that changed?"

"No. He's like another kid with her. There are days when I stand back and watch them together and wonder who the hell he is."

"What does Maddie say?"

"The same thing she's been telling me for years: I need to find a tolerant way of dealing with him." He shook his head. "Honestly, I doubt there will ever be one."

29

BRIAN
1985

BRIAN LOOKED AT his sister's crestfallen face. "Something's wrong. What is it?"

"It's for real this time."

He heard the break in her voice. "What is?"

She picked at the wispy strands of hair on the white pillowcase. "I want this to be over. The cancer medicine isn't working anymore."

Horror-struck, he said, "Jesus, Gracie, don't say that." He pointed to the IV bag. "See those tiny drops? Millions—no, gazillions—are going into your body. They're the good guys fighting those stupid cancer cells. You need to stay positive and not give up on yourself—or us."

After three years of relapses, he knew his reassurances weren't enough. He had to give Gracie a reason not to give up.

Too fatigued to go to Disneyland or the amusement park, they had gone to places she could tolerate. The aquarium and the science museum in Boston. *The Goonies, Alice in Wonderland*, and *Pee-wee's Big Adventure* movies, where they stuffed their faces with Reese's Pieces, buttered popcorn, and Gummy Bears. One of her favorite places had been the beach. On warm, sunny days, their parents packed the car with towels, plastic shovels, buckets, and a picnic basket. They felt the gritty sand between their toes while they filled pails with seashells and sea glass. When they stopped to look at two gray-and-white squawking seagulls perched side by side on a nearby rock, she had asked, "What do you think they're saying to each other?"

"Maybe how much they love each other."

"Like us?"

He squeezed her hand. "Yes, like us."

After lunch, they spent hours building an elaborate sandcastle with fancy towers and moats. Huddled together on the blanket, they admired their masterpiece while eyeing the crown of waves lapping against the shoreline. Gracie had stood and grabbed his arm.

"Brian, please do something. I'm not ready to see it disappear."

No matter how fast he had dug deep trenches, when he failed, he could feel her sense of loss. "I'm sorry Gracie, I tried."

She patted his arm. "That's okay."

He had grabbed the skin between his thumb and finger, pinched it until there was pain. *What if I can't save her?*

Two weeks later, Brian lay next to Gracie, careful not to get entangled with the tubing and wires. The side effects of the new drug worsened. Mouth sores made it impossible for her to eat solid food. Her ribs protruded, and her limbs looked like the jointed segments of a vine stem. Dark, smudged half-moons formed beneath her eyes and stressed the papery, lucent pallor of her skin. Like fluffy floaties clinging to a dandelion, a tuft of red hair fought to survive on her scalp. A second IV bag, filled with a thick white liquid, hung in hopes she would gain weight.

When she started having severe headaches, the doctor told his parents a CAT scan showed cancer cells in her brain. Brian refused to give up as long as she still had a breath in her. He didn't care what they said. She was going to win this battle no matter how long it took. But when the doctor decided three days later that the last cocktail of medications was harming, not helping, he realized all the remissions had been falsehoods. They mocked his belief she would conquer the demons that ravaged her body.

In the room, dark except for the flashing lights of the EKG monitor, his father held his mother while she wept. Nestled next to Gracie, he whispered, "I'm here. Don't be afraid."

"Brian?"

"Yes?"

Her voice was so light it floated up toward the ceiling. "Don't leave me."

"Never, Gracie. Never."

The cadence of her heartbeat slowed. No longer matching his, he could feel their bond weaken. When her frail body gave up its last breath, he buried his head in her chest. For nine years, they'd been bound in an inextricable knot, and now the *we* became an *I*.

30

MADDIE
1985

MADDIE HAD KEPT her eyes closed as a whirlpool of sights and sounds played in her head. Light from the stained glass windows danced across two caskets covered with sprays of white gardenias and pink peonies. Mournful sobbing had interrupted a hush of loss. She had wanted to scream until her vocal cords snapped. "It's all a terrible mistake. Mom and Annie aren't in there."

The words, "Comin' for to carry me home" filled the church and drew her into the present.

Standing next to Brian and Sam, she watched as six pallbearers made their way down the aisle with a pink casket adorned with pink and white roses. When it rolled to a stop, she reached out and touched it. One tear broke free, then another, followed by an unbroken stream. No longer able to contain the extent of her grief, she sank into the pew, rocked back and forth, and keened like a wounded animal. Never expecting to bury her nine-year-old child, death had again defined the order of her existence.

At the burial service, the weather should have been as raw and unforgiving as her emotions. But the birds sang, and the flowers bloomed to show how the world would go on without her daughter. Crouched in front of the casket, the image of her lying in a cold box filled Maddie with a ball of tangled grief. As unchecked tears rolled down her face, she blocked out the condolences, even the heartfelt ones from Julia and the Strathmores. All she heard was the voice in her head repeating, *Not again, not again, not again.*

Sam knelt beside her, cradled her in his arms, and kissed the top of her head. "Somehow, we will get through this."

She dragged her fingers through the freshly dug dirt. "I won't."

His hands on her shoulders, he guided her upright. "Let's get Brian and go home."

She glanced at her son leaning against a nearby oak tree, hands shoved in his pockets. Her heart shattered again at the vacant look on his face. *The magnitude of his despair must be titanic.*

For days, Maddie lived in a maelstrom of disbelief and denial. She continued to pack Gracie's lunch box. Laid out her school uniform and the red buckled Mary Jane shoes. Kept the pink toothbrush in its holder. Cooked for four. But when she opened the itemized bill from the hospital with her daughter's name on it, the motions of daily living became too much.

She cried over the physical voids of her daughter's presence. An unoccupied seat at the table. The fervent, singsong tone of her voice. Her heart-melting smile, and the crushing absence whenever Brian entered a room. A heavy despair wrapped around her heart like barbed wire. To give up would have been less harrowing, because breathing meant to wake up and face another day of hell. She'd been encased in this darkness before, but this was the ultimate violation. Her flesh and blood had been snatched from her arms, and left in its place was a pain and a grief she would endure for a lifetime.

When anger swallowed the anguish, her body burned and shook at the wrongness of the medical profession. She ranted to Sam or whoever would listen. "The doctors should have done more. Offered a different drug. Listened when I pleaded to include Gracie in a new clinical trial. But no. *They* decided she wasn't a suitable candidate." In a downward spiral, sleep became the only refuge. But the moment she woke, reality returned with a vengeance. She had given birth to a life full of promise, and God, in his handiwork, had stolen it.

Curled in a fetal position, she tucked into her chest the nightgown Gracie had worn the night she died. Pressed to her nose in search of a lingering scent, something scratched her chin. Her eyes widened when she saw her mother's Saint Michael pin. She ripped it off, flung it across the room, and thought of the day Gracie held it in her hand.

Gracie had skipped into the kitchen while Maddie set the table for breakfast. "Look what I found."

She had released a troubled sigh at the sight of the Saint Michael pin. "Where did you get this?"

"It was in a blue pouch tucked inside a compartment in Grandma Kate's jewelry box. Can I bring it to school for show-and-tell?"

Angry for not knowing it was there, she unclasped the chain around her neck and showed her a charm fashioned out of baby feet. "Your dad bought me this after you and Brian were born. See how inside the curve of each foot there are two, tiny, emerald-colored birthstones. On the other side, your birthdays are engraved—May 1, 1976. Would you like to bring this instead?"

"Yes. This is so cool."

The request for the pin had resurfaced when Grace was in the throes of her last relapse.

Unable to deny her twice, she had pinned it to her nightie. Despite the mistrust, she foolishly had prayed for the protection denied her mother and her sister.

31

SAM

SAM'S TEARS FELL on the glass top of his desk when he picked up a photograph of Gracie. With an extra-wide grin on her face, her arms were wrapped around his neck. A precious moment, frozen in time, never to be recreated. Death changed everything. Birthday celebrations, holidays, graduations, walking her down the aisle. The list was endless. The unthinkable loss left a Gracie-shaped hole in the tapestry of their lives, and hour by hour, it frayed and ripped further. He wept so much that a drought sidled in, and insomnia became his sole companion.

Maddie was lost to him too. She'd disappeared into a dark abyss. On the rare occasion she left Gracie's bedroom, she paced the house like a penned animal. He'd pleaded with her, "Please, don't shut me out. It's hard for me too. Maybe we should attend a bereavement group, make an appointment with a therapist, or talk to Julia. She's been calling every day and wants to see you." Her response—deadened silence. It would have been simple to join her, sealed off from the world, but someone had to be there for Brian.

Being forced to cut his hours at the firm and work from home made it open season for Brian to push him beyond his limits. His presence buzzed around like a fly he could never swat. Every time he opened his mouth, it felt like crossing a minefield. Any efforts to parent became impossible. Told to clean his room, pick up his dirty clothes, and take out the trash, he'd respond, "That's your job."

Sam tried to focus beyond his hatefulness. "I know you're having a hard time with your sister's death. If it's difficult to talk to me, what about seeing someone who knows how to deal with this? Bottling your feelings makes it harder."

"You want me to see a shrink? Do you hear mom wailing in the bedroom? She's the one you should convince. Are we done with our little chat? I have homework to do."

He tried again. "What about a visit to the cemetery?"

"Why would I want to go there?"

"The priest explained this can be a source of comfort."

"Are you for real? That's not closure. Anybody who stands in front of a slab of stone and talks to it needs their head examined."

"So, this is the way you honor the sister you claimed to love so much?"

"What I feel about her is none of your business."

He itched to slap his face until it wobbled on his neck. In no mood for another ugly clash, he said, "Leave, before I do something you'll regret."

"Go for it. That should get mom out of her self-imposed isolation."

Sam delivered a lethal stare and left, but not before he caught his derisive comment.

"Looks like you lost your nerve. Oh, for the record, your cooking stinks, so how about ordering a pizza for supper?"

Sam had hoped Gracie's temperament would have a lasting influence. Not a huge transformation, but something to show his son had a heart. *Since nothing has changed, maybe I need to see someone.*

In the therapist's waiting room, toys and books were scattered across the floor. Sam felt a twinge when he noticed one of Gracie's favorite books—*Charlotte's Web.* He imagined her on her bed fresh from a bath, hair still damp, wearing pink pajamas, her head resting on his shoulder. *Can you read it again, Daddy?*

The door opened, and a voice interrupted the image.

"Mr. Middleton, please come in."

He sat on the plush, overstuffed, beige leather chair and tugged at his tie.

"You said you wanted to discuss your son's reaction to his twin sister's death."

"Yes. It's been three weeks since she died, and I am at a loss for what to do."

"Let's start with you. How are you doing?"

His shoulders sagged. "It's been hard to accept, and because of the stressful situation with my wife and Brian, there are days I feel as if I'm drowning."

"All that you are dealing with can be difficult, and your feelings are understandable. How is your wife handling the loss?"

"She sits in my daughter's room, crying. Even when she comes out, she walks right by me. I guess it's worse for mothers."

"Not really. Each of us carries and processes grief and pain differently. And your son?"

"He and Gracie did everything together, to the point it was nearly impossible to separate them. The instant they diagnosed her with cancer, he refused to leave her side each time she was admitted to the hospital." His voice wavered. "He laid in bed with her until she died."

"And now?"

"He's never cried. Not after she died, during the services, or since. Everything about him seems flat, unless I try to talk to him."

"How does he respond?"

"Either he walks away or picks a fight."

"From the little you told me, he appears to be coping with her death appropriately. Emotions can fluctuate between denial, anger, depression, and acceptance. This happens when a twin loses their best friend—many say a soulmate. These are all protective mechanisms to numb their pain. And his mother's absence may have added to it."

"How long will this last?"

"Because there are no road maps when someone experiences the loss of a loved one, even for adults, I can't give you a definitive answer."

"What can I do to help him?"

"Be patient and accept whatever stage he's in. If you want to set up an appointment for him, call me. We have a couple more minutes. Anything else you would like to discuss?"

"Not at the moment." *It would take hours to unload all my fears about my son.*

32

MADDIE

MADDIE STARED IN the mirror at her grief-stricken face and disheveled appearance. It was a blunt reminder of how her father had reacted to the deaths of her mother and sister—lifeless, hopeless, and defeated. It had confused and angered her the way he'd disappeared when she needed him most. Now, she was in danger of doing the same thing to Brian. *I won't sacrifice my place as his mother by drowning in my pain.*

In her bedroom, she undressed, stepped into the shower, and let the sensation of warm water wash over her. A towel wrapped around her, she sat on the side of the bed she hadn't slept in for weeks. She could only imagine how Sam must be suffering too.

Hearing movement in the house, she dressed and followed it into the living room. Her heart pounded beneath her rib cage as she searched Sam's face. Without hesitation, he drew her into the space that was hers to fill. "Can you ever forgive me for not being here when you and Brian needed me?"

His hold tightened. "There's nothing to forgive. I'm just glad you're back."

"Do you think we can survive this?"

"Together, I do."

"Where is Brian?"

"He's at a friend's house. I need to talk to you before he gets back."

"Why? What's wrong?"

"It's been rough. He's been acting . . ."

The front door opened, followed by footsteps. Another door banged closed. She kissed him. "I need to see him first."

Maddie wanted to burst in and embrace him but was unsure how he would greet her. Tapping a light knock on the door, she said, "It's Mom." He didn't answer. *Maybe he didn't hear me.* She knocked louder. "Can I come in?" Nothing. *Is he purposely ignoring me? Does he hate me for neglecting him?* She paled at the thought. "I'm coming in." Snubbing her presence, he turned the pages of a comic book. "Brian." When he refused to lift his head, a groundswell of anguish rippled through her. She pictured Gracie—the same heart-shaped face and tiny dimple at the corner of his mouth. *No, I'll prove to him he is not a replacement.* "Honey, I feel terrible that I wasn't here when you needed me, but I promise I'll make it up to you." She reached for his hand. He wrestled it away.

"Whatever. You can leave now."

His tight-lipped glare and biting tone stunned her. "I'm sorry, I . . ."

"I said you can leave now."

Worry lines spread across her forehead when she asked Sam, "How bad has it been?"

"Do you remember how he showed no emotions at the wake or funeral?"

Guilt lay like a rock in her gut. "No, I don't."

"Nothing has changed. He has rejected all my efforts to help him. I didn't know what to do, so I called a child psychologist."

"Was it helpful?

"He refused to go."

She wrinkled her forehead. "You couldn't make him?"

"I didn't want the situation between us to get any more out of hand, so I went."

"And?"

He sighed. "She told me to be patient, but so far it hasn't worked."

"Let's give him a little more time before I make the call."

Two weeks later Maddie waited for Sam in the kitchen.

"Day off, or are you going into work later?" he asked.

She cupped her hands around her coffee cup. "Can you sit for a minute?"

"Is it about Brian?"

"Partly. I haven't been able to focus on what I've been doing. Twice, my brain froze while discussing a piece of art. I've misquoted prices and had a painting delivered to the wrong address."

"Maybe you should cut your hours."

"I'm going to sell the gallery. Home is where I need to be right now. This way, Brian can count on me being here whenever he needs me." Her voice wavered. "I know what it's like to come home to an empty house. No one to talk to about your day."

"You can't be serious. You've worked your tail off to get a place of your own."

"My heart's not in it."

"I get that, but let your assistant take over and revisit the decision later on. While we're discussing Brian, enough time has gone by, and he's still uncommunicative and sullen. We agreed if there wasn't any change, you would schedule a therapy session."

"We need to give my staying at home a chance."

Each afternoon, she had sat at the kitchen table with a plate of baked sweets, hoping to draw Brian into an exchange about his classes, friends, or feelings. When he continued to scorn the attempts, it convinced her his stance had to be the anger stage of Gracie's death. But when he continued to address her with, "Drop the mothering. I'm fine as long as you leave me alone," she made the call.

33

BRIAN

BRIAN WAS SO teed off when forced to go to a therapist, he either refused to talk or his answers came out terse and snarky.

"How are you feeling today?"

"Great, which means this is a waste of my time and yours."

"Maybe so, but while you're here, tell me about your relationship with Gracie. Were you close?"

He crossed his arms. "Aren't all twins?"

"Not always. Do you feel guilty you're alive and she's not?"

"That's a stupid question."

"Why is that?"

"We're all going to die someday." To watch her disappear breath by breath was the type of emotional pain he had never experienced. For the longest time after she died, it felt like his right arm was missing.

"Are you upset with your mom for not being there to comfort you?"

"No." *It was a relief, and my stupid father should have followed her lead.*

"Do you think if you make a mistake, they won't love you?"

"I don't make mistakes."

"Brian, you sound angry."

"That's the first thing you got right in three weeks. Why don't we end this? You can open a spot for someone who wants to be here."

"How would you feel if I talk to your parents so we can all decide how best to help you?"

The last thing he wanted was to have them involved. He realized he needed a different approach, or he would be trapped into coming for who knows how long. "Whatever I say in here is private, right?"

"Some things, but because of your age, not everything is confidential."

"Can we try a few more sessions first?"

"Of course."

The next time Brian walked into her office, he slumped into the seat, a crumpled tissue in his hand.

"How have you been since our last session?"

He hung his head. "I don't want to be like this anymore."

"Would you like to talk about it?"

His eyes were moist, and his voice broke when he lifted his head. "I'm mad at everybody—my parents, you, even Gracie."

"Can you tell me more why you feel this way?"

He sniffled. "I don't even know who I am or how to be without her."

"Brian, twins have a connection that gives them a sense of purpose and being. They have an attachment that is irreplaceable. In fact, it's been known that sharing their lives, even before they are born, is the beginning of nonverbal communication. Their need for closeness is what matters. Does this sound like how it was with you and Gracie?"

He nodded in agreement. The hour was almost up when the therapist asked how he was feeling. "Different. Better. Does this mean I can stop coming?"

"You've made terrific progress this afternoon, but let's take it one session at a time."

His toes curled inside his shoes. "Okay." *Looks like I have to keep up this farce. Maybe I can use this as a challenge to practice my manipulating skills like they work on my mother.*

When Brian slid into the passenger side of the car, his mother reached over and put her arm around his shoulder. Though eager to shrug it off, he sat motionless.

"Everything go okay, sweetheart?"

Ever since his mom reentered the land of the living, he was sick of hearing his name attached to that nauseating word. He fixed a grin and said, "Yes. She told me I'm doing better." He clenched his jaw as she pulled him closer.

"That's wonderful. I know your dad will be pleased."

He fought the urge to laugh. Pleased had never been in his father's realm of thinking when it involved him.

"A fresh batch of double chocolate chip cookies is waiting for you at home."

"Great, I'm so hungry, I may eat all of them." When his mother dropped him off and drove to the store, he ate one cookie and shoved the rest down the garbage disposal. The grinding noise was music to his ears.

Once Brian completed his therapy sessions and his mother decided to return to work, it was a relief he would finally be alone—until she told him about the sitter.

"A high school girl will be here when you get off the bus."

He kicked the chair. "I don't need a babysitter. I can manage on my own."

"That behavior says otherwise. You're nine and not old enough to stay alone."

He thought, *The sitter is going to regret the day she walks through the door.*

When his mother came home, the sitter was cleaning up a mess on the floor.

"Brian, what happened here?"

He pointed at the sitter. "That stupid girl could have killed Lucky. She left some chocolates on the counter where he could reach them. He started to shake and peed all over the floor."

"Mrs. Middleton, that's not true. After I gave your son a piece, I put the cover back on."

He shot her a hostile glare, turned to his mother, and said, "She's lying because she's scared you'll fire her."

"Is Lucky okay? Do I need to take him to the vet?"

Brian said, "No. As soon as I saw a couple in his mouth I covered the box and put it away. He's in his dog bed in the living room."

By the time the next girl arrived, he had another plan. He barricaded her in the bathroom for two hours. She was cussing and banging on the door when his mother walked in. She removed the hooked chair underneath the door handle and let her out.

"Brian, why was she trapped in the bathroom?"

A hand over a self-inflicted red cheek, he moaned. "She slapped me for going outside and riding my bike. I know I'm supposed to stay in and do my homework. I'm sorry I disobeyed, but she didn't have to hit me. I locked her in there because I was afraid she would do it again."

"Mrs. Middleton, your son is not telling the truth. I never touched him, and he never went outside."

When his father asked why she fired both sitters, Brian overheard his mom's explanation.

"They lied to me. I've a good mind to call their parents."

"You *really* believe both girls lied and one of them slapped him?"

"Yes. It was obvious Lucky ate the chocolate, and Brian had a red mark on his face."

"Like everything else with our son, what I think doesn't matter. So now what? I take it you won't hire anyone else."

"I considered the after-school program, but I have another idea. Remember how we agreed to give a sizable donation to the pediatric ward during Gracie's hospital stay?"

"Yes."

"When I brought the check over last month, a nurse approached me and commented on how wonderful Brian had been with Gracie. She felt he would be a great ambassador by spending time with children who are undergoing cancer treatments."

"He may not want to go back there."

"Let's give him a chance and see how he does."

Not only did Brian abhor the idea of being in the hospital with the imbeciles who failed to save Gracie, he detested being told to help someone else's sick kid. When the nurse asked him to sit with a seven-year-old boy, he decided this would be the first and last time. He pointed to the IV bag. "Did the doctors or nurses tell you this kind of medicine can kill you? It happened to my sister."

A ghastly white spread over the boy's face. He took hold of the needle in his arm and tugged at it. When blood spurt from the site, he screamed, "Someone, take it out."

After the nurse rushed in, pressed a piece of gauze to his arm, and calmed him down, she left the room and asked him what happened. He backed up, placed his palms against the wall, and wimpered, "I don't know. Please call my mom. I want to leave."

When his mother arrived, he reached out and grabbed her arm. "I don't want to be here. There are too many bad memories."

"I'm so sorry. I should have listened to your dad."

He lowered his gaze so she wouldn't see the smirk on his face. *She is such an easy target. How pathetic that I can make her feel so guilty.*

"I'll arrange for the after-school program tomorrow. Before we leave, I want to check with the nurse and make sure the boy is okay."

He hung back just far enough to hear the conversation.

"We've called the doctor and his parents. He's scared and doesn't want another IV. When I asked why, he said your son told him the medication would kill him like it did his sister."

"He must be mistaken. My son would never say such a thing." She turned. "Brian, come over here and tell us what you said."

He shuffled over with his head tucked between his rounded shoulders. "He asked if I knew of anyone who had cancer and if the medication made them better. I told him the truth. It made Gracie real sick, and she died anyway." He looked up at his mother with wide, sorrowful eyes. "Mom, you told me never to lie. Should I have this time?"

She drew him close and whispered to the nurse, "He really didn't mean to frighten the boy." The game of seeing how much he could get away with thrilled him. Like the high school girls, and now this kid in the hospital, Brian decided to broaden his scope. Middle school would be the perfect venue to try out more daring schemes. He had issues with how authority figures, like his father, were always making rules. *Take out the trash. Do your homework. Clean your room. Do this. Don't do that.* The biggest offense was the job of taking Lucky out twice a day, picking up the shit, and bagging it. He knew one day it would no longer be necessary.

The new principal, who most kids hated, would be the perfect target. Brian went to school with a stack of note cards. Each one had a sentence made of letters cut from a magazine. "The principal was seen in the back parking lot kissing someone." He left it up to the imagination who it might be. He discussed the plan with Darren, the social freak who became his coconspirator. A runt of a kid who had been ripe for bullying since the second grade, he had an untreated lazy eye that never ceased to wander and two oversized front teeth that made him look like a walrus.

"I'm not doing it," Darren said. "It's too dangerous, and he'll get fired."

Brian torqued his arm. "Listen, you bucktoothed, crossed-eyed creep, you *will* help me. If you don't, I'll rearrange that face even more. Get moving and pass these out."

The rumors churned like a tsunami until the principal found one stuck on the placard outside his office. An immediate message screeched over the intercom. "Teachers, escort the students to the gymnasium."

As they filed into the bleachers, Brian heard the comments from the students behind him.

"What's this all about?"

"Mr. G must have seen the note."

"I wonder whose mouth he was twisting his tongue in?"

"I bet it's a student."

"Nah. It's either one of the teachers or that rad-looking secretary of his."

"Do you think he'll find out who did this?"

"Who knows, but whoever did this is a badass."

Brian grinned at the compliment. The principal's face was warped into a threatening stare as he strode back and forth with clamped fists pressed against his back. When a doomsday silence filled the room, he thought, *Oh boy, this should be good.*

"We will question the entire student body. The person or persons who spread this vicious lie will face a significant punishment."

After days of investigation, they were unable to prove who was culpable. Brian waited until things returned to normal before he organized his next ruse.

In the school's crowded hallways, Brian gave Darren a signal to pull the fire alarm. The loud, incessant beeping and the sound of sirens triggered disorder and panic. A couple of teachers lost control when students pushed and shoved others on the stairwells. While the firefighters searched the building, everyone stood outside for forty-five minutes in a temperature that dropped into single digits. Brian listened with delight to the groans of freezing classmates and faculty. Having layered his clothes this morning, he waited, unaffected.

With no confirmed fire, they were ordered to the gymnasium. A corpse-like chilliness hung in the air when the principal walked in. He stood, legs spread wide and hands on his hips. Anyone sitting close enough could see his nostrils flare and the veins in his neck bulge with each pulse.

The kid next to Brian whispered, "What do you think he's going to do?"

He stifled a yawn. "Get ready for another round of threats, unless he has a stroke."

Every word out of the principal's mouth was layered with frost. "When someone triggers a false alarm, it's a punishable crime. You could be charged with disorderly conduct, disturbing the peace, a fine up to $500, or both. The juvenile authorities will be notified. Someone must have seen who did it. That person can speak to me in private, but if no one comes forward, I'll notify your parents that I'm calling the police in to speak to each of you."

Gasps circulated. Not wanting to risk an interrogation by the police and have his parents involved, Brian murmured to the girl in front of him, "I bet it's that kid Allen. He's the clown who thinks he's better than us because he's going to high school in the fall. Pass it down so we can get out of here."

Shouts of, "Allen did it," echoed through the gym. Brian held his stomach to keep from laughing as the kid was escorted out, yelling, "They're a bunch of liars! It wasn't me."

He contemplated a repeat performance but decided starting a fire would be much more exciting. First, he needed to figure out when and where.

34

SAM SAT AT the table with a cup of coffee, reading the local news in the *Boston Globe*. He scanned the front page until his eyes riveted on a story. A man had been found frozen to death in an alley three blocks from their shelter. It upset him that this still took place after all he and Maddie had done. Their financial success had allowed them to pledge large sums of money to improve the conditions of two homeless shelters in a Boston neighborhood. Several outreach programs were formed. Vans offered food, blankets, warm clothing, and medical help when no spaces were available. They'd planned to pass this legacy on to their children.

He was refreshing his coffee when Brian slid into a chair and poured milk into a bowl of cereal. "Good morning." He watched Brian shovel Cheerios into his mouth and ignore the greeting. Normally he wouldn't bother, but this time, he decided to see what his reaction would be after he read the article. "It happened near one of our shelters. It's terrible when someone dies this way." Sam watched him slurp the remains at the bottom of the bowl before he answered.

"The dude got what he deserved."

"How can you be so hateful?"

"Easy. Remember the cliché, 'You made your bed, now lie in it.' Or as the Bible says, 'As you sow, so shall you reap.'"

Blanching at his scorn, Sam said, "Have *you* heard of the Golden Rule? 'Do unto others as you would have them do unto you.'"

"There's one even better. Karma says everything in life is ruled by cause and effect."

The set of his jaw caused the muscles in his neck to go taut. "You are a pathetic piece of . . ."

Brian wagged a finger at him. "You know it's not Christian like to use foul language, especially around someone as impressionable as me. I'd like to pursue this heartfelt banter, but the air in here is oppressive."

Tempted to wipe the perverse grin off his face, Sam said, "I'm not finished."

"Well, I am. At the moment, I have more important things to do."

"A day is going to come when you will pay a heavy price for your callous attitude." *And I hope I'm around to witness it.* His adrenaline thrummed through his body as he watched Brian swagger out of the room. Every day, he sorely tested his patience and tolerance. Not this time. Unlike other kids, punishment had never worked on him, until today.

Sam marched to his room to give him the news, but when he heard him on the phone, he stopped to listen.

"It's going to be kick-ass."

He rapped on the door. *Whatever he's planning sounds like trouble.*

"I'm busy."

"Too bad. I'm coming in. Who was that on the phone?"

"So now you're into eavesdropping. I guess I need to get a longer cord that extends into my closet. To answer your question, I was talking to a friend, and it's none of your business."

Sam's eyes bore into his. "You better tell me."

Brian flashed a sly grin. "I bet you keep stuff from Mom. Like the time I heard you mumble how you wished I had died instead of Gracie. I wonder how she'd feel about that."

Sam knew she would never forgive him. They were already at deep odds in their assessment of their son. He thought about the time another major skirmish had erupted between him and Brian.

Maddie had come running to Brian's rescue. "Did you hit him? Is that why he's crying?"

"You probably won't believe me, but no. I didn't lay a hand on him. Your son is an impudent brat and . . ." He had flung up his hands. "I've had it."

"Well, so have I. Why can't you see how your behavior sets a terrible example?"

His anger had been swift and hot. "And what does your constant defense say about you?"

"It's simple. I'm his mother, and I love him."

"I can tell you it hasn't rubbed off on him."

35

BRIAN

UNDERNEATH HIS DOOR, Brian picked up the article about the dead guy and threw it in the wastebasket. With no interest in the plight of the human condition—poverty, mental illness, or the destitute, he had more important things to care about.

Propped up against the headboard, he groped through his backpack of books, loose papers, and a snowball of candy wrappers until he found the three-ring notebook he bought after Gracie died. A prized possession, it detailed his thoughts about the turmoil he created. Many of his acts, throughout middle school, were nothing more than childish pranks, others devilish. He decided to read a few entries before dinner.

> *Entry: A kid in my class has asthma attacks whenever he gets overly stressed. I've seen the one thing that can stop it. During recess, he started to wheeze. When no one was looking, I took the inhaler out of his backpack and stuffed it in my pocket. Unable to*

find it, the kid's eyes went wild, and his lips turned blue. Rushed to the ER, he returned to school a week later. I selected him, like all my targets, because he was easy prey.

Entry: This week, I chose my next victim—a teacher who was completely ineffective in controlling the class. Waiting for the right time, every afternoon, I stayed to help him straighten the room. When he told me he had to pick up papers in the principal's office, I snatched his wallet and car keys from his desk drawer and buried them in the trash basket. When he came back I watched him open the drawer. He erupted in a fit of anger. "I am going to find out who did this." The reason he never asked if I did it was because I'm viewed as a polite, unassuming kid who could do no wrong. Charming is my second nature, and I've successfully used it in many of my bag of tricks.

Entry: Two days ago, I was told to get rid of the bird crap that landed on the patio. If I had a BB gun, I would have used them as target practice. The things I could do with a gun like that—our neighbor's cat might be fun. I'm gonna ask for more allowance so I can purchase one. Not to digress, I found a bag of pesticide in the garage and mixed it with the wild birdseed. The next day, across the backyard and the patio, it was a gas to see those birds lying on their

their sides, or their feet up in the air, stiff as boards. When Dad asked what happened, I shrugged a shoulder and said, "How would I know?" His sarcastic response—"I bet you don't." It didn't matter if he thought I was lying. I have a knack for leaving no proof.

Called to supper, Brian despised family dinners since Gracie died, but after reading pages in the notebook, he was in a light-hearted mood. It changed when he sat down and his father issued a directive.

"You're on the volunteer list at one of our homeless shelters during Christmas break."

He held the fork in midair, his tone smacking with defiance. "Not happening." Turning to his mother, he said, "I've got big plans. One of my friends has an extra ticket to the Van Halen concert."

"There will be plenty of time for concerts. It's time you realize how the less fortunate live."

"It's because of that dead guy."

"No. Helping is a way to remind you to appreciate all you have."

Scraping back the chair, he stormed to his room and kicked the door shut. Seconds later, his mother knocked.

"Can I come in so we can talk? I don't like to see you so upset."

Away from his father, he was certain she had changed her mind. "The door's not locked."

"Brian, volunteering at the shelter will make you feel good about yourself. And someday you will look back and be glad you did."

As his anger elevated to rage, it was all he could do not to punch the wall and smash things. Not just because he would miss the concert, but the fact his father bested him. His lips curved inward. *It will be the last time you claim victory over me.*

On his way to the shelter, Brian was a prisoner to his father's non-stop prattle about the homeless.

"The men you'll meet are often mistreated. Society targets them with all kinds of nasty labels—lazy bums, losers, and good-for-nothings. Being homeless is not a choice for them. Besides providing food and a place to sleep, it's important to remind them they're human beings first and deserve to be treated with respect."

Brian blew out a long exhale. *Christ, I wish he would shut the fuck up.*

His father pulled in front of a white stucco building and said, "Look for Bobby McKay. You can't miss him. He towers over everybody. I'll pick you up at nine."

Brian glowered at the haphazard group dressed in moth-ridden layers stuffed with newspaper. *No way I'm going to stand in line with them.* "Where's the back entrance?"

"Only personnel can use it."

Outside, the unforgiving cold struck him. Poking his face like icy fingers, it breached the heavy winter parka. More than the outside conditions made him shiver. It was the idea of being stuck in a room full of impaired social deviants, drug addicts, and perverts. He decided to wait until the last one entered the building before going inside.

The noxious stench of cigarettes and smelly body odor fought to obstruct the oxygen in the room. His mouth and nose covered, he suppressed a gag. *Screw this, I'm out of here.* He dashed outside and saw a pay phone across the street. *I'll call Mom. After I tell her I feel sick, she'll come get me.* One foot off the curb, he turned when his name was called. A soaring height and bulky frame stood in the doorway.

"You must be Sam's son. Come in. Let's get you out of this brutish weather."

When Bobby offered his hand, he ignored it. He hated meaningless interactions with nobodies. He motioned to a bench in the corner. "I'll wait over there until my shift starts."

"We let the men in early because of the weather, but there is still a group heading our way. Sign them in on this clipboard and jot down if they mention a spot they call home."

"Sounds like a bunch of freeloaders if they already have a home to go to." The big lug stared at him with pursed lips and a single raised eyebrow. *I bet he's wondering why my father sent me.*

"Not your definition of a home. During the day, they hang around subways, train stations, and bus terminals. At night, if they can't make it to a shelter, they'll take cover under sheets of plastic or pieces of cardboard. We keep tabs on the regulars. If we haven't seen someone in a while, we check those sites, other shelters, hospitals, and sadly the morgue."

He wanted to say, *The cold storage is a worthy fate for these scumbags.* With a subtle hint of sarcasm, he asked, "Who's bright decision is this?"

"Your parents. They insisted we try it out. So far, it's been moderately successful. After you're done, I'll meet you in the kitchen and introduce you to the other volunteers."

He stood on the steps as a sea of commotion brewed while the men tried to push their way in. "You know the rules. Name and location first."

Someone countered, "Do it later. We're frozen, tired, and hungry."

Peeved, he stretched an arm above his head, waved the clipboard, and yelled, "Are you deaf? No one gets in until you do as you're told." Instead, the herd formed a headlong stampede. He flattened his body against the door to ward off physical contact. Loud enough for them to hear, he said, "What a bunch of dimwits."

After the last man was in, he left the door open, filled his lungs with crisp, clean air, exhaled, and followed the plumes of white steam. By his watch, he had been here less than thirty minutes. *I've got two and a half hours to figure out how I'm going to get through this.*

The noise was deafening as Brian headed toward the kitchen. It sounded as if it reached the level of one hundred and ten decibels. *Dad, someday you're going to regret this night.* His senses balked at the smells when he pushed opened the swinging doors. He inspected the two freaks leaning against a long, butcher-block island. Their appearances were cringeworthy. The woman's dirty white hair was streaked with yellow that matched her pockmarked, sallow complexion. Ample dark fuzz on her face called for a straight-edge razor. With torpedo shaped arms, she had a girth that would take up three seats on an airplane. When she opened her mouth, the teeth looked like rows of chipped, discolored headstones.

The guy was just as gross. The wrinkled skin on his face was dotted with liver spots, and a large, raised scar stretched across his forehead. Cauliflower ears accented a nose that appeared to have been repositioned more than once. The gummy smile showcased missing teeth. At the corner of his mouth hung the remnants of a burnt cigar. He quickly spit it in the trash as soon as Bobby entered. *As long as I have to stay, maybe I can use his secret to provoke a little excitement.*

"How were the men?"

"Like a pack of wild dogs."

Bobby ignored the comment. "Everyone's fear ratchets up being left out in the cold. Ernie, Bertha, I'd like you to meet Brian. It's his first time volunteering. You're in good hands. I'll check in with you later."

Bertha handed Brian an apron covered in splotches and a two-by-two piece of plastic. "Put these on."

He scoffed at what she gave him and threw them aside. "It will be a cold day in hell before I cover my hair with that offensive thing." When she stood in his face, the fetor of her breath made him choke.

Like a no-nonsense drill sergeant, she belted out an order. "It's the law, sonny boy."

His jaw seized with indignity as a black mood came over him. *Don't fuel your rage. When this night is over, you won't be back.*

"Kid, it's time to roll up your sleeves, unless you want food all over those expensive digs. When the water boils, throw the spaghetti in the big pot. Cook only twelve minutes and drain it. Stir the sauce so nothin' sticks to the bottom. I spiced it up to taste extra special."

When the half-wits put on their jackets, he looked at Ernie. "Hey, where are you going?"

"Me and my gal pal are going out back for a break and a smoke. When you're done, we'll take over."

As he stirred the bubbling pot, the apron collected the fallout, but not before it splattered and ruined the sleeves of his Ralph Lauren shirt. Perspiration marks stretched under his armpits as beads of sweat collected under the hairnet and trickled down his temples. Next to the burner was a shaker of red-hot pepper flakes. A sneer followed the thread of his thinking. His idea of payback would come in a different form. He flipped off the top, sprinkled a handful into the inedible pigwash, and hummed while he ladled the swill over the pasta. *This should spice it up.*

As soon as Bertha and Ernie went to set up the food on the tables, he threw the apron and hairnet on the floor and rambled into the room. The guys were already filling their plates when Bobby came up to him.

"Grab a dish and join me and the other volunteers in the kitchen. There will be plenty of leftovers."

"Thanks. Bertha added something different to the meal, and I can't wait to try it."

He took a plate, stayed out of the kitchen, sat in a corner of the room, and waited for the party to begin. It didn't take long. There were men who thrust fingers down their throats. Others peeled off sweaters and hats. And then the shouting began.

"It's too fucking hot in here."

"I'm gonna be sick."

Fights ensued over the water cooler and the pitchers of water on the tables. Some fainted. The rest seized their abdomens and cried in pain. He could hear identical sounds from the kitchen.

This is fantastic, and this must be why my mom only adds a pinch to her cooking. With a last look at the pandemonium, he hustled outside. A desperate tone to his voice, he called his father. "Come get me," and hung up before he could respond. His father arrived, got out of the car, and pointed at the ambulances and first responders leaving the center.

"What happened? Did someone get hurt? Why are you standing out here alone?"

"Everyone got really sick after they ate."

"Get in the car. We're going to the hospital to get you checked out."

"The food looked terrible, so I didn't eat anything. Can you please take me home?"

Brian inched away when his mother hovered over him and tried to place a hand on his forehead.

"How do you feel?"

"Okay, but it was scary to watch everyone get so sick."

"Dad's at the hospital, waiting for more information. Can I get you anything?"

"No. I'm just tired."

"Try to rest. I'll check on you later."

When he heard her footsteps heading toward the kitchen, he snuck into the library, removed the book on poison prevention, scurried back, and read the effects of excessive hot pepper flakes.

> *If your heart beats faster and your skin sweats,*
> *these suggest the body's reaction to the ingredient*
> *is volatile. Too much can cause literal pain. Some*

even faint because of the strength. It's caustic to mucous membranes, can scorch the tongue and burn your taste buds. Reflux and heartburn occur when the hot pepper reaches your stomach and interacts with the acid. This can also result in nausea. As it passes through and out of your system, it can prompt painful, burning diarrhea. The more you eat, the more likely this is to occur. Your first instinct will be to gulp water, but this will only spread throughout your mouth and hasten its way to your stomach. Eat something absorbent, such as bread, but once you've eaten it, there's little else you can do to mitigate the side effects until it passes through your system.

In a fit of laughter, he gasped for breath and almost fell off the bed. *This is priceless. Three loaves of bread were right next to the pitchers of water.* When he overheard his father talking to his mother, he stood outside his door and listened.

"No one knows any of the facts except something extra hot might have been added to the sauce. Bertha will be questioned when she's better."

"God, Sam, do you think she did it on purpose?"

"No way. She's been the main cook for years. One of the best we've had. It had to be an accident. How's Brian?"

"Okay, but since we don't know for sure what really happened, Brian is not going back."

"What about his volunteering?"

"We'll just have to think of something else."

Good ole Mom to the rescue. He started to close his door but stopped when his father grumbled, "Funny how he was the only one who didn't eat."

Back on his bed, he took out the notebook and turned to the index that catalogued his exploits with an elaborate scoring system from one to ten. Everything he had accomplished so far had been a level one, two, or three. But one incident was so comical, he'd assigned it a solid four.

On the school bus, Brian had jabbed Darren. "Look at the fat girl across from us. No one wants to get close, so she leaves her lunch box on the empty seat."

Darren had covered his mouth and nose with his hand. "God, what smells so bad in that bag you're holding?"

He'd found a mouse in the garage, stuck in a trap still breathing, and used a kitchen knife to gut it. "You'll see. Pick up the lunch box, sit next to her, and keep her occupied."

"How the heck am I supposed to do that?"

"Make something up, you wuss. Wait, I know. Tell her she's the most beautiful girl in the school and ask if you can sit with her at lunch. After you have her attention, pass the lunch box to me. I'll give a thumbs-up when I'm ready to hand it back."

In the cafeteria, Brian had picked a table nearby to watch Darren and the girl. The skin on her face whitened when she found out what replaced the sandwich. She'd thrown everything on the floor, shrieked, and upchucked at the same time. Everyone had scattered like roaches. He gestured a victory sign to his pal, who looked like he was going to hurl, too.

With ten more minutes for lunch, he opened the notebook and reviewed the scoring. A five through eight meant planted drugs, ruined reputations, and stealing from classmates. It was a toss-up between seven and eight for authority figures. Nines and tens were allotted if they involved more risk. He read the entry tagged a nine.

> Entry: *At my dad's country club this afternoon, I watched a game of water polo. It pissed me off when I tried to join them and was told to bug off by a freckle-faced pip-squeak. My upper body work-outs and the skill of holding my breath under water came in handy. While the guys were in play, I dove under, grabbed the geek's foot, gave it a hard yank, watched his body spaz out, and released him after twenty seconds. I swam to the side of the pool and resurfaced at the sounds of someone yelling that the kid was in trouble and needed help. The lifeguard pulled him out before he needed to be resuscitated. If only I had kept him under longer. No worries, there is always a next time.*

The shelter had to be a ten because it combined getting even with the staff and his father. The notebook closed, he reached into his backpack and felt the contents inside the plastic bag—Ernie's cigar butt, the one he picked out of the trash, and the lighter left hidden in the kitchen cutlery drawer. His lips curved into a malicious sneer. *Maybe I should up the ante to a ten plus.* He fondled his birthmark with his index finger and thought, *I was born for this.*

36

SAM

HOPING TO SOFTEN the tension between them, Sam left work early to surprise Maddie with flowers and a gourmet meal from her favorite restaurant. He expected Lucky to greet him, wagging his tail, when he walked inside, but he wasn't at the door.

He called the dog's name, listened, but got no response. Nowhere in sight on the first floor, he raced upstairs. The last spot he checked was behind a chair in one of the spare bedrooms. Lucky lay on his side, his tongue hanging out and foam dribbling from his mouth. Pulling him into his lap, Sam burrowed his face into the thick part of his neck and cried. Lucky had been his greatest comfort after Gracie died. When he heard Brian shut the front door, barely able to speak, he called out to him. "I need to talk to you. I'm upstairs in the spare room."

He meandered in and stood in the doorway. "What are you doing on the floor, and what's wrong with the dog?"

Tears in his eyes, Sam's voice faltered. "He's dead, and I don't understand how or why. I took him to the vet three days ago for a yearly checkup, and everything was okay. Was he acting strange or did he seem sick when you took him outside before school?"

"Nope. Pissed and crapped like always."

Irritated by his dispassionate tone, Sam said, "So, you saw nothing unusual in his behavior?"

"Nothing. If you decide to bury him in the backyard, I'd be happy to help dig the hole."

Fury leapt to his lips. "Get out of my sight before I wring your neck."

A hand to his ear, he replied, "Mom's home. How about I re-play how you want to strangle her cherished *only* child?"

Overcome with murderous thoughts, he made a fist with his hand. *If I had it in me, I would.*

Sam chose a spot in the backyard to bury Lucky. He wrapped him in his favorite blanket and held him for the last time. *You were my sounding board. My bedmate when Maddie retreated after Gracie's death, and you defused my teed off moods over Brian. Cheered me up and made me laugh whenever I needed it.* The agonizing loss was familiar to him. He had experienced the same feelings after Gracie died. And like her, there would be no timetable for the grief to pass. He carefully placed Lucky's body in the hole, and gently covered it with dirt. Finished, he trudged back to the house, pressing the dog's collar to his chest. On the patio, Maddie sought to comfort him.

"I'm so sorry. I never had a pet growing up, so I can only imagine what that's like. Not right away, of course, but would you like to get another one?"

What he really wanted was to tell her what his thoughts were about Brian. The fiasco with the sitters. The shelter meal making everyone sick, except him. Lucky's questionable death.

Despite the absence of proof, this latest incident convinced him there had been too many coincidences to ignore their son's involvement. And the ongoing fear, that only he could see, of him doing more harm. "No." He shook his head. "I can't go through this again."

The summer before Brian entered high school, Sam decided to speak to Maddie about sending him to camp. His choice would have been a place for troubled youths, but that suggestion was bound to deliver a flat-out no.

"I'd like to talk to you about Brian." He pulled out the kitchen chair across from her and sat down.

"What has he done to aggravate you this time?"

Ignoring the sharpness in her voice, he said, "You mentioned being concerned about leaving him on his own with nothing to do this summer."

"Sorry, I didn't mean to snap at you. I trust him, but with both of us working, we can't always be available to drive him if wants to go somewhere. What are you thinking?"

"There's this place in the Berkshires offering a wide range of things to do—water activities, sports, wilderness and adventure programs. Here's the brochure."

"This looks wonderful. The best part, they can practice leadership skills. It says here they learn how to resolve conflicts, communicate better, and how to become a mentor. Since it's your idea, why don't you tell him?"

I don't care what it offers if it gets him out of the house. He called Brian into the kitchen and explained the camp. "Your mom and I are sending you there for two weeks."

"You want to wreck my summer like you did Christmas vacation? That worked out well for me. I am not hanging around a bunch of rejects doing arts and crafts or joining lame leadership classes I could teach."

"You don't have a choice, and if you keep up this smart-alecky attitude, we'll send you for the entire summer."

"I'M. NOT. GOING."

When he flounced out of the room, Sam yelled, "YES. YOU. ARE." His voice made him feel as if he had sunk to his son's level.

Sam was reading about the ongoing investigation into the fire at their nearly destroyed homeless shelter when Brian walked back in.

"You reading about the shelter? Anything new?"

"The only evidence is a broken window and a burnt cigar on the floor."

"Do you think they'll be able to find out who did it?"

"We hope so." He watched him pull the camp brochure out of his back pocket.

"I decided to go."

"What's changed your mind?"

"The stuff looks interesting, and there's nothing to do around here."

He didn't buy the sudden three-sixty-degree decision or the unconvincing reason for wanting to go. But it was all he could do not to grab the car keys and take him there on the spot.

Sam could feel the calm the moment they walked into the house. *I can't remember the last time I breathed without tightness in my chest.* He put his arms around Maddie and said, "Let's have some fun and get away for a romantic weekend. Remember how much you loved the White Mountain Hotel in New Hampshire?"

"I do, and it's sounds wonderful, but with Brian away, it's the perfect opportunity to finally make a few changes in his bedroom."

"It's only two days, and I won't take no for an answer. Besides, I already booked the hotel. We leave this afternoon, so go pack a bag." He winked when he said, "Make it a light one. Not sure how much time we will get to spend outside."

The blue sky, dotted with white fluffy clouds, was perfect for a trip on the eighty-passenger cable car that brought them to the 4,080-foot summit of Cannon Mountain. Holding hands, they looked out at the panoramic views of the distant valleys and the mountains of four states and Canada.

Two hours later, they arrived back in their suite with more views of the mountains. Satiated by the delicious meal delivered by room service, they polished off a bottle of the best champagne and rediscovered the passionate lovemaking that had been missing. They slept through breakfast, had an early lunch, and strolled around the grounds before they headed home.

"Are you glad you came?" Sam asked.

"Yes. I didn't realize how much I needed this. How much *we* needed this." She reached up and put her arms around his neck. "I love you, Sam Middleton. Never forget that."

"I hope last night proves how much I love you too, and nothing will ever change that. We could stay longer. Nothing to rush home to."

"We can come back again. Maybe around the holidays. Right now, I want to get home and start redecorating Brian's room."

It was the first time in two days they'd mentioned his name.

When asked to strip the sheets off Brian's bed, Sam tried to open the door but couldn't. "Maddie, the door is locked."

"Get the spare key in the second drawer of the pantry."

"Sorry, no key. Looks like you'll have to wait until he gets home."

"Remove the hinges."

"You're kidding. You know what a fanatic he is about his privacy."

She gave him a light pat on the cheek. "Once you strip the bed, put the sheets in the wash."

After an hour of cussing, he finally removed the door. The room was meticulous. Books neatly stacked on shelves. Pencils, pens, rulers, and paper lined up on the desk. Pants, shirts, and sweaters were arranged in the closet. Everything matched by color. Even the socks in the dresser were in perfect alignment. Nothing was out of order, except his messed-up son. *Don't go there. If you ruminate on him, it will spoil the great weekend we had.*

Maddie came to check on his progress. "Great job with the door."

"Seems I'm a natural at breaking and entering."

She laughed and blew him a kiss. "I am off to Sears and then the hardware store for paint. And thanks again for a wonderful weekend."

The bed stripped, he saw a notebook stuck underneath the mattress pad. Ready to toss it on the desk, he paused when he read the white label on the cover—*Personal Musings by Brian Jacob Middleton.* His fingers itched to read it. Instead, he brought the sheets to the laundry room and turned on the machine. The cyclical agitation matched the stirring in his brain.

He returned and picked up the notebook. *What harm could it do to see what he's writing about?*

The number of egregious acts against classmates, teachers, principals, and animals unnerved him. But the part about killing Lucky with antifreeze coated his throat with vitriol. It grew thicker when he read about the destruction of property—broken windows, tires slashed, cars battered. He sat on the floor, the notebook in his lap, and thought, *Don't read anymore.* Except it was like driving by a terrible accident. You can't help but slow down and stare.

When he got to the page about the shelter, his pupils flared, and a white-hot rage consumed him. *Jesus Christ, he tainted the sauce, planted the cigar, set the fire, and let Ernie and Bertha take the fall.* Horror-struck by his son's state of mind and physical trail of destruction, he turned to the last entry, dated a week ago.

Entry: It didn't take long to determine how flawed humans are. Greed, weakness, and vulnerability make them ripe for intimidation and easy targets to exploit. This also includes people who can't see through my charm and manipulation. When it got out how smart I am, requests came from stupid kids to write their papers and do their homework. I even devised a plan to let them cheat off my tests. Nothing was off-limits if it made them indebted to me. If someone were ever to read this, which will never happen, they may wonder why I do what I do. It's for control, revenge, amusement, boredom, and because I can. I can't wait for high school. I already have big plans to raise the bar.

Sam thought of the camp. *Has he already done something, or is he planning to? Is that the reason he went?* Scribbling a note to Maddie that Joe needed him at a jobsite, he got into the car, shifted into drive, squealed out of the driveway, and raced against the clock.

Ninety minutes later, he screeched to a halt in the camp parking lot. He stepped out of the car and felt the rapid-fire of his heartbeat. Lightheaded, he broke into a sweat and found it difficult to breathe. Hands on the roof, he bent his head and waited until the episode passed.

At the front desk, his words tore from his mouth. "Do you know where Brian Middleton is? He's my son, and I need to see him."

"Are you here because of the incidents?"

His fears spiked. "No, has something happened?"

"Your son is fine. Several campers were traumatized when they found two rabbits maimed in the petting zoo, and the staff found a couple of nonvenomous snakes in the shower stalls. I've been running this camp for fifteen years, and I can assure you nothing like this has ever happened. Thanks to your son, we caught the kids involved."

"Where can I find him?"

"His group is on a hike, but they should be back in twenty minutes. You can wait in his dorm. It's number five. You raised a great kid, Mr. Middleton. All the staff love him. During free time, he entertains the younger kids, and I've been told he's doing fantastic in the leadership program. Unless he wants to go home, I hope you'll let him stay."

Sam noted Brian's inquisitive expression when he saw him standing in front of his bed.

"So, to what do I owe this honor? It can't be because you already miss me."

Sam's eyes blazed as he flung the notebook and missed his head by inches.

"What the fuck? You broke into my room? You had no goddamn right."

"How could you do those despicable things?"

He watched his mouth pull into a fiendish grin and when he spoke, his voice was smooth as glass.

"You read it, so you know the reasons."

Sam clamped down so hard on his back teeth, his head hurt. "I want you say it."

"You sure you want to torture yourself twice?"

"Start talking."

"For entertainment. To settle scores. To prove I could do it. By your expression, I must have hit a nerve."

Sam finally had the evidence his son was a depraved human being and everything he did or said was backed by evil-minded intent.

"What other crimes have you committed?"

"I haven't killed any human *yet*. That would make me deranged."

"I going to report you to the authorities."

"Unless you have more proof, all you have is the notebook."

He grabbed the scruff of his neck. "Get your stuff. We're going home."

Sam took Brian by the arm and shoved him into his bedroom. "You'll get out when I'm good and ready."

"There's no door. What are you going to do? Tie me to the headboard or lock me in the closet?"

"I'm an expert with hinges." Secured in less than five minutes, he took the door key from his backpack and pulled the phone cord from the wall. "You won't be needing these anymore, or this." Brandishing the notebook in his face, he said, "Imagine what your mother will say when she reads this."

"What planet are you on? We both know she's an easy pushover when it comes to me."

"Not this time." He left, listening to him curse.

He looked at the display of photographs on the rosewood hutch. A wedding picture, taken twenty-six years ago, had them standing in an intimate pose. He picked up one of Maddie's favorites that captured the first time the twins stood on their own. His, too, if not for the macabre expression on Brian's face. *God, even back then, there was a sign.* He smashed the frame against the wood, shattering the glass, ripped the picture in half, crumbled Brian's side, and threw it on the floor. *This is going to devastate her. How do I tell her the child she believes is good and kind is a diabolical monster with no heart, no soul, and no morals?*

Maddie walked in and saw the broken glass and the destroyed photo. "Sam, what happened here?"

In the background, the sounds of Brian trashing his room accompanied a string of foul language.

"What's Brian doing home, and why is he acting that way?"

Faltering over his words, "I—he's . . ." When she tried to leave, he held her arm. "First, let me explain."

"Explain what?"

Not wanting to divulge everything in the notebook, he left out some of the gorier entries. "I know it's a shock. When I read it, I . . ."

Acrimony in her voice, she interrupted him. "This is absurd. He told me weeks ago he was writing a psychological thriller."

"Maddie, it's all a pack of lies. He poisoned my dog."

"You must really hate him to accuse him of doing those monstrous things. This time, you've gone too far with your sick accusations."

The bitterness in her voice staggered him. He thrust the notebook in her hand. "He didn't deny any of it. Read it and see if you still think he's telling the truth."

37

MADDIE

OUTSIDE BRIAN'S ROOM, Maddie's hands shook as she read the first three pages. *This can't be true.* She unlocked the door and saw the wrecked room. "We need to discuss this." To control the shaking in her voice, she said, "Your dad insists it's a record of the awful things you've committed. Is it true?"

"Mom, I told you, they're ideas for the book I plan to write. You believe me, don't you?"

She looked at the innocent expression on his face. "Explain to me why you didn't deny it?"

"He's the liar. He'll say and do anything to make me look bad. You've seen how he treats me. Instead of worrying about what I wrote, you should be more concerned about how much he hates me."

When his attitude turned from woeful to vindictive, the back of her neck turned clammy. She turned, shut the door, and went back to Sam.

"This is not who my son is. Maybe it's something physical, like a brain tumor that triggered him to do those dreadful things."

"For God's sake, it's not a tumor. We can't waste any more time. He's sick and needs help before he does something…" He stopped before he said, "Kills someone."

"I'm not doing anything until I call Julia and get her advice."

"I don't think that's a good idea. How can she be objective? She's your best friend."

"Please, let's see what she has to say."

"Fine, but he's not going anywhere until we know what to do with him."

She dialed the number twice before getting it right. The answering machine picked up after four rings.

"This is Dr. Reardon. Please leave a brief message, and I will return your call."

"Julia, please call me right away."

The phone rang ten minutes later.

"Something's wrong," Julia said. "What is it?"

"It's Brian."

"Oh no, is he sick?"

She cried. "Please come. I—we need to talk to you."

38

JULIA

THE DOOR WAS flung open before Julia knocked. Everything about Maddie screamed fear—slouched posture, eyes wide, eyebrows raised. When she hugged her, she felt the tautness in her body. "Tell me what's going on with Brian."

In the living room, she watched Maddie pace back and forth from the couch to the chair. Concerned, she said, "Come sit down." Before she could ask where Sam was, he walked in and didn't waste time with small talk.

"Before we discuss anything, I—we—need to get your take on what he's written in his notebook."

As she turned the pages, her stomach tightened, and her breath quickened. When she looked up, their eyes were glued to hers. "If it's true, this is serious."

Sam looked at her with a clear-cut expression of disgust. "Oh, it's true. He admitted it to me. Even though I've had suspicions, I never considered he could be so . . . so evil."

When Maddie didn't speak, Julia placed a hand on her knee. "Can you tell me what you're thinking?"

"I don't understand how he got this way. Can you talk to him? See if you can find out what made him do these things?"

Because her anguish was so raw and palpable, Julia said, "I'm not sure how much I'll learn from him, but I'll try."

When she rejoined them, Maddie leapt off the couch and bombarded her with questions.

"What happened? How is he? What did he say?"

"He told me the same thing he told you. The notebook references his novel. When I reminded him he already admitted it wasn't fiction, he made it quite clear there was no proof accusing him of any wrongdoing."

Sam raised his voice. "We can't let him get away with this. I guarantee he will not stop—because he can't. Where do we go from here?"

"What he needs is an in-depth evaluation to make an accurate diagnosis, followed by extensive therapy."

Maddie made a strangled sound. "Knowing how much he loved Gracie and how devoted he was to her, I don't understand how any of this is possible. Sam, have you forgotten the way he sat at her bedside to comfort her when the pain was too much? The way he held her hand when another needle pricked her bruised and damaged skin? Swabbed her cracked and bleeding lips until the end? Did you forget all of that?"

"No, but remembering how he was doesn't rule out what he's done. Julia, you must have an idea what's wrong with him. Please tell us what you think. And be honest."

This will not go well. "There is no way to soften what I am going to say. His entries show him as a consummate manipulator and liar. Unable to distinguish right from wrong, he takes great pleasure inflicting pain and suffering. To get what he wants, he uses intimidation, threats, and superficial charm. It's only my opinion, and nothing is definitive until he has the proper testing."

When Maddie's eyes bulged and her mouth went slack, Sam's head drew back. "Come on Maddie. That's enough for now. We need to take a break."

Watching them leave the room, Julia thought, *God, I don't know how much more they can take, and it's only the beginning.*

Julia sat at the kitchen table. After a careful reading of the notebook, she believed Brian's personality illuminated something malignant. Working with children with severe character disturbances, she knew that if left untreated, by age eight, a child would unlikely be able to learn ways to deal with people other than by coercion. Several experts labeled them "fledgling psychopaths" who became more dangerous as they get older.

She understood why Maddie had trouble processing why her son behaved this way and still showed love and kindness to his sister. In her experience, individuals who exhibited strong connections with another person could display these emotions. But, when diagnosed as psychopathic, this side of their makeup prevailed. Even more challenging was the compelling evidence that biology might be the underlying cause of certain personality disorders. She reasoned, *If this is the case, all hope for any change in Brian would be dashed.* Sam's voice startled her.

"Julia, I have something difficult to tell you."

"Without Maddie?"

"She's asleep. In her state, it's better if she doesn't hear this. It's an ugly secret no one knows except Joe and my mother."

She watched him go back and forth as he tracked the wide plank floor, punctuating the words by jabbing his hands in the air.

"Julia, I come from a bunch of degenerates, and the acts they committed are indescribable."

She pulled out a chair. He collapsed into it. "What makes you think that?"

"When I came back from Paris, I found newspaper articles my parents hid from me. My great-grandfather was charged with rape and murder. My drunken grandfather physically and emotionally abused my dad and my grandmother. When my dad couldn't take it anymore, he beat him so badly it left him brain damaged. But that's not everything. Besides an aunt who died, I have an uncle, my dad's twin. At sixteen, he ended up in prison—ten years for murder."

"Where is he now?"

He leaned over and pressed his palms between his knees. "I don't know. I just pray to God he's dead."

"Tell me more about your dad. Other than your grandfather, did he ever threaten or hurt you or your mother?"

"Not her. It was different for me. I withstood the worst of his anger. Once or twice, we came close to a fistfight. I get why he acted that way."

"Why?"

"He was afraid if I lost control, I might hurt someone. He was partly right." His expression twisted with grief and shame. "I wanted to beat the shit out of Brian on more than one occasion, especially after I read the notebook."

"Sam, what stopped you?"

"I didn't want to end up like the rest of those fucking bastards."

She layed on hand on his arm. "When someone is provoked, they can feel anger, even rage. It's called being human. You've clung to these fears for decades, and they have no merit with you."

"Julia, bad behavior doesn't always lead to worst-case scenarios like rape or murder. I tried to convince myself I'm a good person. It worked until Brian was born. What's real is a dark side to his personality, and mine. It's in our DNA. If Maddie and I never had children, this nightmare would have ended with me. But we did, and so many times I wished it had been him who died instead of Gracie."

39

MADDIE

A FLAME OF red-hot fury rose from Maddie's chest as she stood in the doorway. "Anything more you'd like to add?"

Sam's voice splintered. "How long have you been standing there?"

Her words were sharp and acrid. "Enough to find out you've been lying to me since Paris. So much for being honest."

"I wanted to tell you, but I was afraid. It took so long for us to get back together, and I didn't want to lose you again."

"Your excuse is pitiful." She thrust an index finger at him. "How dare you hide your family history, knowing you have a murderous uncle who could still be alive. And you did this despite the risk of the safety to our home and family. The biggest lie—you never wanted children. Were you on your knees and thankful for my miscarriages?"

"God no, but I . . ."

Her voice skidded between octaves. "I'm not finished. After years of denigrating our son, you wished he was the one who died. And now you claim he inherited the ability to do horrible things. Based on what? His notebook? His DNA? I guess I should be fearful of you too."

"Jesus, Maddie, I would never hurt you."

"So it's only Brian you want to hurt?"

Julia spoke. "There's nothing about Sam to support he's anything like his family."

Maddie's words fired like bullets. "Except he wants my son dead." When he opened his mouth to speak, she said, "I'm done listening to you," and stormed out.

On the patio, conflicting emotions tangled in Maddie's head like an unraveled ball of yarn. *How could he do this to our family? Deceive me with such a heinous secret. The only good thing about this relationship was my sweet Gracie and my son.* When Julia came and sat beside her, she handed her a photograph of Brian—smiling with outstretched arms, waiting at the bottom of a kiddie slide to catch his sister.

"What a lovely picture."

Her fingers dug sickle shapes into her palms. "I don't believe he was born bad or inherited a sick gene from one-hundred-year-old ancestors. Despite the things he did, he can't be an irredeemable monster." Her eyes begged for hope. "Tell me, with help, he can change."

"It all depends on the diagnosis and the treatment he gets. I'm sorry. I wish I could give you a more concrete answer."

After Julie left, Sam approached her. "We need to . . ." She got up and tried to brush past him, but he stopped her. "We need to focus on what to do with Brian. I spoke to a physician at a psychiatric treatment facility. They have a spot for him in one of their inpatient programs."

Her eyes flared in defiance. "Typical. *You* decided to take matters into your own hands. Well, you can forget that idea. He's not going to a mental institution. I'm calling the therapist Julia gave me."

"After what he's done, that kind of treatment won't be enough to help him."

"You haven't known what's good for him since the day he was born."

"I've made mistakes and said things I'll never be able to take back, but can't we put that aside for now?"

"No."

Everything tilted sideways, making Maddie's world twist into a sick configuration. Powerless to stop the replay of what transpired during Julia's visit, she called her that evening, condemning Sam for his lies.

"Maddie, there is every reason to be angry. He's made terrible mistakes, said things out of fear. But it's obvious how much he loves you."

She looked at her ringless finger. "His way of showing it is not what I signed up for. If I had been told about his family and the fact he didn't want any children, I never would have married him."

40

SAM

THE MORNING OF the meeting with Brian's therapist, Sam woke in a sweat, as if he walked through the fires of hell. The nightmare he had twenty-five years ago, when he learned about his family history, resurfaced. This time, when he found himself backed against an invisible wall, he wasn't confronted by the savage grins of his family but by the image of dripping blood on his son's hands.

Consumed by the fear of what Brian would do if not sent away, he reconsidered contacting the authorities. But if he suggested it to Maddie, he was certain she would fight him on it. The discord between them had mounted. Besides her purposeful avoidance, a prickly silence draped over them. No matter how hard he tried to make amends, she wanted none of it.

"I want to fix what I did. Please, tell me what I can do to make it up to you."

"Gee, this sounds so familiar. You spoke similar words after you made another epic mistake the way you broke up with me. You can't do anything, so stop asking."

He should have kept his mouth shut and not confessed to Julia. What had he hoped to gain? Confirmation their son was the way he was because of his DNA? *There's not even a trace of proof other than the notebook and my gut instinct.*

The therapist invited them into her office. Sam waited for Maddie to sit and sat beside her. When he tried to take her hand, she pulled it away.

"Brian refused to talk about anything significant. When I brought up the contents of the notebook, he stated it was all fiction. It didn't surprise me when he allowed me to administer one of the standardized tests. The way he spoke, he assumed he could manipulate the outcome. I am sorry to tell you his scores indicate a diagnosis of psychopathy."

"My son has issues, but he's not crazy," Maddie said.

"No, he isn't, but if not treated properly, his insatiable appetite for harm will escalate."

Maddie scoffed. "I've heard enough of this nonsense."

"Please let me finish. There is an adolescent treatment center two hours from here. They oppose using the term psychopath because of the stigma. By trial and error, they aren't able to cure it, but there's been success in training certain individuals. If you agree, I'll call and see if there are any openings."

"Training him? Like taming a lion to act like a house cat? We're leaving. I want a second opinion."

Sam spoke up. "Maddie, a second opinion will only prolong getting him the help he urgently needs. You don't want more delays, do you?"

Her eyes bore into him. "This place better not scar my son."

Ten minutes later, the therapist hung up the phone. "You can bring him after three today."

When Maddie told Brian, he pleaded with her.

"Mom, you can't let Dad do this. It's his way of having me locked up like an insane person. Please, I'm begging you, don't send me away. I know I can change. All I need is your love and support. Just give me the chance to prove it to you."

"Sweetheart, this place will help you get well. You have my word. I am not sending you away for good."

Sam thought, *He's trying to work her over like he always does. Thank God it didn't work this time.*

They met with the intake person while Brian took a guided tour of the residential center. A steady stream of tears flowed down Maddie's face, and twice her hand faltered when it was her turn to sign the forms. Sam tried to drape his arm around her shoulder, but she moved her chair. Sitting through two hours of information about the program, he knew by her constant fidgeting and checking her watch, she was only interested when she could spend time with their son.

"Mr. and Mrs. Middleton, do you have questions?"

"Can we see him before we leave?" Maddie asked.

"I'm sorry, but we can't interrupt our admission procedures with new residents."

"How soon can we visit?"

"Your son needs to become acclimated to the facility, his personalized schedule, and meet the individuals who will render the treatment plan."

"How long will that take?"

"That depends on Brian."

"Our son is exceptionally smart. I'm sure it won't take more than a week."

Sam cringed at her boastfulness. *I guess she needs to hang on to something to make him seem normal.*

On the drive home, Sam asked, "So, what do you think?"

"About the center? Oh, it's perfect. I love having my son in a place where I'm told when I can and can't visit."

The enormity of her anger seeped into every pore of his skin. "I thought you were on board with this. You even convinced him it's where he needs to be."

"He wouldn't be in that place if you'd been a decent father."

The jab felt like a smack in the face. "So, you're telling me his personality has nothing to do with what he did, and it's my fault he's turned out this way?"

"Didn't you confess to Julia it's in your DNA?"

He hit back. "Did you ever consider if you hadn't ignored my repeated concerns and discounted his behavior, we wouldn't be where we are now? Instead, we have a kid who gets off on poisoning people and burning down the shelter. Do you want me to continue? It may take all day." He should have bitten his tongue, because she spent the entire ride home recounting all his deceit and lies.

41

MADDIE

IN FRONT OF Maddie lay the twins' photograph that Sam tore the day he found the notebook. Unable to glue them together, she placed the unmarred side of Gracie next to Brian's. *What if I lose him too?* Her head filled with self-blame, she called Julia. "I feel so ashamed and guilty."

"Why?"

"I'm his mother. I should have been the one to give him the help he needs."

"You can't blame yourself. His diagnosis warrants a structured environment with professionals."

"But it will ruin his entire life, being in a place like that. How is he supposed to deal with that?"

"What did he say when you visited him?"

"It's been two weeks, and I've heard nothing about when I can visit. I'm afraid when I do, he's going to tell me he hates me." Her voice was tremulous. "Maybe he won't even want to see me."

"I can't tell you how he'll react, but I know he needs your love and support, even if he doesn't show it. What about you and Sam? How are things going?"

"Our relationship is at an impasse. When I blasted him for being a terrible father, he got angry and accused me of overlooking Brian's behavior." She let out an exasperated sigh. "I wonder why I'm still here."

"Don't make any drastic decisions while you're under so much stress. You shouldn't be alone and without support. No matter how you feel, the entire situation is difficult for Sam too."

"So what's the answer?"

"Call a truce. Put your anger aside, and if you need a referee, get professional help. It's a healthier way to air your grievances, and maybe you will both have a reason to meet halfway."

When Maddie got off the phone, she slipped on a raincoat. Under a light drizzle, she walked to the farthest corner of the backyard and stopped in front of the playhouse Sam and Joe had built. It had scalloped rooflines, gables, balconies, a wraparound porch, and a working doorbell with a brass door knocker. Covered with extra-wide tarps, it had been a well-kept secret until its completion. She remembered the shock and awe when they unveiled the miniature replica of their house.

Because no one had stepped inside since Gracie's death, Sam wanted to tear it down, but she wouldn't let him. Her heart couldn't handle another vacant space—inside or out. Feeling an ardent pull to go inside, she paused on the scuff-marked hardwood floor. In the center of the room was a large, worn-thin, light-green rug. On top was a round maple table surrounded by four chairs padded with gingham patterns of pink and blue. Undisturbed sat four place settings with the tea set she'd passed down to Annie and then to Gracie on her fourth birthday. She heaved a sigh. Her entire life was filled with the mingling of sadness and happiness.

In the far corner, a sizable wooden three-tier bin held toys and games. Next to it was the Easy Bake Oven. The cake pan still had hardened crumbs along the rim—remnants of the chocolate cake the twins baked on Sam's birthday.

Undone in the middle and heavy on the yellow frosting, Sam's nose had puckered when he took a full bite. With a rub of his stomach, he'd said, "This is the best cake I've ever tasted." His lips, teeth, and tongue tinged a bright yellow, he whispered, "Do I have to eat the whole thing?" A mischievous grin had splayed across her face. "Do you have to ask?"

She thought about the fault line that had solidified between them and wondered, *What happened to the man I married?*

She placed her hands against the textured walls, painted a satin ivory and smudged with tiny handprints. Her eyes closed, she visualized one of Sam's hands holding Gracie's while the other supported a tottering Brian. His voice materialized. "You're a big boy. You can do it." A forlorn sigh escaped. *There were moments it hadn't always been bad between you and Brian. You just don't remember.*

She climbed the ladder to the cozy loft. Twin beds were arranged under a skylight. Handcrafted by Sam, personalized toy chests with delicate finishes stood at the foot of each bed. Lifting the lids, she selected their cherished possessions: a surplus of candy and bubble gum bought at a local sweetshop; sea glass and shells of all shapes and sizes collected at the beach; boxes filled with acorns, leaves, and feathers gathered during long walks in the woods; and a glass jar packed with spiders and insects meant for afternoons of counting legs through magnifying glasses.

Palming an acorn, she reminisced about the time Gracie posed a question. "Daddy, if Brian and I dig holes and plant acorns, will they grow into trees?"

"Well, it starts with God," Sam had said. "He creates a special power inside them, and then a miracle happens. They take root in the ground and need to be cared for to grow strong and sturdy."

He had helped Brian and Gracie plant two acorns. They watered them daily and eagerly waited for sparks of life. Eight weeks later, when the shoots sprouted, the twins wanted to celebrate. Each year, the ritual had continued. By the time Gracie died, the northern red oaks had grown eight feet. The parties had ended, but the plantings didn't. To pay reverence to her nine years of life, Sam had planted seven more.

Through the skylight, she could see the tops of the oak trees glistening from the rain. The November weather had turned the vibrant red leaves into desiccated brown. Sam once said, "In thirty years, their full height will be sixty feet." She wondered, *Will we still be the couple to witness their beauty and strength?*

A sudden downpour hammered against the metal roof as if it tried to cleanse the pain and clear a path to an open heart. She reconsidered what it must have been like to be saddled with the despicable deeds of his family and forced to hide it. She understood how situations changed who you were and colored your thinking. It made her realize she didn't want to give up on him. At least not yet. But he needed to accept their son could change and be willing to support him. Julia's suggestion made sense. To see a therapist would be critical to help remove the boxing gloves.

Maddie struggled to smooth the nonexistent wrinkles from her skirt. So much of what happened next with Sam depended on the outcome of these sessions.

The therapist said, "I understand you are having issues with your son and how it's affected your marriage. How old is he?"

"Fourteen," Maddie said.

"Is he living with you?"

"He's in an inpatient facility."

"Why is he there?"

"He has psychological problems."

"Would you like to discuss them?"

"No. We are here because my husband refuses to visit him, and he needs to see firsthand his progress. He's taking classes for academic credit toward his high school diploma. When he graduates, he wants to attend college."

"I hope my wife is right, but no one can guarantee he won't ruin more lives. Even if he learns to control his actions, it won't change the fact that when he's released, it will be with the same diagnosis."

Maddie crossed her arms and said, "This is what I mean. I need a partner who can show empathy for what our son is going through. It's obvious my husband can't get beyond the negative attitude."

"Sam, do you want to respond to what she said?"

"I love my wife, and I'd do anything for her, but it's a struggle to forget what he's done."

"It's clear both of you have difficulty seeing Brian in the same light. The constant bickering and fighting isn't helping either of you or your son. My advice: take a step back. Not from the support of your son, but from your disagreements about him. Maddie, you mentioned on the phone you've been married twenty-four years. Try not to fixate on what's wrong, but the reasons that have kept you together. It will give you the strength to handle whatever the future holds for your family. And Sam . . . you need to see your son."

42

SAM

SAM SAT ACROSS from Brian in the visitors' lounge. Skipping the small talk, he asked, "How are you handling being here?"

"Can't complain. Three squares a day, and I don't have to listen to my misguided mother telling me how much I've changed and we will be one big, happy family. You and I know it will never be the way she imagines."

He eyed him with icy contempt. "If it weren't for her, I would put you away for good."

"Since that won't happen, let's move on to something more momentous. Seems like my genetic makeup comes from your colorful family."

When he extended his hand and said, "Thanks, Dad, for bringing me into your world," Sam slapped it away. "How do you know that?"

"Your pathetic confession to Julia about your nefarious secrets and the upshot of lying to the woman you claim to love. And, there's the fact whenever you look at me you see yourself. Not to mention all the times I've watched you stand in front of the mirror and try to hide the birthmark with your hair. Or press it hard with your knuckles as if you could obliterate it. Get real. You and I come from the same mold, and we can't change who we are. My advice: embrace it the way I have. It's a hell of a lot more fun."

"You disgust me. Sending you here is a waste of money. I've got a good mind to drag your sorry ass out of here."

He got up. "This visit went well. Next time, come on Saturday with Mom. It would be interesting to see how you speak to me when she's around."

"Not if I can help it."

"Better rethink that. On more than one occasion I told her it upset me that my own father won't come spend time with me."

After his visit with Brian, Sam came up with an ongoing excuse that the firm was too busy managing the influx of new business. Maddie, tired of hearing it, laced into him.

"Did you forget what the therapist told you at our last session?"

"No, but work has been—"

"Stop right there. We both need to show a united front for his recovery. Either you come this afternoon or I'm finished trying to improve things between us."

He would have liked to counter the attack by reminding her of all his attempts to reminisce about their days in Paris and the early years when they were happy despite their career struggles. But her concern and focus stayed on Brian.

In the center of the lounge, Sam stood back and watched Brian rush over to Maddie. In a false display of affection, he told her how much he loved her. When he left her side, he came up to him with a sanctimonious grin on his face.

"Dad, thanks for being here. I've missed you, and there's so much I want to tell you."

Brian said it loud enough for everyone in the room to hear, and he had to restrain himself from yelling, "You're such a fucking liar." For the next forty-five minutes, he listened to him lather up the charm.

"This place is so cool. They've asked me to work with the kids who've been struggling with their schoolwork. Who knows, maybe it's a sign I'll become a teacher someday."

Sam winced when Maddie placed her hand over Brian's and said, "Have I told you how proud I am of you?" He thought, *What will it to take for her to see through him?*

"All the time. There's something else. I am doubling up on classes and will have my high school diploma before I leave. Once I ace the SATs, I'll be ready to apply to several Ivy League schools. Dad, in case Mom didn't tell you, Harvard's my first choice. Since it's close to home, you and I will have plenty of quality time to spend together. Won't it be great?"

When he winked, Sam pulled his lips into a tight smile. "Can't wait."

Maddie asked, "How are your therapy sessions going?"

"Great. Because I'm doing everything I'm supposed to do, they're happy with the changes I've made."

"That's wonderful, isn't it, Sam? All the progress he's made."

Her praise left him wordless.

"And, get this, I even earn points for positive behavior."

Sam thought, *Points? Did he actually say points? For the love of God, the next thing he'll say is he has a chart covered in gold stars for all the times he's able to fake it. Am I the only one who sees the truth that he'll leave here the same or even sicker?*

When Sam got back, he went to the office and called Joe. Standing with his head pressed against the window, he wondered what his reaction would be when he learned Sam's son was corrupt to the bone.

"I went through every red light and ignored the speed limit to get here," Joe said. "The sound of your voice scared the hell out of me. Did something happen to Maddie or Brian? Jesus, look at me. Tell me what's going on."

"He's a goddamn psychopath."

"Who is?"

"Brian."

"Come on. Where would you get an absurd idea like that?"

"You'd better sit." He wrestled to get the words out. "I found a notebook he kept filled with pages of repulsive acts. The earlier ones might have been seen as cruel pranks, but the older he got, the more destructive and deviant they became. The sickest part— he gets a thrill out of what he does and has no remorse."

Joe's eyes widened to their fullest extent as he took in his words. "Not in a million years would I have thought he was capable of such violence. I don't get it. He was always so personable and soft-spoken whenever I saw him."

"That's Brian. It's all a calculated disguise to win people over. He's done it with Maddie and every therapist involved in his rehabilitation, except with me. Early on, I saw right through the facade."

"What are you going to do?"

"I can't do anything until he's discharged."

"I hate to say it, but if he was my kid, I would be afraid one day he would flip out and do something like . . ."

"Murder someone. He already did—my dog."

When Maddie returned from a visit with Brian, she gave Sam the good news he was being released in a couple of hours and she wanted him to go with her. He lied. "I'm meeting with a client to review the final blueprints on a new building. Construction starts on Monday."

"Can't you let Joe cover for you?"

"It's his daughter's birthday."

"So much for your promise to be supportive. You've already failed by your infrequent visits."

He caught the petulance in her voice. *Maybe I should have told her how he demeaned her when I saw him. Forget it. She wouldn't believe me, anyway. I swear, if he ever kills someone, she'll say it was self-defense.* The sick notion that both could be real possibilities scared the living shit out of him.

"I guess that's a no. In case you're interested, I have a copy of his discharge summary. It's on the kitchen table. I'm planning a special dinner with all his favorites. Perhaps you can break away from your busy schedule and join us."

After she left, Sam looked at the date Brian entered the facility. The doctors had reasoned he was well enough to go home even though it'd been a little over two years. "So much for years of documented brutality." He read that on admission, they confirmed by standardized tests and the psychopathy checklist, his diagnosis was manifestations of psychopathy. When he first got there, it said he exhibited episodes of callousness, lack of empathy, lack of remorse, and periods of grandiosity.

His course of treatment had been a structured environment, group therapy, and intensive psychotherapy used to help him understand his diagnosis and how it affected his life and his relationship with others. A therapist actively worked with him to develop strategies and coping skills for more constructive behaviors to decrease the severity of his symptoms. And then he came to the discharge summary.

"Brian has successfully redirected his impulses to make better choices for healthier outcomes. To reduce recidivism depends on a strict adherence to twice-weekly sessions with a local therapist. Based on his progress as an outpatient, this will determine when he is ready to socialize. It is also imperative the parents recognize an individual with this diagnosis gives little thought to punishment. Because it won't discourage criminality, positive reinforcement is key."

His hands unsteady, he had to clasp them together. *Those fucking quack doctors may have colored his diagnosis with fancy medical terms, but they can't sugarcoat the unmitigated truth—he's an unalterable psychopath.* The idea of going to the police never felt so strong. But the option was no longer valid. The discharge papers stated he'd changed.

43

MADDIE

AFTER FOUR WEEKS of Brian's therapy, the subtle changes in his behavior encouraged Maddie. He volunteered to help around the house, showed his affection, and engaged in long conversations. She even caught hints of Gracie. "Brian, your therapist must be pleased with how well you're doing."

"She is, and I'm glad you feel the same way, but there's something important I want to talk to you about. Do you remember the deal about positive reinforcement and how it needs to be part of my therapy?"

"I do."

"My therapist knows it's one of the best ways for me to improve. I haven't seen my friends since I got home. I want to be able go to the movies, the mall, and maybe bowling."

"I need to discuss this with your dad and see if he agrees."

"Why? He's hardly ever around, and he doesn't seem to care what or how I'm doing."

She knew he was right. "Okay, but on one condition. I'll bring you to meet your friends, and when you're ready to come home, call me."

"But—"

"No buts. One more thing." She went to her room and came back with a copper tag attached to a sterling silver chain. His initials and date were engraved on the back. "Read what it says."

"May you always see yourself as I do and know how special you are." He hugged her and said, "I love it . . . and you."

She watched as he clasped it around his neck. *Things are coming together.* She sighed. *Except with Sam.*

An attempt to soften the friction between them, before he left for work, Maddie handed Sam a steaming mug of freshly brewed coffee. "I thought I would give you a warm send-off." When he glanced at the door and his watch, she said, "I need to talk to you."

"Can't it wait until later?"

"It could if you didn't leave before I get up in the morning and come home too late to eat supper with Brian and me." She touched his arm. "I'm worried about you. I know you're not sleeping or eating well. Have you looked in the mirror lately? Your clothes are hanging off you."

"Joe and I need to hire more architects, but the recruiters haven't sent the talent we're looking for."

"What's the point of taking on more business if you end up flat in bed or the hospital?"

"That won't happen. If that's all . . ."

"There's another reason I'm concerned. Maybe it's not only work that keeps you away."

"What do you mean?"

"Your absence since Brian's been home is too much of a coincidence."

"I was around when he got back."

"Scarcely enough time to foster a stronger relationship."

"According to who?"

"Our son and me. I told him you would stay this morning, have breakfast with him, and plan something you can do together on Saturday. If you're going to work, it's something you can do together. Take him to one of the sites. Let him see how the business operates. He was excited when I mentioned it last night."

"You believe him?"

She held back a frosty look. "Yes, I do. You'll be amazed to see how different he is. There are omelets in the microwave. Heat them up while I get him. There's something he's been wanting to tell you."

44

SAM

SAM WONDERED IF Brian would be the authentic version or the one who duped Maddie and every doctor he'd ever been to. He got his answer the second he came into the kitchen and spoke in a snide tone.

"Look what we have here. Breaking bread with my father. I would give you a hug, but I need to preserve my bogus affections for Mom. You know how she eats it up."

He slammed the plate with the omelet on the table. "I hope you choke on it."

"Normally, I'd tell Mom, but I'll cut you a break this time because I'm in such a good mood. Life is great when you're not around. In fact, I've convinced another therapist how quickly she's helping me become a success story. One that's sure to be written in one of those medical journals. It'll be a blast to see my name in print."

"If that happens, how are you going to feel when your name is attached to the word psychopath and what you did to deserve such an honor?"

"Maybe the question should be how it will affect you and mom. Moving on, I gather you didn't hear my exciting news. I took the SAT and completed the application for Harvard. I start in January."

"That's not going to happen. I won't pay for it or any other college. You'll have to work for it."

"Do you still think you're the one who makes all the big decisions about me? News flash: you're not. There's something else that's been going on when you're not here."

"Like what?"

"I'll let Mom do the honors."

Sam found Maddie in the living room. "What's this deal with Brian?"

"Because he's been doing so well, I let him go out with his friends. You would have known if you were—"

His voice exploded in decibels. "Goddamn it. You had no right to make that decision without my input. Did you at least get the okay from the therapist?" Her look said everything. "How the hell do you know what he's doing and getting away with it?" He caught the sharp intake of her breath as she backed away. "I'm sorry. I didn't mean to get so angry, but you need to open your eyes and accept the facts. He hasn't changed."

"Since *you're* the authority, I guess I'm supposed to disregard his discharge report from the treatment facility and the therapist he's seeing now."

"Yes. Let me tell you about the two conversations I had there and the one this morning." When he finished, he said, "You don't need to be an expert to recognize a consummate liar and schemer who has a history of committing criminal acts. The notebook is in my desk. You should read all of it this time."

"I don't need to. It's not who he is anymore."

He looked around to make certain Brian wasn't within listening distance before he said, "I give up." Maddie's face went chalk white when he added, "He's not going to change, so I bought a gun."

"Why would you do that?"

"For our protection. It's locked in a metal box in our closet with the key taped underneath."

"You've lost your mind. I want it out of the house."

Sam continued to find himself on shaky ground with Maddie. Whenever they were in the same room, she shunned him or left. The added withdrawal of physical intimacy was her obvious message to have him sleep in another room. Brian's derisive attitude amplified his dejection.

"Have you noticed how much she hates you?"

Sam's eyes narrowed to slits. "What's between your mother and me is none of your damn business."

"But it is. Were you aware I got you driven out of your own bed? I convinced her I was petrified you would try to send me away. You should've seen her response when the tears dripped down my face and I whimpered, 'Promise you won't let that happen. You're the only one I can count on to protect me.' It was quite the performance, and looking at the forecast, it won't be long before you're kicked to the curb."

Sam remembered the first time he held the gun. *Would I ever have it in me to aim it at my son and pull the trigger.* For the right reason, he would. He hissed, "One day, you'll make a colossal mistake you won't get away with, and I'll be right there to make sure you pay for it."

"Time to give up on those idle threats. They make you look weak and insignificant. All these years, you've struggled to stop me and failed. But kudos to you for maintaining the status as a pushover adversary. This stimulating conversation has made me hungry. Perhaps we can pick up later, after I meet the guys at the Pizza Pub. Do you want me to bring you a slice in case Mom doesn't make you dinner?"

Sam cornered Maddie. "Brian won't be going to Harvard. I'm calling the bursar's office tomorrow to have the offer letter withdrawn. He can live at home and work at McDonald's until he can afford to go to one of the local community colleges."

"How dare you go behind my back. He *is* going to Harvard."

"I won't pay for it."

"You won't have to. He's getting early admission and a free ride because of his grades and entrance exams."

He turned to see Brian in the doorway with a superior grin on his face. "We can't go on this way, always at war over him."

"No, we can't. We need . . . I need a break."

"You want me to move out?"

"Yes."

"For how long?" Every muscle in his body tensed as he hung on to her answer.

"I don't know."

Sam moved into one of the firm's furnished, renovated brownstones in the North End of Boston and left a message for Joe to tell him where he was and why he needed time off. It took less than two days before the place was cluttered with unwashed dishes and half-eaten containers of takeout. Unable to sleep and desperate to numb his feelings, he bought a case of beer and drank himself into a stupor. Only a temporary fix, he would wake up with hangovers that exacerbated the pain and grief.

After two weeks of refusing to see him, he heard Joe bang on the door. Unshaven, hair standing on end, and dressed in sweats, he kicked aside an empty beer can, a pizza box, and used chopsticks. "Watch where you step."

"Man, you're a mess, and so is the apartment."

He rubbed his head where a tight band had formed. "I feel worse than I look."

"What you're going through is terrible, but at least she hasn't asked for a permanent separation or a divorce."

"Not yet, but with Brian pulling the strings, I…"

"Have you spoken to her?"

"Twice, I checked on her to see how she was doing and if she needed anything."

"And?"

"And nothing. She said she would call if she did. That whole idea of us seeing a therapist and calling a truce over Brian—it never worked." He kicked another beer can. "I don't know what to do anymore."

Joe gripped both his shoulders. "I do. Move your butt, get yourself and this place presentable, and come back to work. The firm needs you. I need you, and right now, you need me."

During the holidays, the crowded streets with happy couples made it difficult for Sam to hold it together. When Joe called to invite him to Christmas dinner, he said, "Thanks, but I'll pass. I'm not good company these days."

"I won't take another no. You refused to come over for Thanksgiving. This time, I'm not letting you stay alone. Besides, the kids will be excited to see you, so don't disappoint them."

On the drive over, Sam was glad he hadn't refused a nice, relaxed, quiet dinner with Joe's family. As he walked up the steps with a pecan pie in hand, the eruption of noise from the house took him by surprise. He opened the door to a rotund, gray-haired woman with a corrugated face. Dressed in black, she wore maroon scuffs and an Italian apron imprinted with *I Don't Need a Recipe. I'm Italian.* "*Accedere, accedere.* Come in."

She kissed both cheeks and crushed him with a muscular embrace. The pie almost slipped from his grip until Joe grabbed it.

"Nonna, let him go before he suffocates."

Sam walked into a large gathering already seated in the dining room. Filled platters of Italian cuisine from appetizers to desserts spanned the length of a long table. When they spoke over one another in broken English mixed with Italian, he understood the focus was not to race through the meal. Joe turned to him and elevated an eyebrow as if to say, "Sorry, I should have warned you." As the hours passed, it took every ounce of strength to overcompensate with a false front of happiness. Wherever Maddie was, he wondered, *Did she pretend as I did?*

Back in his apartment, he decided to call to wish her a Merry Christmas and ask if he could stop by with some gifts. After four rings, the answering machine picked up. "Hi, it's Maddie. I can't come to the phone. Please leave a message." His name missing, he couldn't believe she had already managed to rearrange her life.

45

MADDIE

MADDIE FAILED TO come up with a valid excuse the day Bill called to invite Brian and her to Christmas dinner. When he greeted her with extended arms and kissed her cheek, it felt like being comforted by her father.

"I'm glad you came. Rita and I have been worried about you. We missed you at Thanksgiving. How are things going with Sam?"

"Okay." She deliberated over the word. "Just okay." He nodded, turned to Brian, and put a hand on his shoulder.

"I hope you brought your appetite."

"I did. All I had this morning was toast and juice. I'm warning you not to expect any leftovers."

At the dinner table, Maddie was relieved when Brian kept the conversation going about passing the test for his learner's permit and attending Harvard in January. When she stared at the empty chair across from her, all her thoughts were on Sam. Her heart told her she could never shake the truth—she would always love him, but . . .

Rita's voice broke the chain of her thinking. "Everyone ready for dessert? It's warm apple pie topped with vanilla ice cream. Brian, you're getting an extra-large piece and two scoops."

"Everything was delicious, and I bet the pie is, too. Sorry, Mom, but it's getting late. One of my friends is going to pick me up to go to the movies." He laughed. "It'll be our third go-round of seeing *Batman Returns.*"

Bill pulled her aside and handed her a covered dish and two pieces of pie wrapped in tinfoil. "You scarcely touched your dinner."

Bright spots of color formed on her cheeks. "It wasn't the food. I asked Sam to leave."

"Because of Brian?"

"And me."

"Oh, sweetheart, I'm so sorry. Promise you'll call if you need anything or want to talk."

Her chin quivered. "I will."

He turned and gestured to Brian. "Take care of your mom. She depends on you."

"No need to worry, Mr. Strathmore. I've got everything under control."

Maddie sat with an unopened book in her lap, thinking about the next big holiday. No amount of persuasion from Bill, Jason, or Julia could convince her to spend the evening ringing in the New Year. She heard the doorbell and figured Brian had forgotten his key, but when she opened the door, Sam was standing there.

"Hi, Maddie. I wanted to stop by and wish you a Merry Christmas. Can I come in for a minute? I brought some presents."

"You should have called before you came. I would have told you . . ."

"I tried, but no one was home. Were you with the Strathmores today?"

"Yes, and you?"

"Joe's. Pretty hectic with his entire family and all the kids."

"Sam, it's been a long day, and Brian will be home soon."

"How is he?"

"Fine."

"I wasn't sure what to get him, so I bought a watch. The receipt is in the box if he doesn't like it. I also bought a book on painting. It's one I know you don't have. There is another reason I came." His chin dipped when he spoke. "Maddie, I want to come home."

She knew she crushed his heart by his stricken expression when she said, "I need more time."

"More time for what? To live separate lives?"

"You need to go before this turns into another argument."

"I'm sorry. I shouldn't have said that. It's just . . . I miss you."

She looked at the clock. *Brian could walk in any minute.* "Please take the gun with you this time."

"It stays for your protection."

"I told you, I don't need it."

"Let's hope not."

The minute he drove away, Brian appeared. "He's no longer wanted in this house, so what the hell was he doing here?"

Hearing the insolent tone he always used on Sam, a flush of bewilderment crossed her face. Recently, she'd noticed a dramatic change in his behavior. He refused any physical affection, and the daily mother-son chats ended. There were moments when she would catch a glimpse of a disquieting expression flash across his face. She had tried to wheedle him into an explanation. "Is something bothering you? Have I done or said anything to upset you?"

"I've never felt better—as long as he stays away."

Unable to seal off the worry, she made an appointment with his therapist.

As if her fingers had a mind of their own, Maddie played with her coat zipper. "I'm anxious about the way Brian is acting toward me. Has he said anything in therapy?"

"I can only tell you he's mentioned your separation and said if you ever take your husband back, he will never forgive you."

"I overheard him tell a friend a couple of weeks ago that things would get bad if we got back together. This must by the reason for the difference in his behavior. But how can I convince him if he won't talk to me?" Shocked by her admission, she realized, no matter the fallout, the only thing that mattered was to ensure a safe and happy environment for her son.

46

SAM

SAM WISHED HE had never gone to see Maddie. The visit only proved to remind him how far apart they were, and any consideration of a reconciliation seemed bleak. But when he arrived at the office the next day, the answering machine light blinked. Maddie's message asked if they could meet this afternoon. Replaying the recording, he fixated on the softness of her voice and thought, *Maybe she realizes she wants me back.*

In a café in town at a time with fewer patrons, he ordered a coffee. When he lifted the cup to his mouth, his hand wobbled. *Get a grip. You're letting your nerves take over.* He drew in a deep breath, held it, blew out a slow exhale, and let the uneasiness in his chest release.

But, as soon as she walked in, his heartbeat rocketed. Afraid his legs might give out, he stayed seated and waved. When she sat at the table, she looked awful, like she hadn't slept in days. *I hope it's because the strain of being apart is wearing on her too.* Unsure of what to say, he let her speak first.

"I didn't want to tell you over the phone, but the house is too big for Brian and me. I'm looking for a smaller one near the Harvard campus. This way, I can take him back and forth until he gets his license."

Near panic, he said, "Is this your way of telling me you want a permanent separation?"

Her chin trembled. "No."

"What then?"

When she spoke, the words sounded alien to him.

"It's best we end it now."

His shoulders fell. "Just like that? No trial separation, right into a divorce?"

"It's not as if I didn't struggle with the decision. I can't see any other way. Remember what you said? You can't change. I can't change. And in your mind, neither can Brian."

"Look at me and tell me you don't love me anymore."

"I love you, but it's not enough."

Tears pressed against his words. "This can't be the end of us."

Sam found himself launched into uncharted territory—there was a for sale sign on the front lawn of their forever home, and soon he would no longer be married to the woman he'd never stop loving.

Joe became the rock he clung to. No need to offer unsolicited advice, he never made him feel hurried to get through the pain. Absent of judgement, he gave him the space to express his feelings. But Sam still had to tolerate the persistent comments made by colleagues and friends who assumed they were being helpful. "You're better off without her. Your gloomy mood is ruining your chances of another relationship. Let me set you up with my girlfriend's sister. You'll get along great." The most injurious, "It's not the end of the world."

And it wasn't. Although the divorce had yet to be finalized, he stopped the wallowing and conceded, *I can't go on like this. I need to try to focus on the future.*

At the end of the day, Sam agreed to meet Joe and a half dozen architects at 5:30 p.m. for a round of drinks. He shivered at the memory of the short walk to the office this morning. The bitter air seeped through the layers of his thin jacket and made him swear about not dressing warmer. He thought about the punishing cold in Paris and quickly fended off the memory.

When the phone rang he decided to let the answer machine pick it up. Halfway out the door he heard Maddie scream. He stumbled over his feet, hit the button and froze. Her words sounded garbled. "Something terrible . . . Brian. He—I . . ." The last sound was the clatter of the phone.

He used the heel of his hand and banged on the button for the lobby. The state of his panic mounted when the door opened on the eight floor. "Why the Christ did we lease offices on the fiftieth floor?" He wrenched the door open to the stairwell, bolted down the stairs, and ran outside. The second he jumped into the back seat of a cab, he yelled, "Get me to 1232 Glendale Road in North Reading. This is an emergency."

"Mister, in case you didn't know, the roads are like sheets of glass and there's been several traffic jams and accidents in and around Boston."

Inhaling quick, raspy breaths, he balled his fists. *If Brian's done anything to hurt her, I'll fucking kill him.* When the driver stopped in front of the garage, Sam paid no attention to the meter. He pulled a hundred-dollar bill out of his wallet and tossed it on the seat.

Sam tried the door and realized he no longer had a key. "Screw it," and grabbed a loose paver, brought his arm up, and smashed the floral glass. He shoved his hand inside to release the dead bolt, and flinched when a shard of glass stabbed the back of his hand. Wiping the blood with the sleeve of his jacket, he tore through the first floor yelling, "Maddie, where are you?" It was unusually quiet.

He took the stairs two at a time. When he entered Brian's room, the image of his son nearly leveled him. As if he was surprised, his eyes were wide open. Three tiny, blood-tinged wounds pierced his chest. Sam's heart beat like a bass drum when he saw the gun wavering in Maddie's hand. He forced his voice to remain calm. "Maddie, please give me the gun." Unable to release it, he carefully pried it from her fingers. She gave him a blank look and tried to scrub the spattered blood off her face and clothes. *I need to get her out of here.*

Like helping a toddler learn to walk, he held onto her. But before they left the room, he stared at his son. *I should have been the one to do this years ago.* He washed the blood off her, helped her change clothes, and laid her down on their bed. The gun wiped clean, he turned to go downstairs to call 911 when she released a low pitched moan.

"Is Brian okay?"

He brushed his lips across her forehead. "Stay here. I'm taking care of everything."

Hunched over, arms wrapped tight around his chest, Sam heard the doorbell ring. Anxious of what he was about to do, he drew in a deep breath and answered the door.

"Hello, sir. My name is Officer Morgan, this is Officer Braddock and Art Burgess, the medical examiner. Are you the person who called to report your son was murdered?"

"Yes."

"Your name?"

"Sam Middleton. Come in."

"Where is your son's body?"

"Upstairs in his bedroom."

"Is there anyone else in the house?"

"My wife, Maddie."

"Where is she?"

"Upstairs in our room."

"Can you take the medical examiner and me to your son's room while my partner checks on your wife?"

On his way upstairs, he said, "Please don't disturb her. She's traumatized by what's happened." He stayed in the hallway while they went into Brian's room. When Morgan came out alone, he asked, "Is there a place we can talk?"

"In the kitchen."

"Mr. Middleton, who owns the gun on the table?"

"I do." Sam's shoulders curled forward when Morgan picked it up with a gloved hand, placed it in a plastic bag, sealed and label it with his initials, and documented the date and time along with a description of the evidence.

"Who shot your son?"

Hoping to sound convincing, he said, "I did."

"Was it an act of self-defense?"

"No."

"I need to advise you of your Miranda rights."

"I want to waive them."

"Before I question you, do you want a lawyer present?"

"No."

"Are you sure?"

"Yes."

"I noticed blood on you hand and sleeve. Where did that come from?"

"I ran out of my office with out my house key and had to break the glass.

"And the reason you came home?"

"I heard my wife's voice on the answering machine crying out for help."

"What did you find when you got here?"

"My son had her pinned against the wall and was screaming at her. He told her if she didn't do what he wanted, she'd regret it." Until now, he remained impassive, but suddenly he became livid. "He's a known psychopath with a long history of cruelty. He even bragged how he could get away with murder. I wasn't going to wait until he physically harmed my wife, so I shot him."

"We need to take you down to police headquarters to be processed."

"I can't leave my wife alone. Can I call someone to stay with her?" When he sensed movement in the doorway, he turned and froze. The officer who'd checked on Maddie stood by her side.

She was gripping the bloody sweater and blouse in her hand. *Oh sweet Jesus, I should have gotten rid of them.* "Maddie, what are you doing?"

"My husband is trying to take the blame for what I did. He wasn't even here when I shot my son. These clothes prove it."

"Before you say anymore, I need to read you your rights."

She shook her head.

"Are you refusing?"

"Yes."

"We need to take you both to the station to be processed."

"Why? My husband didn't do anything wrong."

"It appears he tampered with the evidence and gave a false report."

Sam saw the fresh pain flash across her face when she spoke to him.

"I'm so sorry. Every atrocious thing in the notebook is true. I should have listened to you instead of blaming you."

He reached out to cradle her in his arms when Morgan put up a hand.

"That's not allowed."

"Not allowed? She's my wife."

"Sorry, it's the rules."

"Maddie, don't say anything else until we both get lawyers. I love you, and I know you had a good reason." He still didn't know what had made her shoot Brian, but whatever the reason, it had to have been self-defense.

Sam walked over to the phone, gripped the handle, and thought, *Everything is falling apart, and our future might have arrived at its end.* He dialed Joe's number and told him to call their law firm and find two high-profile criminal lawyers—one for him and one for Maddie. He said they would be at the Cambridge police station." When Joe asked why, he said, "No time to explain," and hung up.

285

47

MADDIE

WHEN MADDIE WAS brought into the station lobby, the unforgiving florescent glare and the aroma of burnt coffee and stale cigarette smoke made the nausea and fear of fainting force her to grab the police officer's arm. Taken to a small white cinderblock room with only two chairs, a desk, and a camera, she stared at the blinking red light in the upper left corner. Her life had been tormented by the tragic losses of her parents, her sister, and her miscarriages. It had been easy to accuse God, the angels, and anyone else she felt was responsible. But this time, the stain of murder was on her. The door opened, and a tall strapping man with smoky gray eyes that matched his hair stepped in.

"Hello, Maddie. My name is Carl Bergeron. I'm here to represent you."

"Does Sam have a lawyer?"

"Yes. He's meeting with my partner in another room."

"He was only trying to protect me. How much trouble is he in?"

"Although he made a false statement to the police, I'm fairly confident, in this situation, his lawyer will get him off with a fine and no jail time. Can I get you anything? It's late, and you must be hungry."

She gave him a tired look. "No, thank you."

"If you change your mind, let me know."

"Mr. Bergeron. I—"

"Please, call me Carl."

"Carl, I'm going to plead guilty. I want to spare my husband the pain and embarrassment of a trial."

He turned on his recorder. "Why don't you start from the beginning and tell me everything."

"Late this afternoon, I heard someone pounding on the front door, yelling my name. The second I opened it, a woman started shrieking. I thought she or someone else was hurt or in an accident, so I reached out and touched her arm to calm her down. She yanked it away, got in my face, and shouted terrible things about Brian. How he dragged her innocent daughter Bella into the woods and repeatedly raped her. She said my disgusting son and our family would pay for what he did. I struggled to explain he would never do anything so hideous. Then she dangled the silver chain I had bought him in my face. Her daughter had it in her hand. Shocked, I stood there, and watched her leave."

"Let's take a break while I get you something to drink."

Eyes squeezed shut, she pressed her hands against her ears to crush the incriminating voices in her head. *I hate myself for what I did to you, Brian. Killing you wasn't the answer.* When she opened them, Carl had come back and placed a paper cup of hot tea and a bottle of water on the table.

"I have a few more questions. Are you up to answering them?"

"Yes."

"Where was Brian when Bella's mother came to the door?"

"In his bedroom."

"Did he overhear the exchange?"

"No. His room is upstairs in the far corner of the house."

"Did you confront him right away?"

Her throat felt like sandpaper. Before she could continue, she took a large swallow of water. "No. I had to sit because I was afraid I would faint. When I was steady enough on my feet, I went to his room." Her body trembled as she remembered the conversation she had with Brian.

Maddie had stood outside the closed door and tried to deal with the accusation that her son was capable of rape. She had given him everything. Loved him unconditionally and would have laid down her life for him. Her hand had tremored as she opened the door and walked in.

"Hi, Mom. I've been going over the list of majors in the Harvard catalogue. I was thinking about something in business that might lead to a CEO someday. Remember how well I did in the leadership program at the summer camp you sent me to? Hey, why are you standing in the doorway, and what's with the strange look on your face? Was Dad being an asshole again?"

She had felt the pressure and heat behind her eyes and tried not to cry. But the tears still came. "Why, Brian? Please tell me why?"

"What are you talking about?"

"Bella, the girl you raped. How could you do something so heinous?"

"I never raped that girl. She wanted it. I can't believe you're accusing me of something like that."

Outraged, she had thrown the chain at him. "Then explain how she got this?"

"The clasp must have come undone while we were having sex. I guess she decided to keep it. You know, as a souvenir for the great time we had."

She screamed, "Stop lying to me. All those times your father tried to tell me you were sick, and I wouldn't listen or believe him."

"You were such an easy mark and so gullible. I won't hold that against you, especially when all of those pompous therapists were fooled. One other important thing to consider: it's her word against mine."

Her eyes had hardened. "You're not getting away with it this time."

When the walls in the interrogation room felt like they were caving in, she started to hyperventilate.

"Maddie, I want you to breathe deeply through your nose. Then breath out the same way, but through your mouth."

When her breathing stabilized, Carl asked if she was okay to continue. To keep from coming unglued, she folded her arms over her chest. "It was my fault he raped Bella. I had to stop him before he destroyed another life."

"What happened next?"

She angled her head downward. "I don't know if I can say it out loud."

"There's no one here to judge you."

A haunted expression crossed her face. "I left, intending to call the authorities to report the rape, but when I overheard him on the phone telling his friend that his mother had gone crazy, I got the gun Sam hid in our bedroom closet. My hands shook so much it took me a few minutes to figure out how to load it. Back in his room, I pointed it at him, but all he did was laugh and say, 'Don't be a fool. You're shaking like a wet dog. You can't even aim straight.'"

"I didn't stop to think as he came toward me. I just pulled the trigger. When the bullet hit the wall, he called me a fucking bitch and demanded I give him the gun. The hatred in his eyes scared me. I fired again. This time, it hit him. I remember the dazed expression on his face, how he put a hand on his chest and stared at the blood on his hand. He looked up and tried to grab my arm. I pulled the trigger, and another bullet struck him. He still wouldn't go down, so I shot him again. He staggered back and collapsed." Pressing her fingers into her temples, she muttered, "I killed my son. I'm so sorry for what I did."

Carl reached over and touched her shoulder. "It's okay Maddie. Would you like to take another break?"

She looked up at him. "No, I just want to get this over with."

"Is that when you called Sam?"

All she could do was nod as hot, shameful tears clung to her jaw.

48

SAM

WITH WINTER IN full swing, the snow covered the grass, and the trees stood naked. An icy wind was blowing, and Sam's hands and feet were chilled to the marrow. He stood alone in front of the flat, nondescript marker inscribed with Brian's name, his birthday, and the day he died. Any meaningful epitaph would've contradicted what he had become. He imagined his son's satanic grin as he looked down at the carnage he left behind. *There will be no grief or tears to shed. Your memory will never be a blessing, only your death. May you rot in hell.* From the fringes of his vision, a group of cameramen shuttered their ceaseless rounds.

Behind him, a hoard of predatory journalists pelted him with offensive questions. "How did you discover what your son had done? Did he get any psychiatric care before he was murdered? Is your wife sorry for what she did it? Was it self-defense?" The local channels had a field day carrying the story of the well-respected architect who lied to the police to protect his wife, the famous artist, who murdered her only child. Perfect for heady news coverage, it played out in all the local papers. Except for close friends and long-standing clients, the city that once held them in high esteem blamed them for all of their son's ills. Driving off, he thought about his morning meeting with Maddie's lawyer.

Sam's anger rose like boiling water. "It's not fucking fair she has to pay because she feared he would commit more sadistic acts."

"I know, but I need to prepare you for what comes next. Because she pleaded guilty, she'll have to remain in the county jail until sentencing."

"What the Christ for? She's not a flight risk and never even got a parking ticket. Whatever the cost, I can afford the bail."

"Because it's a felony crime the judge denied it."

"That's bullshit."

"So now everyone thinks she's going to get another gun and . . ."

"No, but it is safer to keep her there. After the ordeal she's been throught, she may try to harm herself. You've seen her. She's not holding up very well."

Her lawyer had let him see her before they released him from the station. Her head had been pressed into the crook of her elbow, and she kept crying, "I should be the one who's dead." He knelt beside her and had tried to reassure her it wasn't her fault. But when she looked up at him, her face reflected the immense self-loathing for what she had done. Knowing he would never forget the scene in Brian's room and the smell of blood in his nostrils, he had wondered if she'd ever be able to live with what she had done.

Sam asked Carl, "What happens next?"

"I spoke to the DA after he read the notebook, briefed him on Brian's psychopathic diagnosis, the questionable release, and summary report from the treatment center. We agreed, if he can convince the judge your son's murder resulted from mitigating circumstances, we may get her off on voluntary manslaughter. Because of her upstanding character, I'm asking for a three-year sentence."

"Three years shut away in prison? That's the best you can offer?"

"Yes. When she admitted she waited before she confronted him about the rape and fired the gun four times, they would have convicted her of first-degree murder and given a life sentence."

To hear that was like a physical blow to his body.

Sam's sole experience watching TV court dramas made him sick to think they would handcuff Maddie with leg shackles, make her wear a hideous jumpsuit, and parade her in front of a media circus and perverted spectators. When he got to the courthouse, he was thankful the judge had restricted access to the proceedings because of the high-profile case. But nothing prepared him for the waking nightmare of being in a room that smelled of centuries of fear.

He sagged into a seat, braced his elbow on his knees, and clawed at his scalp until his skull hurt. The pain made it easier to tolerate that, in a matter of hours, his beautiful, kind, loving wife's fate would be sealed, along with their lives.

The door by the jury box opened, and a deputy shepherded her out. She was dressed in the navy-blue suit he had given to her lawyer. He jumped up and said, "Maddie, I love you." The second the words charged from his mouth, he heard a loud bang of wood on wood.

The judge said, "Mr. Bergeron, have the individual behind you sit and remain quiet."

Escorted to the chair in front of him, her eyes were wounded hollows, and her face bone white. Alarmed, he attempted to touch her shoulder, but she moved away from him.

Ordered to approach the bench, they placed her under oath. He held his breath as the judge read the indictment.

"In the Suffolk County of Boston, Madelynn Marie Middleton, age forty-eight, on January 10, 1992, is accused of deliberately and with willful criminal intent shooting and killing the deceased, Brian Jacob Middleton, age sixteen. Do you understand the charges, the penalties, and trial related rights?"

The yes sounded so feeble, Sam had to bend forward to hear her.

"How do you plead?"

"Guilty."

Even though he had been prepared for her answer, his body jolted. When she staggered, he scrambled to catch her, but a guard detained him and led her back to her seat. This time, the judge admonished him directly.

"If you can't control yourself, security will usher you out of my courtroom. The two attorneys, please approach the bench."

Like he never had before, he bartered and prayed to God the judge would show leniency and give her a lighter sentence. He hoped to catch a positive sign from Carl when he returned to his seat, but his expression was clean as a blank slate.

"Everyone, please stand. Madelynn Marie Middleton, I am sentencing you to three years in prison with no right to appeal a verdict based on a guilty plea. This court is adjourned. The bailiff will escort the prisoner into custody."

As he tight-fisted the railing in front of him, the last shred of hope died as the door closed behind her.

49

MADDIE

HANDCUFFED, WITH HER feet bound, Maddie shuffled to the transport vehicle. A guard walked in front of her, holding the chain to the handcuffs. She teetered on the wet cement floor and had to fight to stay upright. In stony silence, she sat with three other women on the two-hour ride to a state penitentiary in Massachusetts.

As her bent head grazed the cold metal truss on her wrists, she thought of Sam in the courtroom. She could still hear the desperation in his choked voice when he called out, "I love you." Misery had shredded her insides when she forced herself to resist his touch. At that moment, she needed to show him there would never be a future with a wife convicted of murdering their son.

Last in line to go through the jail's formal interview, Maddie faced a stout, no-nonsense woman with a black buzz cut and petulant eyes the color of granite glaring through horn-rimmed glasses. Her beefy, tattooed arms narrowly squeezed through a beige, short-sleeved shirt under a bulletproof vest. The snug-fitting, khaki cargo pants had a leather belt with a clip that drowned in several keys. Compartments were filled with gear, including a flashlight, two-way radio, handcuff keys, pepper spray, and cut-resistant gloves. She considered the outfit with indifference, but ice crept through her veins when the guard tapped a gun in a holster.

"You better memorize the list of rules and what we expect from our inmates. I'm adding my own. Don't take up with no gang ring. Don't do no drugs, and if you're straight, best you stay away from those other weirdos."

Unmoored, Maddie wondered if she could brave the reality of living behind bars. She knew she wouldn't when she had to disrobe, be strip-searched, and undergo an intimate visual inspection. Scared and trembling, it was demeaning and traumatic to have a stranger enter the deepest part of her. Violated and no longer feeling safe, she stifled a cry when she thought of the fear and pain Bella must have endured being repeatedly raped by her son.

The examination over, she sat through a health assessment before being assigned inside the prison. Asked a series of questions about her physical and mental status, they informed her the emotional pain of being incarcerated could be so intense there had been individuals who considered suicide. When asked, she said no. She thought, *If the time came, she would consider it.* By the time they took the prison picture, finger printed her, gave her a number and identity card, she tried to dissociate from the revulsions and humiliation she'd endured the last twelve hours.

Maddie entered cell block 142 and was greeted by a gangly girl with a waist-length strawberry-blonde braid, flawless skin, and wide-set hazel eyes. *She doesn't look like a criminal, but neither do I.*

"My name is Sandy. Welcome to our six-by-eight digs. We're among the privileged because we have a window. But this is where feeling special ends."

When she pointed to two metal-frame beds and an exposed toilet–sink combo in a corner, Maddie shook her head in disbelief.

"Sadly, the prison food is like playing Russian roulette. You never know what's gonna land on your plate except for the beans." She scrunched up her face. "Stay away from them or they'll come back to curse you."

In the hallway, the guard said, "Sandy, enough of your personal descriptions. Dinner is in fifteen minutes." His tone got cheeky. "You don't want to miss tonight's jailhouse special— creamed chipped beef over mashed potatoes."

Maddie clutched the bedroll, prison uniform, and a box of toiletries to her chest.

The guard looked at her. "You can settle in after you eat."

Her voice slight, she said, "I'm not hungry."

He slammed shut the fortified door and said, "Suit yourself."

The merciless sound of being locked in made her jump.

After she tossed her things on the upper bunk, she took three steps and looked through the steel bar window. The barbed wire fence surrounded a depressing plot of dirt and not one patch of green. *It would have been easier not to have a window.* She turned and let everything sink in. For three years, she would never have the luxury of deciding where she wanted to go, what she wanted to wear, or what she wanted to eat. *None of that matters because I deserve this and more.*

Maddie didn't need to be woken in the morning. The night had been pierced with the sounds of wailing, coughing, flushing toilets, whispers between cells, and angry catcalls.

"Stop the fucking crying. We're trying to sleep."

She turned away when Sandy sat on the toilet.

"Modesty is dead on arrival. You'll eventually get used to squatting in front of me. As far as the smell? It can be pretty gross, but I learned if you put a sheet of fabric softener in the air vent, it'll blow in a pleasant scent."

"Can't they put up a curtain or a sheet?"

"That's a no. Someone could hang themselves with the rod or the sheet. Trust me, you'll get used to it. Guess not, by the odd color of your face. If it makes you feel any better, I'll try to remember to turn my back when you go. Anyway, on to another topic.

As a newbie, you'll wonder where it all went wrong and how you landed here."

She thought, *Those are questions I'll never have to think about.*

"If it gets too bad and you have trouble adjusting, you might need to see the shrink. But for now, I can help you learn the ropes in this joint. The cell doors unlock at 5:00 a.m. Being an early riser has its perks. More hot showers, less inmates giving you the once-over or approaching you with wandering hands. Stay with me until you get the hang of how things operate in Disneyland. Okay, so far?"

No, it's not. "Yes."

"After breakfast, we go to our work duty. The good news—I work in the laundry room, so we'll never run out of fabric sheets. Did you get your assignment yet?"

"Today."

"Sheesh, you're not much of a talker. I guarantee, in a week, you'll crave conversation. Besides our jobs, it's what gets us through doing time in this stink hole."

Prison became a struggle. She suffered repeated episodes where she woke up short of breath, as if her ribs had tightened around her lungs. Eyes halfway open, the inability to move for the first one or two minutes was terrifying. When she tried to get Sandy's attention, only a whimper came out. Examined by the doctor, she was told, "The cause might be nighttime panic attacks, anxiety, depression, or a combination." She put her on a mild antidepressant, along with weekly sessions.

The self-hatred remained a constant shadow. The piercing memories were like a needle on a record player stuck in a groove: the hatred on Brian's face before she pulled the trigger, his expression after the first two bullets hit his chest, him lying dead on the floor, and the blood spatter on her face and clothes. Everything was a devastating reminder she was the mother who murdered her child at point-blank range.

Since she'd arrived, and no desire to make any friends, she made a point of keeping to herself during mealtimes. In their cell one night, Sandy finally had given her a stark warning.

"Maddie, it's safer if you sit with me and my friends. Everyone in this place needs some protection. If you're alone every day, you'll be the perfect target for a group of no-gooders who are just waiting for the opportunity to hurt someone."

The truth of what she said materialized during her work assignment in the library.

A brazen-faced woman with red-inked droplets under the tattoo *Blood Out* on her cheek sauntered up to Maddie waving a newspaper. "Hey, girls, wanna know what this snake with the curly mop of red hair is in for?"

A chorus rang out. "Yeah, is it something juicy?"

"Better than that. Here are the headlines. 'Woman Artist and Humanitarian Murders Sixteen-Year-Old Son.'"

Maddie's heart began to beat wildly when the entire article was read. Lewd name-calling followed.

"You're a cold-blooded killer. They should've belted you into Old Sparky and let you fry like a roasted pig. You're not a mother. You're a heartless piece of shit."

Another woman ambled up to her, just as freakish looking, spit in her face, and jabbed at her chest. She tried to step away but found herself up against someone else. When fingers squeezed and jerked back her neck, she cried out, "Please, someone help me."

"You scared, Red? It ain't nothin' compared to what you did to your kid. Imagine how he felt, staring down the barrel of a pistol while the person he thought loved him gunned him down with three bullets to the heart."

The women chanted, "Make the she-devil pay for what she did."

From her peripheral vision, she could see the shiny tips of a pair of scissors. She tried to reach up and stop what was about to happen, but someone pinned her arms down. She begged and cried at the same time. "Please, don't hurt me."

The uproar brought three guards running. Weapons drawn in one hand, pepper spray in the other they yelled, "Bitches, if you don't back off, it won't be pretty how this ends."

It was too late. A chunk of her hair was gone.

At first, Maddie was angry when she had looked at her hacked hair in the barber's mirror, until she decided it might help to keep her under the radar. But the crude remarks and threats, along with the prods, trips, and shoves, continued. She quickly discovered the guards chose to turn their backs unless there was a real threat to her life. How stupid to even consider her crime wouldn't become public fodder inside prison.

If the humiliation could do her in, she envisioned what Sam was going through. The affronts he faced because his wife was a murderer must have been beyond difficult. She didn't want him to see what a mess she was, so she continued to refuse his calls or let him visit. The only person she let in was her lawyer, and at every visit, he implored her to reconsider Sam's feelings.

"Maddie, he's worried about you. All he wants is to be there for you, but he can't unless you agree to put him on the visitors list."

What is there to talk about? The food is terrible. Seeing a therapist is going nowhere. The medication does nothing. I work in the library and got attacked. I'm scared all the time, and there are days I wake up and want to end it all. She had nothing to say that would assuage the reality of being locked up for what she had done.

"Don't shut him out. He's the only family you have."

Maybe a visit is the only way I can make him see he's better off without me. She gave him a mournful look. "I'll think about it."

Sam wasn't her only family. For years, the Strathmores provided a haven of stability when she needed it. How could she expect them to love or stand by her after what she had done? It was too big a sin to accept. And Julia. No matter the situation, she always knew if she needed her, she would be at her side. But the last time they spoke, she had mentioned wanting to divorce Sam. It was the first time she didn't support her.

Julia had asked, "You're going to walk away from a man who loves you because of Brian?"

She had told her she didn't have a choice. "My son's feelings and well-being come first."

"I should have been honest with you from the beginning. Treatment at his age doesn't work, but you were so desperate for hope, I let my personal feelings cloud my professional judgement. If you had known . . ."

"Known what?"

"A psychopath hides their true intentions, and they are masters at faking who they truly are."

She had insisted he'd changed. "Just ask every therapist who's treated him and how well he did in the treatment center."

"No, Maddie, he hasn't. He's been savvy enough to put on a false self even with them."

"That's absurd. You sound like Sam."

"I believed him when he told me how Brian manipulates you to get what he wants—and even gloated how easy it was to convince you Sam had to leave."

"Nice to know my best friend has been having secret conversations behind my back."

"No secrets. The only reason he came to me was because you refused to listen."

"It's obvious whose side you're on."

"There are no sides. I'm trying to get you to see the truth."

"And *your* truth is a lie. Attacking my son—you're no different then my husband. I'm done with him and you. Brian and I can manage on our own."

50

SAM

WEEKS HAD GONE by since Sam watched Maddie being led out of the courtroom by the guard, and it killed him when she refused to see him or take any of his phone calls. Hungry for contact, he wrote to her every day and poured out his heart. *I love you. I need to see you.*

He tried to take comfort in the support from Joe, Julia, and the Strathmores. *She'll come around. Give her time to adjust.* But to him, time was the enemy. If . . . the word made him sick to think it. If she survives the three years in prison with no outside support, how would it affect her emotionally and physically when they released her?

Each time he met with the lawyer for updates, he handed him the unopened letters. "Why won't she let me visit her or read my letters? Did you tell her I love her and I don't blame her?"

"I conveyed all your messages, but she's still refusing your requests for a visit."

After another unproductive day at the office, Sam left earlier than usual. He walked into the apartment and took out the two-day-old pizza and a beer. Collapsing in a chair, he pressed his forehead against the cold open bottle, then flung it and watched it splatter across the floor. Afraid to get drunk again or break things, he grabbed his jacket and left. Up and down the block, he kept rambling on how he would lose his mind if he never got to see her until she was released.

The weather turned foul, and by the time he got back home, he was drenched and had a miserable headache. Peeling off his clothes, he grabbed sweats off the chair, headed to the bathroom and stopped. The light flashed on the recorder. Alarmed, he thought, *What if something bad has happened to her?*

"Sam, this is Carl. Maddie has agreed to let you visit. Meet me in my office at six. I need to give you the paperwork to fill out."

Sam scrambled up the one flight of stairs and blew into the office. His voice breathless, he said, "When?"

Carl looked at him. "Hopefully, after you clean yourself up. You need to complete this paperwork—the visiting application and a criminal record release authorization form. I'll have to notarize them before they're dropped off at the prison."

"How soon can I make an appointment?"

"Unfortunately, the process can take a while."

He explained what to expect when he arrived, but all Sam heard was the voice in his head. *That's too much time to let her change her mind.*

Sam stood at the end of a long cement walkway. The gray sky pressed down on him as he looked up at the austere architecture. The high walls of a behemoth brick structure were connected to four one-story buildings on either side. Spools of razor wire and multiple fences delivered a harsh, silent message—an inescapable loss of freedom. A sense of foreboding seized him. The belief he could support her through three years of imprisonment seemed implausible.

He entered the check-in office, showed the staff his driver's license, wallet, car keys, and cell phone, and emptied his pockets. Each item was carefully scrutinized and searched for hidden drugs or other contraband. As if time had no purpose, the man moved at the sluggish pace of a turtle while he dawdled over the list he made and stored the items in a locker. Sam glanced at the desk clock. His anxiety level rose and escalated when someone else led him to another area. *I'm going to be late.* A fingerprint card and an ink pad rested on a table with a camera in front of a blank wall. His eyebrows shot up. "Is this for me?"

"All new visitors are required to have a photograph taken. We scan the prints and include them in the identification process."

When he finished, he was told a guard would take him to the main prison, where he would be searched and passed through another metal detector. His last stop was the visitors' center. He put up both palms. "Where do I wash these?"

"Sorry, mister. The ink stains will come off eventually, but it will take a week. The best thing is to let your natural oils do the work and gradually rub it off. This will cause the least amount of damage to your skin."

Sam could only imagine what they'd put Maddie through.

Standing inside the doorway, he let his eyes search the crowded room. After three tries, his face dropped. *She changed her mind or thought I wasn't coming.* He turned to leave when the guard at the door stopped him.

"Are you on the visitors list?

"I'm supposed to be."

"What's your name?"

"Sam Middleton."

"Yep, you're on here. Who are you visiting?"

"My wife, Maddie—Madelynn."

"Pretty crowded today. Lots of kids here. Check out the room. I'm sure you'll find her in a corner."

No wonder he hadn't seen her. The long, vibrant hair had been replaced with a chopped-up cut. As he got closer, he saw the birdlike shoulder blades poked out from underneath the issued blue-and-white shirt. *My god, is this what prison is doing to her?* When he sat down, his heart seized. She had a deathlike quality to her. The ghostly color of her skin had the texture of parchment paper. Her cheeks were sunk in, and the emerald-green eyes that could light up a room had dulled.

"Maddie, I . . ."

She placed her hands over her face and shook her head—a signal she didn't want to talk.

Don't force her. Be patient. Give her the space she needs. "You don't have to say anything. We can sit here until you're ready." He looked around the room and noticed the relaxed body language, cheerful smiles, and laughter. He knew it hadn't been their first visit. Carl had warned him seeing a loved one or a friend for the first time might be a demoralizing experience. He didn't care. He just wanted to be with her. When she finally spoke, her eyes were wet with tears, and a flash of anguish spread across her face.

She stood. "I'm sorry. Being with you . . . it's too difficult."

His body drooped against the chair as he watched her slowly walk across the floor—head bent and arms dangling at her side. Everything about her appearance and manner told him a vital part of her life had been stripped away. Fear ballooned in his chest. *What if there's not enough left to keep her going?*

Before he left, he met with the correctional supervisor. "I saw my wife. She's a mess, and I'm scared of what she might do. I've read self-harm is prevalent in prison, especially among women."

"Readjusting to daily life is more challenging for certain individuals. I've been told she has resumed her therapy sessions and there's been a change in her medication."

He was unable to keep the heat out of his voice. "Apparently, none of it is working." *If she wanted to hurt herself*—he paused before he could complete the thought—*or kill herself, she would find a way.*

51

MADDIE

AFTER SEEING SAM, Maddie's guilt and shame intensified, and she found herself incapable of eating, sleeping, or taking a shower. She spent her time staring at the ceiling or robotically counting the number of gray cinder blocks. Her roommate tried everything to get her to move. "You need to stop this before they get on to you."

"I appreciate your concern, but I just want to be left alone."

"You've got until dinnertime. If I don't see you there, I'm gonna tell a guard. and he'll notify your therapist. Who knows, she might put you on suicide precautions. Do you want that to happen?"

Her answer: she turned and faced the wall.

That evening, a guard stepped into her cell and ordered her to shower and get dressed for a meeting with the therapist.

"Hello, Maddie. I was told you haven't been feeling well. Want to tell me what's going on?" the therapist asked.

Her tone was lackluster. "I feel nothing."

"Can you describe what that means?"

"It's like a deadness or emptiness inside. I can't cry or get angry. Does that sound like I'm going mad?"

"Not at all. Numbing yourself is the body's way of coping with being in prison and the reason you're here. I'm going to start you on a stronger medication and schedule mandatory meetings three times a week. In between, you can always schedule more. I read in your file you're an accomplished artist."

"Was."

"I'd like you to paint again. Materials will be sent to your room. Like therapy, it will help you process your feelings and reduce the stress and anxiety that's creating upheaval with your mind and your body."

"Do I have a choice?"

She smiled. "No. Try it even if all you do is smear paint on a canvas. One other thing: you need to eat and get outside. The rest of the time, you can choose where and how you want to spend it."

For weeks, all Maddie did was hold a brush and stare at the canvas. All she could think about was her former self—a wife, a mother, and an artist. But when the medication finally kicked in, she painted. Unlike anything she has ever done, she worked with acylics. Using warm and cool colors, painting hard and soft lines in various shapes and patterns, she liked how the color combinations played off one another. When she stood back and considered the walls of art in the cell, each piece defined an emotion—anger, fear, sadness, and confusion. The feelings, along with the therapist's safe and nurturing environment, provided a slow path to feeling lighter and more in control of her life.

Maddie considered their recent conversation. The therapist had told her there was still more work to do, but said she was making excellent progress. Along with the art work, she wanted her to start socializing more than just with her cell-mate Sandy and her friends. "I understand you have refused visits from your family and friends. Reaching out may seem difficult, but it's critical to seek their support." It had taken her weeks of back and forth before she had contacted Julia.

Maddie fiddled with her hair and clothes and wondered if Julia would come. She kept looking at the clock as it moved past the start of visiting hours. *I knew it. Why would she want to see me after the way I treated her?* She got up to leave but stopped when Julia walked toward her. Her face puckered with tears when Julia pulled her into a fierce hug.

"My sweet, precious friend, it's okay. I'm here now."

She held on longer than she should have before releasing the embrace. "I'm sorry for how I treated you the last time we spoke. I would have understood if you never wanted to see me again."

"No way that could ever happen. Don't you remember the night we celebrated our graduation and agreed that no matter where life took us, we would be in it together?"

"Yes, but I didn't think murder and a prison sentence would make the cut."

When Julia reached out to touch her short hair, she asked, "Can you talk about any of it?"

"Maybe when I'm out of here, but all I want to do is look at you and reminisce about all the fun times we shared."

52

SAM

AS HE WENT through all the checkpoints at the prison, Sam thought about Julia's call last night. She'd talked about how happy Maddie was to see her. When he asked if his name came up and it didn't, it left him with a strong premonition this visit would be the last. He could never close his mind to the last words Maddie said to him. "Being with you . . . it's too difficult."

He entered the visitors' room. This time, she was sitting in a chair by the window and not hidden in a corner. Having not seen her in weeks, he realized how healthy she looked. The withered appearance had disappeared, along with the sunken cheeks and the deadened look in her eyes. When she saw him, she walked toward him. No closer than arm's length, neither one spoke, until he broke the quiet and said, "Thank you for agreeing to let me come."

A smile radiated across her face. "I'm glad you're here."

Sam visited every weekend, and eventually the conversations became less stilted. She talked about her job in the library, her roommate, the friends she made, and how she eventually got used to the food. The one time he wanted to know about prison life and how she was dealing with the hardships of being incarcerated, she changed the subject. But her eyes lit up when she told him she started to paint again.

"That's terrific. It must feel good to be doing something you're so passionate about. What made you start?"

"My therapist. It's another safe space for me to express my feelings."

"Is it helping?"

"Yes, more than I imagined. You would never recognize it as my work, but I think what's emerged is exciting."

He placed a palm under her chin and lifted it a fraction. This time, she didn't resist his touch. "Sounds as if your therapist knows exactly what she's doing."

1995

Pulling into the parking lot, Sam remembered how a looming darkness had settled around him the first time he'd stood in front of the prison building. But today, the sun cast its brillant glow—the kind meant to lift the spirit. Despite his excitement, he wondered how she would feel reentering the outside world.

When she walked out the door, accompanied by a guard, the drab, ill-fitted uniform was replaced by the rose-colored, scalloped blouse and beige slacks he brought the week before. He broke into a run and enveloped her as if she were a piece of fine china. When he released her, he could tell by the way her eyes flicked from side to side that she was anxious. He took her hand, threaded his fingers through hers, and said, "Let's go home."

Alarm crossed her face. "I can't live there. Not after . . ."

"You won't have to. We're staying in my apartment until we decide where you'd like to live."

Sam was warned to expect emotional challenges, but their severity blindsided him. Daily life was shadowed by what was unspoken. There were days Maddie retreated and became impossible to reach. As if her body was in fight-or-flight mode, he watched her fall into disruptive sleep patterns of tossing and turning. When she kept crying out the word *murderer,* he felt his own sobs before he heard them. Her pain and grief came in cycles, and the fragility of their marriage followed the same course. It moved up and down on the scale of her suffering. With nowhere to turn, he reached out to Julia.

"The first two weeks, Maddie seemed happy and excited about looking for another house. She talked about returning to the gallery, working part-time for the new owners, and going out with the Strathmores, Joe, and his wife. I don't even know what triggered the change. She's acting the way she did after Gracie died."

"This is not the same. She didn't cause her death."

He raised his voice in a in flurry of anger. "It wasn't her fault."

"But, Sam, she believes it is. There's no quick and easy way to recover from what she's experiencing. And remember, she never got to say goodby or grieve at Brian's gravesite. Give her a few more days. If she doesn't improve, I'll give you the number of a colleague who has experience working with people dealing with adjustments outside of prison. You should see someone too."

He stared at the receiver. Twenty-nine years of marriage, and in almost half, they narrowly made it through the searing pain of losses and misery. He waited a week, then made the appointment, and under light pressure, Maddie relented. He took Julia's advice and set up one for himself.

53

MADDIE

MADDIE MET WITH the therapist at Sam's insistence. But in her mind, she no longer believed anyone could fix what was sorely fractured. Her sins were packed too deep in her heart. Between the self-hatred and critical voices in her head, she saw no way to forgiveness.

"From the prison notes, it states you felt good about the progress you made before they discharged you."

"I was wrong. Wrong for killing my son and wrong how I treated my husband. I don't see how I will ever be able to put my life back together with before and after prison. This is going to sound absurd, but I wish I was inside again."

"It's not unusual to feel a loss of security when you leave a place of confinement. This can also lead to major setbacks. It can be disorienting without a schedule of being told what to do and where to go. And when you're out, dealing with other people's reactions and the discomfort in social settings, it can play havoc with your emotions. Maddie, listen to me carefully. It won't be easy, but being able to forgive yourself calls for compassion, kindness, and understanding. It also requires you to accept that forgiveness is a choice. Your debt was paid, and you don't have to live a life of punishment."

She blinked back the sting of tears. "I don't know if I'm strong enough to do that."

"You are. You survived three long years of incarceration, and it's not a situation you should handle alone. I'm here, and so is your husband, if you'll let him. When he called to make the appointment, he said he felt like he was failing you. Did you share with him how you felt before you went to prison and how being in confinement affected you?"

"No. I've made his life miserable enough without hurting him with the gruesome details."

"Do you believe he loves you?"

She blew her nose. "Yes."

"Then it's time to trust he can handle whatever you tell him."

Maddie finally found the courage to tell Sam every sordid detailed she experienced in prison, including the guilt and shame she felt after murdering Brian. He let her talk with no interruptions, and when the deluge of tears fell, he spoke in a comforting tone.

"I know how difficult this is to talk about, but I'm so glad you told me."

She took the tissue he gave her, wiped her eyes, and said, "Me too."

"Maddie, we both need to stop replaying what happened and blaming ourselves for what we should or shouldn't have done differently. It serves no purpose, and it will bury us in grief."

"What do you mean by *we*?"

"I blame myself for passing on the evil that corrupted our son."

The soulless sound of his voice tugged at her heart. It was the first time she realized he'd lived with this indictment since the day Brian was born. To her, it had nothing to do with Brian's DNA and everything to do with how she enabled him to become who he was. "The way he turned out has nothing to do with you."

He looked at her and stroked small circles on the back of her hand. "I say it's time we work on letting it go."

After weeks of searching, Maddie fell in love with a small, newly renovated farmhouse on a remote country road. It offered the tranquility and privacy she craved. Unlike the massive, ornate Victorian with its grand entrance, three fireplaces, and crystal chandlers, this was a place with the warmth of natural wood, soft colors, and beamed ceilings. Standing on the wraparound porch, Sam asked if she was sure about living here.

"This isn't your preferred style."

"I've never been more certain in my life, and it's not only the charm and coziness of the interior." Her arms spread wide. "It's all of this. What do you hear?"

"Birds chirping."

"Anything else?"

"Nope."

When he came up behind her and wrapped his arms around her waist, she leaned against his chest. "It's the perfect home for us."

While Sam still worked at the firm, Maddie stayed home and continued to paint by commission. Taking long, solitary walks around the property, she discovered being among nature was one of the simplest remedies to heal and recharge the spirit.

54

SAM
2008

SAM SAT ACROSS from Maddie on the waterfront terrace of their favorite restaurant overlooking Boston Harbor. A pleasant summer breeze tousled her wavy red hair, now fringed with silver streaks. At sixty-four, she was slender, with the same allure he'd felt the first time he saw her on the plane going to Paris. Though she'd been freed from prison fourteen years ago, he was never able to forget his first visit. She had become a shell of the woman she once was. He recoiled at the memory.

"Everything okay?"

He lifted the back of her hand to his lips. "How did I get so lucky?"

"Luck has nothing to do with it. I might add, you're looking pretty spiffy at sixty-nine. Even with specks of gray around the temples, you haven't lost a lock of your hair." She held up a glass of wine. "To us."

Clinking hers, he grinned. "To us."

When she excused herself to go to the ladies' room, he thought, *It's a miracle we've made it.* Their marriage had been tested many times over. While they both worked to forgive themselves, they still experienced weeklong stretches of heavy silences and days and nights when the passage of words was difficult. Sorrow lingered over them, waxing and waning, until it lessened to a degree they could accept it as part of their marriage.

When she returned, there was a sparkle in her green eyes. "So, when are we going back to Paris to renew our wedding vows?"

He drew out an envelope from his suit pocket and handed her two airline tickets. "How about a week from Saturday?"

Sam smiled as he watched Maddie repack two suitcases for the millionth time. Her euphoria was limitless.

"I can't believe we'll be there in three days. Tell me it's not a dream."

Holding the small of her back, he dipped her backward and placed a lingering kiss on her mouth. "This should prove you're not dreaming. What are some places you want to visit once we've settled in at the hotel?" The list was like a run-on sentence. She could have kept going until he chimed in, "Whoa, you realize we're only there for two weeks." Her expression was like a disappointed child.

"Oh dear, I guess I need to prioritize."

"Nah. Now that we're retired, I suppose we'll have to stay until you see everything on that list."

"If that's the case, I'm off to do more shopping. Anything you need me to buy?"

He lifted her up and swung her in a wide arc. "I've got everything I need right here."

The trip would be a renewal. Another reminder of their love and commitment and how they battled and won against every curveball life had thrown at them. One of the marriage vows he recited forty years ago remained true. "I promise to cherish and protect you and never stop showing you how much I love you."

The doorbell rang and stirred him out of a dream state. When he opened the door, his body arched, and he stumbled backward. He would have lost his balance if his hand hadn't gripped the doorknob. Nothing prepared him for the shock of what he saw staring at him—a carbon copy of Brian and himself.

"Hi, I'm Justin. I've been wanting to meet my grandparents for quite a while. Looks like I'm in the right place."

"That's absurd. We have no grandchildren." He tried to shut the door, but Justin wedged his shoulder inside.

"Remember Bella, the girl your son raped sixteen years ago? She's my mother."

He's lying. We would have known about him years ago. "You're wasting your time. Get out of here, or I'll call the police and tell them you're trespassing."

"Why would you want to do that? I mean, look at us. Hey, if you want to make a fool of yourself, call them, but while we're waiting, here's the proof."

Justin held out a scrapbook, but Sam refused to take it.

"Come on, Gramps. It's pretty rad stuff. Boy, my father was a real wacko. No wonder Granny knocked him off. I'd sure like to thank her."

He fought to gain control of his emotions. *I've got to get him out of here before Maddie returns.* "I don't see a car in the driveway. How did you get here?"

Justin stuck out his thumb. "An old geezer picked me up. Why don't you invite me in? The three of us can have a nice chat about all the newspaper articles. Plus, I'm eager to get the lowdown from Granny on what it was like in the slammer."

His eyes took on a hostile glare. "She's not home."

"Then invite me in and we can look at the scrapbook together. It'll be a great way to kick off our relationship."

"Not here." Steering him into the car, he shifted into gear and peeled down the street.

"Hey, Gramps, you'll kill us both if you don't slow down."

He stepped on the gas harder. Swerved off the highway and screeched into a truck stop. A self-assured grin played on Justin's lips when he gave him the scrapbook.

"Look. I'm sure you've seen it all, but it will be a nice reminder."

Without looking, Sam tossed it back and said, "So what's the point of all this?"

"Before I get to that, let me fill you in on a few important details of how my life has been. I was five when my grandparents died and left me with my nineteen-year-old mother to fend for us. No money for a college education, she had to work in fast-food joints, dry cleaners, and grocery stores. We eventually lost the house and didn't have enough money for a place to live. So we ended up in a homeless shelter. How does it feel to know your only grandchild spent weeks in one?"

Sam slammed his fist on the steering wheel. "Is that all?"

"Nope. I'm just getting started. My mother finally scraped enough to rent a broken-down apartment from a slum landlord in a rough project in Boston. Unlike you, we never lived in a big fancy house in a high-class neighborhood, or out in the country, or wore expensive clothes and dined in fancy restaurants. As you can see, I got the lowdown on you, Gramps."

The steel tone in his voice reminded Sam of Brian. He squared off in his seat. "What do you hope to gain by telling me this?"

"For starters, new wheels would be great after I get my license. Something slick and sporty like yours. A free ride to a classy college. No need to worry about making a bad investment. I won't have any problem getting in. Early on, I tested for a genius IQ. I figure it's in my DNA, which I'm sure I got from you and my father. Any Ivy league school that's close to you would be perfect. This way, I can give you updates on how my life is going and whenever I need more of your help. Oh, I almost forgot. New digs for my mom and me. I'm sure you'll agree we deserve better than the rattrap we're in now."

Justin smirked. "You don't look so good. What's that saying, 'green around the gills'? Better get a hold of yourself or you'll make a mess on these nice leather seats."

Every goddamn enraged emotion he had felt with Brian made him want to grab the kid by the neck and . . . He checked his anger and said, "Why did you wait until now?"

"My mother was the one who saved all this stuff. I wasn't aware they existed until I found them in a box in her closet. When I asked why she lied about my father being in an accident, she said she didn't want me to know she'd been raped. It's one of the reasons she refused to go to the police. But now, she regrets not settling the score. That's when I decided it was time to use the information to our advantage. Who would've believed it would turn out this way."

"Blackmailing me won't work. Now, get the fuck out of my car. If you ever, I mean *ever*, show up where I live again or try to speak to me or my wife, I'll . . ."

"Kill me? No, you won't. Wanna know why? How do you think your wife will react when she reads in the paper her loving husband murdered her only grandchild? If that's too radical, and you decide to contact my mother to stop me, forget it. She's in on the deal."

Sam's eyes narrowed. "For the second time, get the fuck out of my car."

He slithered out, rambled over to the driver's side, and leaned against the door. "The clock is ticking. If I don't hear from you soon, my next move is to speak to Granny. I can only imagine how happy she'll be to see how her son has risen from the dead."

In a cold sweat, Sam sat on the steps of the porch, his head reeling with terrifying thoughts. *Justin's personality suggest he is more than a physical clone of Brian. If there is the slightest possibility evil exists inside him, I need to end the cycle.* But was there any way to be certain? The psychopathic behavior had skipped two generations—his and his father's.

What if he's just an angry kid who feels he deserves better? If I go along with the blackmail, it will never end, and there will always be a risk Maddie could find out. If I tell her, she will do everything she can to make up for murdering Brian and what he did to Bella. And what if he's already engaged in some gruesome acts and no one has caught him? Do I stand by and wait? Live in a state of fear? What if I make the wrong decision? He dropped his head in his hands and thought, *Christ, what do I do?*

When Maddie returned, she sat beside him and snuggled against his shoulder. "Hey, you. The thought of packing already giving you a headache? Maybe this will cheer you up." She dug into one of her shopping bags and pulled out two berets—a green one for her and a black one for him.

He felt the full extent of her joy as she went on about experiencing Paris for the second time. Her voice receded into the background as he struggled to figure out his next move. No matter what he decided, there wouldn't be any turning back.

AUTHOR NOTES

THE GENESIS OF this novel began with a longtime fascination with past centuries of horrific examples of evil: The Holocaust, Stalin's extermination of over 30 million people, atrocities in Syria, global terrorist attacks, religious pedophiles, and serial psychopaths like Ted Bundy, Jeffrey Dahmer, and John Wayne Gacy.

The noun *evil* is defined as "morally objectionable behavior." The adjective: "having or exerting a malignant influence, or morally bad or wrong." In less dramatic ways, it's a known fact evil, or a dark side, resides everywhere human beings are connected. In subtle, bigoted remarks, sexual harassment, bullying, physical and mental abuse, animal cruelty, unethical business practices, and the turmoil of our political climate.

As a professor of human biology and anatomy and physiology, with in-depth lectures on genetics, I wondered if it was a farfetched idea that an evil gene exists. Not only are our physical attributes hardwired into our genes, so are many of our personality traits. Various experts in the fields of psychology, psychiatry, and neuroscience researched documented cases, and the psychopath's brain does not operate as it does with normal individuals. It is also anatomically different in conjunction with associated emotions.

This lent creditability to my story of a father forced to face the fear that his newborn son was preordained for evil.

In the end, we are still left with the confusing question: Are we born this way, or do we behave according to our life experiences? The nature versus nurture debate goes on, but it is a fact that we have traits that are predetermined by our genes.

Below are three links I came across in the course of my writing:

Heitler, Susan. "Evil Genes? An Unconventional Perspective on BPD." Psychology Today (website). Posted December 9, 2013. https://www.psychologytoday.com/us/blog/resolution-not-conflict/201312/evil-genes-unconventional-perspective-bpd

Hagerty, Barbara Bradley. "A Neuroscientist Uncovers a Dark Secret." NPR (website). Posted June 29, 2010. https://www.npr.org/templates/story/story.php?storyId=127888976

Simon, George. "Is Psychopathy Genetic?" Dr. George Simon (website). Posted August 24, 2012. https://www.drgeorgesimon.com/is-psychopathy-genetic/